We were standing at the bottom of a hill ringed by a line of bonfires, and between the fires, there were shadows dancing to music that made the back of my neck prickle. They weren't human shadows. Some of them were tall and thin, wearing beautiful long dresses, or hats with long feathers, and capes fastened with clasps that shone in the firelight. Others were short and wiry, and had bells on their toes and ears. But most of them were animal shadows: dogs with horses' hooves, cats with gleaming eyes and tails that bristled three times their size, pigs that danced gracefully on legs much too long, sheep that pranced like horses, and cows with enormous shoulders and necks.

'Where on earth are we, do you think?' I shouted in Colin's ear.

'No place on earth,' he shouted back. 'This has got to be Faerie – and not just the Outskirts either. You *did* it! You got them to bring us . . . !'

In memory of
John C. Cooley
Dorothy W. Copeland
and
Geraldine Henderson O'Connell

Dignitatem amissam redintegrat amor

It is no doubt very strange that faeries should desire to have a mortal king; but the fact is, that with all their knowledge and power, they cannot get rid of the feeling that some men are greater than they are, though they can neither fly nor play tricks . . . [But] it is only between life and death that the faeries have power over grown-up mortals, and can carry them off to their country. So they had to watch for an opportunity.

—George MacDonald, 'The Shadows'

LAURA C. STEVENSON

ALL THE KING'S HORSES

Illustrated by David Wyatt

CORGI BOOKS

ALL THE KING'S HORSES
A CORGI BOOK : 0 552 547182

First publication in Great Britain

PRINTING HISTORY
Corgi edition published 2001

1 3 5 7 9 10 8 6 4 2

Set in 12/14.5 Bembo by
Phoenix Typesetting, Ilkley, West Yorkshire

Corgi Books are published by Transworld Publishers,
61–63 Uxbridge Road, London W5 5SA,
a division of The Random House Group Ltd,
in Australia by Random House Australia (Pty) Ltd,
20 Alfred Street, Milsons Point, Sydney, NSW 2061, Australia,
in New Zealand by Random House New Zealand Ltd,
18 Poland Road, Glenfield, Auckland 10, New Zealand
and in South Africa by Random House (Pty) Ltd,
Endulini, 5a Jubilee Road, Parktown 2193, South Africa

Printed by
Cox & Wyman Ltd, Reading, Berkshire

1 Samhain

It began the day Grandpa escaped. I know that makes it sound as if Grandpa was in jail, but it's the only word to use. He wasn't in jail, of course; he lived with us, which meant it was dangerous when he got out, because of the neighbourhood we'd just moved to . . . if you could call it a neighbourhood. The place we were renting – a run-down house with a stained-glass window in the hall and a nifty pointed tower – faced the T where the street that crossed the train tracks met a dirt road that didn't go anywhere. Once, that road had led from town to the ferry, and it was still called Ferry Road, but the way to town was blocked off by a pile of dirt and the new 125 Connector now. As for the ferry, it had gone out of business at least sixty years ago, Mom said – and she must have been right, because Colin and I couldn't even find the old dock when we went down to look. The trains were still in business, naturally; they ran half a block from our front door. In the old ferry days, they'd stopped for loads at the two warehouses that stood between the house and the tracks; but later, they'd just whizzed by, and the warehouses, which had been pretty grand once, like our house, had gotten sadder and sadder; now they had paper and boards in the windows instead of glass. People lived in them – old men, mostly, with bottles in paper bags under their beat-up coats, and a few women, not as old, but with the same washed-out look. We weren't allowed to call them bums, and we wouldn't have anyway, because they always said hello as we walked back and forth to the school bus. But anybody could see they were too far gone to stop Grandpa from wandering out on to the tracks and playing with the rocks between the pilings. He always wanted to do that. So we could never let him go out by himself.

Grandpa wasn't crazy – at least, he wasn't crazy the way the warehouse people were. Obviously, a grown-up doesn't sit down on railroad tracks if everything is OK upstairs; but with the warehouse people, you could say what was wrong (even if you weren't supposed to be old enough to know words like DTs or Heroin Addict), and with Grandpa, you couldn't. The doctor couldn't, anyway; all he could say was that Grandpa was old, and that old people got forgetful. I explained, very politely, that Grandpa wasn't just forgetful, he was losing whatever it was that made him Grandpa, but it didn't do any good. The doctor gave me the look vets give you when they've just told you a horse is permanently lame, and he said 'Sarah, I know it's difficult to accept things like this, but even with the advanced medical knowledge of the 1950s, we can't cure everybody,' which is exactly what vets say. So Colin and I knew what we had to do. Grandpa had said you should always listen to vets carefully because they knew things you didn't – but many a time, if you had a horse worth saving, it was up to you to find out what the problem was. Grandpa had cured a lot of horses that vets had said would never jump again, just by using his head. So we started using ours. Because, boy, was Grandpa ever worth saving.

Until whatever it was happened to him, Grandpa lived on a big horse farm in Pennsylvania, and even though he was so old and had only one good arm, he was the head trainer. Every year, Colin and I took the train down there to spend the summer, and when we had to go back to Massachusetts to school, we counted the days until summer came again. The people who owned the stable had two hunter ponies, and since their kids were grown up, they let us ride them. Grandpa gave us lessons every day, and after we got good enough, he let us work bigger horses. He only let us ride six hours a day, but during the other hours, we got to watch him train young jumpers or work with famous people who brought Olympic-level horses to him for advice, so even when we were on foot, we learned a lot. Then at night, we would sit out on his doorstep, smelling the roses that grew up trellises on his cottage, looking at the stars (unless it was raining, of course). Sometimes, we'd just lean against Grandpa and dream off, but most nights, he'd stretch his good hand out to the darkness and chant:

Come away, O human child!
To the waters and the wild
With a faery, hand in hand,
For the world's more full of weeping
    than you can understand.

We'd chant with him, feeling tingly all over, because that poem meant Grandpa was going to

8

tell us faerie stories. You'd better understand right away that the faeries in Grandpa's stories weren't Disney fairies, with plastic wands and tiny wings; they came in all shapes and sizes, and they lived in hollow hills until they rode out at night to visit mortals. When Grandpa told us about them, his eyes shone, and his hand moved, and we could almost see what he was describing: the Sidhe[1], who were so powerful they could spirit bards into the Otherworld, or bewitch the spears and swords of great heroes, or put whole armies to sleep by playing enchanted music – and elves and firbolgs and other little faeries who teased foolish people that didn't believe in them. Sometimes, he got so deep into his stories he'd go on until dawn, and we'd doze off with our heads in his lap, dreaming we were with him in the Otherworld.

Then whatever it was started. It was the summer before I was in fourth grade (I'm finishing sixth, now). Grandpa started forgetting things, like when our riding lessons were supposed to be. He would promise to give us one, but when we had gotten the ponies tacked up, he'd be off doing something else, and he'd get angry if we reminded him. Sometimes he forgot

[1] Pronounced *Shee*.

9

lessons for the famous riders, and *they* got angry and told the Smithes, who owned the stables. But the Smithes said that Grandpa was still the best trainer in the U.S., and people in their seventies were allowed to forget things. The next summer, though, they weren't saying that any more, because it wasn't just lessons Grandpa was forgetting; it was really important stuff. One of his jobs was to supervise the horses in Barn One – those were the top showjumpers, and he wanted to be sure the stable boys treated them just so. But that summer, sometimes he told the boys to feed the horses twice in a row, and sometimes he insisted they'd been fed when they hadn't, and if the boys argued, he'd holler at them. We tried to explain he was wrong, but that just made him holler at us, which he'd never done before.

Half-way through July, Mom turned up at the farm. I was glad to see her, because I knew Grandpa needed a doctor and nobody else could persuade him to see one. But as I said, the doctor was a bust, and instead of thinking about ways to cure Grandpa, the grown-ups made an 'informed decision' about what he should do – which meant that the Smithes decided he was going to retire, and Mom decided he was going to come live with us, and nothing he said (and nothing Colin and I said) was going to make any difference. The only thing that got us through the rest of the summer, while we were saying goodbye to the farm and the ponies and moving Grandpa to Massachusetts, was that we'd have lots of time to figure out what was wrong with Grandpa, and when we did, he'd be able to go back.

The trouble was, Grandpa got worse and worse, and no matter how much we read or how hard we thought, we couldn't figure out why. He was upset and confused after he moved, and he began forgetting more and more things. Then, two nights before Christmas, when he was telling us the story of Finn Mac Cumhaill[1] and the misty faerie monster that burned Tara, he jumped to his feet, the way he always did in the part where Finn throws a faerie spear at the monster – but instead of acting it out, he stared around the room, frowned, and wandered away. After that, no matter which story he started on, he couldn't finish it, even if we helped him along. We begged Mom to take him to another doctor, and she took him to a specialist in Boston, but the specialist just said it was 'dementia', which meant, Mom said in a funny tone of voice,

[1] Pronounced *Finn Mak Cool*

'tough luck'. That's not what it meant; we looked it up, of course. The dictionary said it was 'Irreversible deterioration of intellectual faculties with concomitant emotional disturbance resulting from organic brain disorder. Synonym: insanity'.

We looked at each other. I thought Colin was going to cry (he'd just turned nine, for Pete's sake), but he blinked and set his jaw. 'We're not licked yet,' he said. '"Irreversible" only means the doctor has run out of ideas. Remember that horse that had "irreversible arthritis" that Grandpa cured? Well, if he can do it, we can.'

But we couldn't. No matter how hard we tried to help him, he forgot more and more things; by spring, he'd started putting a kettle on for tea and leaving it on the burner until all the water boiled away and it melted down into the stove in stalactites. One day, he started a fire that way; there was black gunk all over the kitchen walls when Colin and I got home from school. The next day, Mom quit her job so she could be home with him all the time. And soon after that, she put our house on Maple Street on the market. It sold in October. That's when we moved to Ferry Road. Mom said she loved the new place – Victorian houses were so romantic. But I heard the real estate lady telling her the rent was very low because of its 'less desirable location', so I knew we hadn't moved because of the romance.

Anyway, Grandpa escaped, and it was our fault. What happened was, after we got home from school, the two of us kept track of Grandpa so Mom could go shopping or visit her friends. It wasn't too hard, usually. Sometimes we could get him to play Go Fish with us (he taught us to play poker when we were little, and in Pennsylvania we'd played a lot, but he couldn't remember the rules any more), and sometimes we went for walks. But that day was Samhain (Hallowe'en, if you're not Irish), and we told Grandpa, hoping he'd remember his Samhain stories. He didn't, though; he just kept pacing around the living room, the way he often did. We didn't want him to see how sad that made us, so we decided to make some pancakes and invite him to celebrate by eating them. When we make pancakes, we make a whole stack, and Colin mixes up all sorts of interesting things to spread between them. If you don't ask what the interesting things are, they're the best pancakes in the world.

I had just flipped the first pancake, when somebody knocked at the side door – the one that used to be the servants' entrance from the driveway.

Colin looked up from his mixture. 'Listen to that! I *told* Mom nobody would pay attention to the law about not trick-or-treating in this part of town, but she was so freaked that she didn't buy any candy.'

I shook my head. 'It's too early for trick-or-treating – and besides, who would come here? It's not as if we were on the way to anyplace else.'

Whoever it was knocked again, a little louder this time. Colin started to the door.

'Hey, come on!' I said. 'We're not supposed to let anybody in when we're by ourselves.'

'We're not by ourselves,' he said over his shoulder. 'Grandpa's here. And besides, I'm not going to let anybody in. There's a chain.'

I turned off the burner and ran down the hall to stop him, but he had already slipped the chain into the socket and opened the door a crack. He took a quick look, then gulped. 'Um, Sarah . . .'

I shoved him to the side and peeked out the crack, and I saw why he had looked so funny. It was one of the women from the warehouses – not that I recognized her, but the smell of cigarette smoke, old people cooking, and whatever she'd been drinking couldn't have come from anywhere else. Her face was a maze of lines, and her hair was so stringy and dirty that it was matted where it touched the collar of her coat.

The coat had probably come from the bottom of a box at a Salvation Army store, and since it didn't have any buttons, you could see that she had a ripped skirt and a bunch of different length sweaters on underneath it. As she took a step forward, a little white dog with red ears poked its head out from behind her and growled. She scooped it up and looked at me over it.

'Hello, honey,' she said, with a smile that didn't have any teeth. 'Your mother at home?'

'No, she's out right now,' said Colin from behind me.

I gave him a back kick. 'He means she's at home, but she's busy. Can we help?'

The woman stroked the quivering little dog. 'One of the men down the road is sick. I want to make him some gruel, but there isn't any oatmeal. Do you think your mother would let me borrow some?'

Oatmeal. It seemed a funny thing to ask for, but I couldn't think of any reason she would be lying. 'I guess so,' I said. 'Um . . . let me go see if we have any.'

I left the door chained and went back to the kitchen. Colin had already gotten the box out of the cupboard; I took it and stared at the smiling Quaker on the side, wondering if he knew where he was going. 'Do you think we should do this? Mom said not to give those people anything.'

'But one of them's sick,' said Colin. 'And it's not like she asked for anything expensive.'

'That's true. And if Mom notices it's gone, we can just say we ate it, or something.' I walked down the hall, shaking the box; there was a lot left. 'Here you go,' I began . . . but it wouldn't fit through the gap. I had to undo the chain so I could hand it to her.

'Thank you,' said the woman. 'I'll get some oatmeal at the store first thing tomorrow morning and bring it around.'

Colin poked me, but I already knew what Mom would say about that. 'That's OK,' I said. 'Don't bother.'

The woman gave us a funny look. 'You sure?'

'Absolutely,' I said. 'We're glad to help.'

'OK,' she said. 'But listen, honey – if ever you need something, I live at the right-hand warehouse, and my name is Jenny. You got that?'

'Sure,' I said.

The woman smiled her toothless smile once more and turned away. It was foggy outside, and by the time she'd taken two steps, she'd disappeared.

I shut the door. 'She was sort of all right, wasn't she?'

'Yeah,' said Colin. 'You have to wonder . . .'

On the other side of the house, a door banged. We took one look at each other and dashed into the living room. It was empty, and the door that led from the front hall into the foyer was open.

I stared at it. 'Didn't you lock the front door when we came in?'

He shook his head. 'I thought you did.'

That couldn't have been true; he'd stopped in the yard to look at something, and when he'd come in I'd been talking to Mom. But there was no point arguing about it then, and anyway, it was my fault for not checking. 'Well, we'd better go find him,' I said.

We grabbed our jackets and ran out onto the porch, but the fog was so thick that we couldn't even see the big maples at the edge of the yard – which meant, of course, we couldn't see Grandpa. I started down the front steps. 'I suppose we'd better head towards the tracks.'

Colin shook his head. 'I don't think he went that way.'

'I don't see how you can tell,' I muttered, but I followed him until he started up the hill behind the house. Then I grabbed his sleeve. 'Don't be a nerd – he never goes towards the highway!'

'Shut *up*!' he said, stopping. We both listened,

but all I could hear was the roar of trucks on Route 495, which was the other reason our neighbourhood was 'less desirable'. It wasn't a regular highway; it was one of those new four-laners, with bridges and exits instead of cross-roads. The exits were called cloverleafs, because that's what they looked like, and one of them (to the 125 Connector that cut off Ferry Road from town, if you care) was just over the little hill behind our house.

Colin nodded. 'That's where he is – we'd better hurry.'

I never argued with Colin when he was absolutely sure about something, so we ran towards the cloverleaf. But after we got over the top of the hill, it got harder to hurry. The Connector dead-ended at 495 (it was going to be replaced by a big four-laner that went north, but they hadn't gotten around to building that yet), so the entrance ramp of the loop on our side was blocked off. When people figured that out, they started using the area as a free dump, so there were always beer cans, bottles, paper milkshake cups from the new McDonald's hamburger stand, and even dead cars and old refrigerators lying in the grass on both sides of the ramp. By October, when choke vines had grown over everything and the tall grass had started to fall over, it was really slow walking there, and the fog didn't help.

'Maybe we should call,' I said. 'He might stop.'

'Fat chance of that.'

'Yeah, but what else can we do? Come on – one, two, three – GRANDPA!'

We called three times, but when we listened, all we heard was the trucks.

'Criminy,' I said. 'What are we going to do? If he gets up on the highway, they won't be able to see . . .'

Colin climbed onto a dead car. 'There he is!'

I scrambled onto the car, and there he was, across the entrance ramp, standing in . . . well, the only thing I can think of calling it is a clearing in the fog. That is, all around us, it was just as thick as it could be. But where he was, there wasn't any fog. Just Grandpa and two other people about Colin's height. They weren't kids, though; they were the wrong shape.

'Brother,' muttered Colin. His voice told me he was scared, but of course he slid off the car when I did. Together, we crossed the ramp, climbing over the guard rails. The short people had turned away; they seemed to be upset about something, judging from the way their hands were moving as they talked. We both hurried forward, hoping they were going to go on their way, wherever that was, but all of a sudden there was a little zing, like you feel if you run into an electric fence. It didn't hurt; at least, it didn't hurt us. But it seemed to have given the short people a real jolt – they both leapt about a foot into the air and came down facing us. We stopped, staring at them. They were like nobody we had ever seen; their ears were pointed, and their eyelashes flickered with something that glowed murky orange. Behind the glow, their eyes were huge and dark and dangerous.

'Grandpa!' I gasped. Then I remembered we had to help him, not the other way around. I walked slowly towards him, carefully looking just at his confused face. 'Grandpa,' I said in the voice he'd taught us to use with young or frightened horses. 'Grandpa, come on home, now.'

Behind me, I heard Colin step forward too. 'Yeah, Grandpa,' he said soothingly. 'You'll get cold out here without a jacket.'

'Ha!' said one of the little men. 'Somebody's trained them well.'

'There's training and training,' said the other, with a laugh that made me shiver. He strode through a pile of milkshake cups and stood in front of us. 'Do you see me?' he asked.

I reached for Colin's hand, and I found it

sooner than I expected to, because he'd grabbed for mine. That meant he'd remembered the story Grandpa had told us when we were really little. It was so awful, Mom had told him never to tell it to us again, but neither of us had forgotten it.

Once upon a time, long ago, there was a midwife who was so skilful that her fame spread through all of Ireland. One dark night, a strange man knocked at her door and asked if she would deliver a baby at his cottage. She didn't like the looks of the man, but he said his wife had been in labour for hours and was in great pain, so she agreed to go. He set her on his horse (a great black horse it was, bigger than any she had ever seen), and they rode like the wind to a cottage she had never seen before. There was his wife, just as he had said, in great pain. But the midwife knew what to do, and in an hour she had delivered a fine boy. After the baby was born, the man's wife gave her a flask of oil and asked her to rub it into the baby's skin. As she rubbed, her right eye began to itch, and without so much as a thought, she gave it a rub and went on with her business. But when she looked up, her right eye saw not a cottage but a palace bedroom, and not a poor couple but a lord and lady. She was frightened, to be sure, so she said nothing about it – not then, and not later, after the man had galloped her back to her own cottage on the great black horse. A week or so later, when she was at the market, she saw the man whose cottage she had visited walking between the stalls. She stopped when she came to him and asked how his wife and baby were doing.

'Very well,' he said. 'But tell me, which eye can you see me with?'

'This one,' she said, pointing at it.

'The right eye, is it?' he said, drawing his dagger. And before she could say another word, he stepped forward and put out her eye.

Colin and I held hands very tightly, and neither of us looked at the little man. 'Grandpa,' I whispered, 'Grandpa, you'll get hurt out here all by yourself. Come home with us.'

The little man took a couple of steps closer. 'Supposing I were to tell you that he is ours, and he can't come?'

I started to argue, but Colin squeezed my hand just in time. 'Grandpa,' he said, and I could hear the tears in his voice. 'Grandpa, please, please come away. You can have some pancakes with us. You always liked pancakes.'

The second little man tapped the first one on the shoulder. 'This is beyond us,' he said. 'Especially with the Old One. As for the young 'uns—'

'—There'll be trouble,' said the first one. 'They'll say we let them in, and They'll be right! More than our lives are worth, if They find out.'

'They've *already* found out,' said the second man glumly. 'A jolt like that, and They'll be here any second. Best thing for us to do . . .' he glanced at us, then pulled the first man behind a doorless refrigerator.

I gave Colin a poke. 'Quick,' I whispered. 'Before whoever it is gets here.'

We ran through the pile of milkshake cups, and I grabbed Grandpa's good hand. 'Come on, now,' I said. 'Let's go.'

His eyes looked from us to the little men as if he couldn't tell us from them.

Colin tugged at Grandpa's sleeve. 'C'mon, Grandpa,' he said. 'We'll make you a whole batch of pancakes of your own. And a cup of tea too, if you want.'

Grandpa smiled. He'd always had a beautiful smile, and now it was even more beautiful in a funny sort of way. Usually, I felt sad when he smiled like that, but not this time. It meant he was listening, and he'd go with us.

As we helped him over the guard rails, I looked back to see if there were more little people coming, but there was nobody there. At least, I didn't see anybody – it might have just been the fog. Anyway, they didn't follow us. We guided Grandpa across the entrance ramp and up the rise, steadying him when he tripped over the junk. It felt like it took for ever, but it must not have, because when we finally got back into the house and went to the kitchen, the pancake I had flipped was still warm.

Colin and I didn't really feel like pancakes now, but that was all right. Grandpa ate all of them.

2 The Changeling Theory

Dinner was awful – not the food, I mean, but everything else. Mom had got meat for the first time since we'd moved, and I guess Grandpa had forgotten how to cut things, because he couldn't handle his piece. It had always been tricky for him to cut meat, because his right arm ended in a hook, not a hand, but he had always managed before – and you can bet nobody had ever dared to help him. None of us dared to help him this time, either, because we could see how frustrated he was, and we knew he'd get really upset if he thought we'd noticed. I quickly cut up my meat, and I tried to signal Colin to distract Grandpa, but Colin was too upset to notice. Finally, Mom saw what I was doing, and she jumped up and rushed to the window. It worked like a charm; Grandpa got up, too – and when he and Mom came back, there was a heap of cut-up meat on his plate and a whole piece on mine.

That took care of that, but it didn't take care of Colin; he was watching Grandpa carefully, and thinking so hard that Mom had to ask him to pass the salt three times before he heard her. When she finally got the salt, she shook her head and smiled. 'Your mind's in Fairyland again, Colin.'

'No, no!' said Colin, sitting up straight. 'No faeries at all!'

Mom looked puzzled; ever since Grandpa had made up the expression, we'd all used it to describe the way Colin drifted off into his ideas, and usually he just looked sheepish when we said it. 'Is anything wrong?' she asked.

I swallowed a bite of potato too fast, and I coughed for what seemed like for ever. When I finally got my breath back, I said, 'Of course nothing's wrong!' Then I realized the coughing had made it too late to say that, and my face got so hot my glasses fogged up.

Mom looked from Colin to me. 'You two didn't have trouble with Grandpa while I was gone, did you?'

'Of course not,' I said, getting a grip on myself. 'We're just a little down about not being able to go trick-or-treating. It used to be so much fun planning the costumes.'

Mom stopped looking suspicious and looked sad instead. 'Oh, is it Samhain? I guess it is . . . well, you're getting a little old for trick-or-treating costumes anyway. Pretty soon you'll have new friends, and we can make costumes for a real play. That place in the attic where the tower comes to a point would make a wonderful stage.' Then she glanced at Grandpa, and she looked even sadder, so we both knew she'd noticed we'd stopped having friends over, even on Maple Street.

After that, nobody said much. I was feeling bad for Mom; Grandpa was fussing with his food; Mom was trying to act as if everything were fine; and Colin – well, if his mind wasn't in Fairyland, it was somewhere close.

With all that thinking, I was sure he'd come right into my room after we'd finished dishes, but he didn't. I was almost through with my home-work by the time he turned up, and even then, he didn't say anything – just stood behind me, watching me finish my math. I hate that.

'You goofed up number seven,' he said as I folded the paper down the centre. 'When you divide fractions, you have to stand the second one on its head, remember?'

I sighed and slid the paper out of the book. 'Why didn't you tell me sooner?'

'Wanted to see if you had the sense to look them over.'

Remarks like that don't deserve attention, so I just erased number seven, waiting for him to spill what was really on his mind. It didn't take long.

'Look,' he said. 'We have to tell Mom what happened this afternoon.'

I dropped my pencil into the pile of eraser bits. 'You're kidding!'

'Would I kid about this? It explains what's wrong with Grandpa.'

'Oh, sure.'

'It does, I tell you!' Colin sat down on my bed, which is strictly against the rules of my room, but I let him. 'Think of what that man said: *supposing I were to tell you he is ours.*'

'Yeah, but he was only—'

'No, listen! If Grandpa belongs to them, the person who lives with us isn't really Grandpa, but somebody else. And that makes sense of everything that's gone wrong.'

'Doesn't either.'

'It would make perfect sense if you screwed your head on right!' said Colin. 'Remember the stories Grandpa used to tell us about changelings – the leftover faeries the Little People put in cradles after they'd stolen people's babies? Well, it wasn't just babies the Little People stole. It was grown-up women, and men, too, I bet, only nobody tells stories about men who aren't princes or heroes. Why couldn't the Little People steal an old man like Grandpa and leave some faerie that looks just like him here with us?'

'Because it's 1957, for Pete's sake! The only Little People left are in stories.'

'Who says? Not Grandpa, that's for sure. I asked him once if faeries were real, and he said "Of course. Who do you think tips over the water buckets?" I thought he was just kidding — you know how he was — but suppose he wasn't? When you think about it, there's no more reason not to believe in faeries than there is not to believe in Relativity.'

'There is too! There are equations and things proving that Relativity . . . happens. You're just making up a story, like Grandpa.'

'Yeah? Then what did we see this afternoon?'

'Well, um . . .'

'Come on, say it! They were Little People, right? They couldn't have been anything else, with that weird stuff around their eyes. We both saw them. If that's not evidence, what is?'

'OK, it's evidence,' I said. 'But what's it evidence of? Seeing things doesn't make them real. If it did, what we see in our dreams would be true, and you know that isn't so. Maybe we sort of accidentally saw the things Grandpa sees when he dreams off.'

Colin shook his head. 'You can't believe what we saw was really there, but you can believe that we got inside Grandpa's mind and saw what he sees?'

The trouble with arguing with Colin is that you always lose, even when you know he's wrong. 'All right. Maybe we really saw them. What then?'

'Then we should tell Mom. Think how happy she'd be to know it's not really Grandpa who's giving us all this trouble.'

'Baloney. Think how upset she'd be to think we'd gone crazy. And there'd be no way to prove we aren't. Nobody saw them but Grandpa and us.'

For a moment, I thought I had him, but then he shook his head. 'There's just got to be some way we can prove it.'

'Name one.'

'I will, if you just give me a minute to think.'

I went back to work with my eraser; and as I brushed the pile onto the floor, I heard Mom and Grandpa in the hall.

'My thing,' said Grandpa. 'My brown thing.'

'What thing, Dad? You have a lot of brown things.'

If they went on that way, they'd be there all night. 'Think quick,' I said to Colin. 'What brown thing would Grandpa be looking for?'

Colin shrugged. 'His comb, probably.'

I opened the door and looked out. 'Is it your comb you're looking for, Grandpa?'

'Comb,' he said, smiling and holding out his hand.

'I saw it downstairs. Let's go find it.'

He followed me down the big staircase, past the stained-glass window – and I noticed for the first time that there were faeries mixed in with the trees and flowers that made the border of the window pattern. They weren't at all like the Little People we'd seen that afternoon; they were tall and graceful and wearing beautiful clothes, and when you looked at them carefully, they almost seemed to be going somewhere, not just around the edges of the window.

The comb was sitting on the telephone table, right where he'd put it, probably. When I gave it to him, he ran it through his hair, which was long for a man and really thick. 'Comb?' he said, looking at me anxiously.

'Right – comb,' I said, and I gave him a hug. He felt just like Grandpa always did, and as I went back upstairs, I began to wonder if we'd really seen what we thought we had. I mean, it had been awfully foggy. 'Colin . . .' I began as I came into my room.

'Listen!' he interrupted. 'Here's the plan. Tomorrow, we'll let Grandpa get out again, and we'll follow him. He'll probably go to the clover-leaf and meet up with the faeries.'

'Colin, you've gone—'

'—No, I haven't. Think of what they said: *This is beyond us. Especially the Old One.* Now, doesn't that sound like they were going to give a changeling back, but they couldn't?'

'Nope. Who ever heard of faeries *wanting* to give a changeling back? You've got to *make* them do that: throw the changeling into the fire, or pour holy water on it, or—'

'OK, OK,' he said. 'Maybe that's not what he meant. But suppose we let Grandpa out. And suppose he goes where he went today, and we follow him. And suppose he meets the Little People.'

'Yeah, and—?'

'And suppose we say to each other (not to them, of course) that we know Grandpa has been stolen and the one with us is a fake – which is like the holy water, sort of, because it lets them know we know what's happened. So. If we do that, isn't it possible that they'd have to switch

32

what we have now with the real Grandpa, and we could bring him home to Mom?'

I don't know why what he said made me feel so sad, but it did. I looked down at problem seven so he wouldn't call me a cry-baby. 'Things don't work out in real life the way they work out in stories,' I said. 'Even Grandpa said so.'

'I *know* that!' He ran his fingers through his cowlicky hair. 'But we *saw* those people! And we've been doing just what the people in stories do: going to doctors and books and everything we can think of, and Grandpa still isn't Grandpa. If we *were* in a story, wouldn't you be waiting for us to see the obvious solution?'

'Colin . . .' I couldn't go on, because Grandpa came in, without knocking, as usual.

'What name?' he said, holding out his comb.

'Comb,' I said.

'Comb,' repeated Grandpa, smiling his beautiful smile. He stepped out into the hall, but when he got to the top of the stairs, his footsteps turned around. In a minute he was standing in my door again. 'What name?' he said, holding out the comb.

'Comb,' I said, sighing.

'See?' said Colin as the door closed. 'He isn't our Grandpa – he just *can't* be.' His voice was chokey, and when I turned to look at him, I saw two big tears slide down his cheeks.

'OK, OK,' I said. 'When we get home from school tomorrow, I'll leave the door unlocked, and we'll see what happens.'

School always takes forever to be over, but some forevers are longer than others, and the next day was one of them. That was because I'd forgotten my books. Not school books – real books. At Wheelock School, which is where we'd transferred after we moved to Ferry Road, the sixth grade was doing stuff I'd done at the end of fourth in my advanced class at Maple Street School, so I could do the work in five minutes without listening to the teacher. That left time each day to read one whole book and most of another, if I remembered to bring them. But that day, like I said, I'd forgotten them, so I sat there with nothing to do but wish I hadn't let Colin talk me into letting Grandpa out. By the time we'd gotten to reading comprehension, the Grandpa in my mind had run up the entrance ramp a thousand times, and each time, he'd been hit by a different kind of truck.

I sighed and looked around the classroom, hoping the other kids were finished so I wouldn't have to think any more, but they were still bending over their workbooks – all except

Tiffany, the girl at the desk across the aisle. She was the only girl in the class that looked like the no-perm, no-lipstick, no-fainting-over-Elvis Presley friends I'd had at Maple Street School, so I'd started sitting by her on the bus. But she was really shy; it had taken ten days for her even to say 'hi', and she still stared out the window instead of talking. She was staring out the window now, for that matter, smiling to herself the way you do when you're daydreaming after your work is done. Only her work wasn't done; her workbook was lying on her desk, and the checkmarks on it stopped halfway down the first page. Just then, Miss Turner, the teacher, walked our way, and Tiffany jerked out of her dream and started filling in the empty boxes, making a little pattern down the page. I had never seen someone fill in the answers without looking at the questions before, and I was so interested that I forgot all about Miss Turner until she tapped me on the shoulder. 'Sarah, have you finished already?' she whispered.

I didn't say I'd finished half an hour ago. I just nodded.

She looked over my answers, nodded, then wrote neatly in the margin, 'I forgot to send the attendance sheet down to the office this morning. Could you take it for me?'

I nodded and slipped out the door. It was two flights down to the office from our room, really different from Maple Street School, which had been all on one floor. The classrooms were different, too; instead of having moveable desks in clusters and cheerful bulletin boards, they had desks and chairs that were bolted to the floor in rows and huge windows with yellow shades. I was still trying to decide whether it was the classrooms that made the teachers look so worn out or the teachers who made the classrooms look so dingy, when I got to the office.

'I have Miss Turner's attendance sheet,' I said to the secretary. 'Do I give it to you?'

'Sure, hon,' she said, not looking at me as she reached for it.

I was just starting back, when the door to the principal's office opened and Colin came out with Mr Beeker. Colin didn't look very glad to see me.

'What are you doing here?' I asked. 'Did Mom call?' She would only call if something was really wrong.

''Course not,' he muttered.

'Then what—?'

'Sarah,' said Mr Beeker, 'would you come and talk to me, please?'

When a principal says that, you really don't

have much of a choice, so I went into his office. He sat down on the edge of his desk, which meant he was going to try to be friendly.

'Did your mother get the two notes I've sent home about your brother?' he said.

'About Colin?' I said blankly.

'That's right. I asked your mother to make an appointment with me, but she hasn't. I called several times, but nobody answered.'

Nobody answered because Grandpa had begun to pick up the phone and shout into it when it rang, so we left it unplugged unless we made a call out. But I couldn't tell Mr Beeker that, and besides, explaining wouldn't have helped me find out what was going on, which was what I had to do.

'I'm sorry you've had so much trouble,' I said. 'If you'd like to send a note home with me, I'll take it.'

'That's what I was going to ask you,' he said, looking relieved. 'But I thought maybe . . .'

'Oh, no,' I said with my nicest smile. 'Glad to help.'

'I'll bring it up this afternoon, then.' He stood up and opened the door for me.

'Thank you,' I said, and hurried back up the dusty steps, feeling I had handled the thing pretty well.

But I didn't feel so great when I read the letter on the way home, which I could easily do because Colin had started sitting in the back of the bus with a bunch of boys whose hair was greased back into duck tails. I guess he thought they were cool, or something.

Dear Mrs Madison:

I am sorry to report that your son's behaviour has been consistently disruptive since enrolment in Frederick J. Wheelock School this October. We have consulted the school social worker, and it is his opinion that Colin is disturbing the class-room environment due to stress in his home situation. Colin's teacher, Mr Stegeth, and I would like to arrange a meeting to discuss that possibility with you. Please contact me at your earliest convenience

Yours truly,
James Beeker, Principal

I looked out the bus window, watching the gas stations and used-car lots slide by, and wondering what I should do. Obviously, I wasn't going to show the note to Mom; that would be squealing, and we never squeal on each other. Besides, Mom was upset enough about Grandpa without having to think the way he was had any effect on us. But what if the social worker was right?

Of course, he probably wasn't; the social worker at Maple Street School talked about 'home situations' when any moron could have told him kids acted up because they were bored. Especially Colin. He hated being bored, and it made him really fresh, which was why Maple Street School had skipped him. But at Wheelock – heck, even if they skipped him into my grade, it wouldn't help; he knew the stuff we were studying as well as I did. Of course, he should know better than to act up, but . . . the boys in the back of the bus laughed so loudly that the driver had to tell them to shut up.

I bit my lip and turned to Tiffany. For a change, she was looking at me. What a break. 'Tiffany, you know those boys who got kicked out of class today for acting up?'

Tiffany smiled. (Tiffany always smiled when you talked to her, but it was the kind of nervous smile that made you think she wanted you to like her, not a regular smile.) 'Yeah.'

'Did they get sent to the principal's office for the whole day?'

'Oh no,' she said. 'There's a special detention room for people who smoke or mouth off or leave class without a pass, or don't do their work.'

39

'What happens to them? Do they just sit there?'

'They work with Miss Fitzgerald,' she said. 'At least, they're supposed to. But she's . . .' She stopped and smiled again.

I began to feel sick. 'Not very good?'

'Well, she's awfully busy.' Her smile suddenly turned into a real one. 'But there's Mr Crewes. He's one of the fifth-grade teachers, but usually he spends his coffee break in the detention room, helping out. He's great. Even the boys in the detention room like him.'

I was going to ask her how she knew that, but then I realized there was only one way she could, and I blushed. Luckily, the bus stopped at our stop, and Colin and I got off.

'What do you have there?' he asked suspiciously as I stuffed the letter in my pocket.

'Just some dumb note about preparing for junior high,' I said.

'Oh,' he said, and he started up the hill, which wasn't like him at all – I'd been expecting cross-examination. Something about the way he walked let on that he was miserable but trying to cover it up, and I suddenly realized he'd been walking that way quite a bit lately. So I thought again about that social worker . . . and about Colin's changeling theory, which might just mean he was upset. And about the trucks on Route 495. 'Look,' I said, stopping at the top of the driveway. 'About Grandpa. I really don't think we should risk—'

Before I could finish, Mom burst out the side door. When she saw us, she tried to act as if everything was all right, but it obviously wasn't. 'Did you two see Grandpa when you crossed the tracks?'

Colin and I looked at each other. 'No.'

Mom reached back through the door for her jacket. 'I was washing my hands, and all of a sudden, he wasn't there,' she said. 'I'm afraid I wasted a lot of time looking around upstairs, because he usually doesn't try to go out at this time of day.'

Colin tossed his backpack into the house. 'Why don't you go to the warehouses and see if any of those guys have seen him? We'll go down to the river.'

Mom nodded and hurried down the road. Colin and I waited to make sure she wasn't going to look back; then we ran towards the cloverleaf.

3 Outskirts and Sock Limbo

We got to the entrance ramp in record time, but when we climbed up on the dead car to look around, we couldn't see anybody.

'Rats!' said Colin. 'We missed them!'

'Maybe he didn't come this way. I was just starting to say . . .'

'Why else would he have escaped?' said Colin, jumping off the car.

I jumped off too, and we climbed over the guard rails, but there was nothing in the place where Grandpa had been standing the day before. 'See?' I said. 'There's no sign he came here.'

'There are signs and signs.'

I looked at Colin. 'Did you say that?'

But he was staring at something behind me. When I turned around, I stared too. The man

standing next to the wrecked refrigerator wasn't at all like the Little People we'd seen the day before, but you could tell he was one of them. He was tall, and he was dressed in a long, hooded black robe. What I could see of his hair was grey, but his beard was long and white, and his face looked thousands of years old. When he stepped towards us through the plastic bags and newspapers on the ground, though, he didn't walk like an old man. 'Greetings, Children of Lugh,' he said, holding out his hands. 'I am Cathbad, and I have come to meet you.'

We looked at each other. He seemed to know why, because he smiled an ancient smile. 'You may speak without fear,' he said. 'You are under Protection.'

I knew Colin was going to ask, right off, what Protection was, so I nudged him and dropped the best curtsey I could manage. He took the cue and bowed. Grandpa always said terrible things happened to children who were impolite to people from the Otherworld.

Cathbad bowed so gracefully that I was ashamed. 'Tell me – what brings you here?'

The real question, of course, was what had brought *him* there, but something about him made that impossible to ask. 'Um . . . we live just over the hill,' I whispered.

He looked at me, and I shivered; his eyes were as deep and grey as a winter ocean, and his smile seemed to come from the end of time. 'Are you sure?'

'Of course,' I said. But then I looked around.

If we were still in the cloverleaf, it had gotten much bigger. I couldn't hear any trucks, and all I could see was a field sloping downhill to the river. The grass was very green, mixed with red and yellow flowers I'd never seen before. Along the banks of the river, big trees hung over the water, and they were covered with leaves, not bare the way they should have been in November. It was pretty, but I couldn't help thinking of the stories Grandpa told about people who came home after a night of dancing with faeries, only to find they had been gone for a hundred years. They turned to dust the minute they took a step. 'Can . . . can we get home?' I whispered.

'Hush, dumbbell,' hissed Colin. 'We don't *want* to go home! If we're where I think we are, this is our big chance to get Grandpa back.'

Cathbad turned to him. 'I advise you not to talk to your sister like that,' he said. 'You are only in the Outskirts of the Otherworld, but you would be wise to adopt its manners.'

Colin isn't that easy to shut up. 'What are the outskirts of the Otherworld?'

Cathbad sighed. 'I forget how much has been lost in your world,' he said, 'even to the few mortals who are fit to educate the young. Listen well, then. We – the Faeries, or the Faer Folk, as some call us – used to be gods who walked the earth. There were many of us: Manannan, who ruled the sea, Lugh, who ruled the sun, and many others as well. But long years ago, the Sons of Mil, wicked, unbelieving men, drove us from our lands, and we retreated to Faerie.' He glanced at us to be sure we were following, and we both nodded. 'You must not think of Faerie as a place, or at least what you call a place. There are parts of it everywhere, but none of them are in your world; they merely touch it, as they touch other worlds, here and there. And where Faerie touches other worlds, we can go back and forth. For centuries of mortal time, long before men made the wide roads with the strange names you give them, the spot where I met you has been such a place. Those who know the Faer Folk call it a faery ring.'

'A faery ring!' I said. 'That doesn't make . . . I mean . . . we know there've been faery rings in Ireland for centuries, but we're *here*, in Massachusetts – or at least we were before we came to the . . . umm . . . Outskirts. And, see, Massachusetts belonged to the Indians centuries

45

ago, and Indians didn't believe in faeries.' I gulped. 'Did they?'

'No,' said Cathbad, with one of his strange smiles. 'But a Way is a Way to all who know it. In the days of the great trees, Indians called upon their spirits in that place. In the days of the mills and iron roads, people pining for the Old Country they'd had to leave because of the Great Hunger saw it, recognized its power, and called upon us.'

'And still do, sometimes,' said a laughing voice behind us. Turning, we saw a man about Colin's size, sitting on a boulder I was sure hadn't been there a few moments ago. He was wearing red breeches and a leather tunic, and he was smiling in a way I didn't quite trust. 'That's what saved the Ring, though Cathbad's too grand to tell you.'

Cathbad gave him the kind of look grown-ups give people they don't really get along with. 'It was luck alone that saved the Ring,' he said gravely.

'In a pig's eye!' said the other faerie. 'Listen, little ones, and I'll tell you the tale. A troop of men came with big machines and started digging near the Ring, and we thought it was lost for sure. But one day, the head engineer walked a little way across the wounded earth and stepped into the Ring, which, of course, meant we could

46

make him do whatever we chose. I was for making him route the road into the river, or for making the whole crew run mad, but the others said, No, those days were over. All we could do now, things being as they were, was make the engineer design a cloverleaf around our Ring, and then make it difficult for his workers to build it.' He settled himself more comfortably on the rock and crossed his pointed feet. 'Kept us busy for a year, as mortals count time. We drained the gasoline out of their tractors. We moved the white wands they planted to mark the roadbed. The fiery ones among us − the drakes and the will-o-the-wisps − circled around them on winter afternoons, and they ran away, screaming about creatures from outer space. We thought we'd won, but then . . .' He sighed. 'One of the bosses came to look things over, and I'll be blessed if he didn't know a Ring when he saw one. "If things keep going wrong, tell me, and we'll dynamite spots there, there, and there," he said, pointing to three places around the edges of the Ring. That night, midnight, he came back alone and left a dish of milk at each of those places, looking neither right nor left and careful not to step in the Ring. Left with nary a glance over his shoulder. We took the milk − and the hint with it − and let them finish.' He jumped off the boulder and shook hands with us. 'Mongan's the name.'

'Pleased to meet you,' said Colin, and his smile told me he really was. Oh, great. Kid In Trouble At School Meets Faery Prankster.

I looked at Cathbad. 'This is a beautiful place, sir, and it's really . . . um . . . great talking to you, but we *have* to get home. Our grandfather is lost, and—'

'—Your grandfather,' said Mongan warmly. 'Now there's a fine mortal if ever I've—'

Cathbad cut him off with a glance that would have knocked anybody else flat. Then he turned to me. 'You may indeed go home,' he said. 'And therein, you are fortunate. Generally, those who have seen us in our true form must stay in the Otherworld for ever. But the Protection you have been granted enables you to go back and forth between worlds, just as we do.'

Colin leaned towards me. 'What the heck do you suppose we *did*?' he whispered.

I put my finger on my lips. If Cathbad was going to send us home, the last thing I wanted was to slow him down by asking about details.

'There are Rules in the Otherworld, however,' added Cathbad. 'And they grant the privilege of continuous visits under Protection only to those who have a mission.' His grey eyes locked onto ours. 'There is always a chance that mortals may stumble upon powers greater than they understand. The Rules allow such mortals to go and return once, but they can never come again.'

'But if we have a mission,' asked Colin, 'what then?'

'Then,' said Cathbad gravely, 'you may travel back and forth between worlds as many times as it takes you to fulfil your mission. And, furthermore, the Sidhe and all the lesser faeries of the Otherworld must do all that is in their power to help you accomplish it.'

Colin looked at me, and his lips said 'Grandpa.' I nodded, but when I turned to Cathbad, I realized all over again how grand he was, and how little we were – and I remembered how wicked faeries were about giving changelings back. I shivered again, swallowing over a dry place in my throat. 'We *do* have a mission,' I croaked.

'Right,' said Colin, in a voice as dry as mine. 'It's Grandpa. The *real* Grandpa.' He took my hand and held it hard while he finished. 'We want him back. So we need you to take us to where he is.'

'Please,' I added. 'If you'd be so kind.'

Mongan whistled.

'Peace,' said Cathbad. 'They don't know what they're asking.'

49

'We do, too!' said Colin. 'And it's the only thing we want, right, Sarah?'

'Right,' I said firmly. 'No deep secrets, no magical powers – just Grandpa.'

Mongan raised an eyebrow at Cathbad. 'Has it ever been done?'

'Not willingly,' said Cathbad. 'And never by the young.'

'*Please* don't say that!' said Colin. '*Everybody* says we're too young to understand things, and it's *not true*! If you think we're too young or too chicken to get Grandpa back, your Protection is just like everybody else's – it saves you the trouble of taking us seriously!'

'The child has a point,' said Mongan. 'And even if he didn't, the Rules don't permit us to deny them what they ask.'

There was a long pause – like, forever – while Cathbad thought it over. Then he sighed and turned to us. 'Very well,' he said. 'We will help you accomplish your mission.'

'Hot diggity dog!' exploded Colin. 'That's so *cool*!'

'*Thank* you! *Thank* you! *Thank* you!' I said at the same time.

Mongan stirred uncomfortably on his rock. 'Surely, you may not be thanking us later, little ones. It's no holiday trip you've asked for.'

'That's all right,' I said. 'So long as Grandpa's at the end of it.'

'So be it,' said Cathbad. 'But because of your youth, we cannot take you to where your grand-father is directly. Instead, we will take you for short journeys along the road he has followed. If you find things on that road which threaten to harm you in mind or spirit, you may stop your mission, and we will help you return to your own world – as safely as we can.'

I caught Colin's eye, and I could see we were thinking the same thing: they were planning to take us for little 'journeys' into the Otherworld and scare us so much that we'd never want to go back. That way, they could say they'd *offered* to take us to Grandpa, but that we'd called the whole thing off, so they'd taken us home instead.

'Er . . . if it's all the same to you,' I said as politely as I could, 'we'd like to meet up with Grandpa right away.'

Cathbad looked at us, and suddenly he seemed taller and darker. 'You are in a poor position to bargain,' he said softly. I looked away from the mist that swirled in his grey eyes to the endless green of the Outskirts – beautiful, silent, and miles from Mom, with no way of getting home on our own.

'I'm sorry,' I whispered.

'We won't bargain any more,' whispered Colin. 'Short journeys are fine.'

'That's my sensible ones,' said Mongan. 'There's dangers enough along the way without asking for more.'

'Dangers!' said Colin, his face lighting up. 'You mean, real Faerie dangers, like Finn's monster at Tara, or heroes screaming their battle cries, cutting their way through battles in those chariots with enemy heads hanging on the sides? Streams running with blood? Enchanted music? Ravens in dead trees? Don't worry – we know all about those kinds of dangers!'

'It's other kinds I was thinking of,' said Mongan, glancing at Cathbad, who was somehow the right size again. 'No stories about them, to be sure, but none the less fearsome for that. With battles, enchantments and such, the Rules are still the Rules. But—'

'—That's OK,' said Colin, though anybody could tell he'd prefer battles and enchantments. 'Grandpa's taught us to use our heads as well as our fists. No matter what kind of danger there is, we'll pitch in, won't we Sarah?'

'Sure,' I said firmly. 'And once you've taken us to Grandpa, you won't have to worry about us any more; he'll help us find our way home.'

'The way home's the problem, surely,' said Mongan, shaking his head. 'Worse and worse, the further you travel. Suppose when you find your grandfather, he can't help you?'

'Oh, but he will!' I said. 'He's not afraid of *anything*!'

'He surely wasn't,' said Mongan, 'but – well, on your heads be it. Shall we begin?'

Cathbad's white eyebrows rose. 'I'm surprised you want to accompany them, my lord. I had planned to summon a minion for these early stages, there being so little danger.'

Colin stared at Mongan. 'You're a lord?'

'Surely – one of the great Sidhe, son of Manannan mac Lir[1] himself,' said Mongan. 'But I try not to let that little accident of birth get in my way. The other Sidhe miss a lot of fun being too proud to leave the Otherworld. So if you'll have me, I'll guide you, Children of Lugh.'

'Why are we Children of Lugh?' said Colin. 'Our father's name was Peter.'

Mongan grinned. 'Lugh is the faery of light, and you two – thanks to your grandfather – have been enlightened. Come.'

He stepped forward and held out a hand to

[1] Manannan mac Lir is pronounced *Monn-un-aun Mak Leer*

each of us. I hung back, not feeling enlightened at all, and listening to something in me – the part that Grandpa said you should *always* listen to – that said there was more to be afraid of than some monster they might throw in to scare us. There was something we didn't understand.

'Come *on*!' hissed Colin. 'If we chicken out now, we'll never find Grandpa!'

Maybe we didn't *have* to understand. Many a time, Grandpa had always said, people thought so much they never did what needed to be done. I looked at Mongan and Colin, took a deep breath – then reached for their hands. 'OK,' I said. 'Let's go.'

The minute our hands touched, there was a whoosh of something that sounded like music; when it ended, we weren't in the Outskirts any more. We were standing in the living room of our house on Maple Street, only it was the Burkes' now, of course, so it had their furniture in it. Totally ordinary. What a come-down.

'What on earth are we doing *here*?' said Colin, sounding disappointed.

'Beginning your mission,' said Mongan. 'What else would we be doing?'

'Shh!' I whispered. 'Mr Burke is snoozing on the sofa. We'll wake him up.'

'No, we won't,' said Mongan. 'Not being heard is part of being invisible.'

'But we're not invisible,' I objected. 'I can see you.'

'That's a little effect I throw in for beginners, because they find it hard to work with people they can't see.' He turned to Colin. 'Now, down to business. See those keys?' He pointed to the table next to the kitchen door. 'Pick them up.'

Colin gave me a 'what's-going-on?' look and scooped the keys out of the ashtray that was sitting on the table. Just as he shoved them into his pocket, Mrs Burke hurried downstairs. 'What time did you say you'd meet Harry for that round of golf?' she asked, jiggling Mr Burke.

Mr Burke sat up with a snort. 'Huh? Oh, golf. I said 3:30.'

'You'd better hurry, then. It's 3:15.'

'Three fifteen!' Mr Burke jumped up, grabbed his golf bag out of the corner and started for the door, glancing at the table, feeling in his pockets . . . 'Um,' he said, looking a little sheepish, 'you wouldn't happen to remember where I put the car keys, would you?'

'Oh, no,' said Mrs Burke, 'not again!'

She sighed, and they started hunting. After a minute, Mr Burke frowned and hurried back to the table where the keys had been. 'Funny,' he muttered, moving the magazines next to the ashtray, 'I was *sure* I'd put them . . .' He went on into the kitchen.

'Quick, Colin,' said Mongan. 'Put them back.'

Colin plopped the keys down just before Mrs Burke got to the table herself. She clicked her tongue. 'Here they are, dear.'

He hurried back into the room. 'Where were they?'

She pointed to the ashtray. 'Right under your nose.'

Colin laughed as Mr Burke dashed out the door. 'That's what Mom says when she finds things we've been hunting for. But when she forgets where she's put her glasses, we have to turn the house upside—' He stared at Mongan. 'Oh! Is that what happens? You guys . . . ?'

'Strictly speaking,' said Mongan, 'that's out of our realm. Now and again, of course, we filch something from somebody that's annoyed us, which has the same effect. Most of the time, though, mortals forget things all on their own – Come.'

He reached out a hand to each of us, and next thing we knew, we were near the centre of town, on a street that had laundromats and stores with 'Goods Bought and Redeemed' in their windows on one side, and garages on the other. It was OK

– Mom took our car to one of the garages, and sometimes the mechanic gave us each a third of his Three Musketeers bar – but it wasn't a place you'd want to walk without a grown-up, unless you were invisible.

Colin glanced at three teenagers in black jackets who were leaning against a boarded-up shop and looking at the hubcaps of a parked car. 'Why would a faery come here?'

Mongan grinned. 'Because this is prime territory. Here, take my hands.'

We did, and I thought we'd start to spin again, but he was just keeping track of us as he wove his way across the street. There were a lot of cars, and of course, nobody could . . .

'Mongan?' I said. 'Are you *sure* they can't see us? The guy in that green Chevvy . . .'

Mongan grinned. 'He just feels us. Some mortals know when there are faeries around.'

'Oh,' said Colin. 'Like at night, when you don't hear or see anything, but you know?'

'Surely,' said Mongan. 'Though it's not always us. Ghosts have their rights, too – This way now.' And he opened the door to a laundromat, letting out a smell of soap and steam.

I wiped off my glasses and looked at the clock on the wall. It said 3:15. Of course, clocks in laundromats never work, but still . . . I hurried to catch up with the others.

Mongan was opening a dryer door. 'Now,' he said, 'each of you pull out a sock.'

We each did; the socks must have been in there a long time, because they sort of snapped, and their fur stuck out. 'These OK?'

'Not them,' said Mongan. 'They match.' He frowned. 'Colin, m'lad, you're a mathematical one, they say. What're the odds of forgetting to put two *matching* socks in a dryer?'

'That depends on how many socks were there in the first place.'

I swapped one of the brown socks in my hand for a blue one and shut the dryer door. 'It looks like about a week's laundry. So say, seven pairs.'

'One in thirteen,' said Colin. 'If each pair was a different colour to start with. But if there were four brown pairs and three blue pairs—'

'—You're making my head spin,' grunted Mongan. 'Take my hands, and we're off.'

'What about these?' I said, holding up my socks.

Mongan grinned, took the two socks and threw them high into the air. As they started to come back down, they disappeared. 'There,' he said, chuckling. 'Off to sock limbo.'

'Where's that?' I asked.

'It's where all the forgotten socks go – and a fine time they have of it.'

'Wow!' said Colin. 'I've gotta try that!' He opened the dryer, but Mongan stopped him.

'No you don't, lad. That was just a demonstration; any more's against the Rules.'

'Aw, come on,' said Colin, reaching in. 'Just one!'

Mongan grabbed his hand. 'I said, that's against the Rules!' He grabbed me, too, and I braced myself for the whoosh.

But this time, there was no whoosh. First, there was nothing at all – just me, sort of floating. Then slowly, slowly, things began to appear, floating too, but just out of reach. For a moment, I thought, my gosh, he's shut us into the dryer! But it was much bigger than a dryer, and the things around me were moving too slowly . . . no, *I* was moving, in sort of a spiral, and going the other way was everything we'd ever hunted for – riding crops, curry-combs, boot pulls, lead-ropes, homework papers, library books, lunch money, spoons, mittens, barrettes, Tinkertoys, safety pins. I began to get dizzy and sort of sick, but I didn't dare close my eyes, because something kept telling me that in the middle of all that stuff there was something I *had* to find, but I couldn't remember what it was. So

I stared, hoping that something would remind me . . . but gradually, everything faded, and there was nothing again, and suddenly I had a terrible feeling that Mongan and Cathbad had forgotten *us*, and we were lost for ever, like all the other stuff, which meant no matter how hard Mom looked, she'd never find us, and we'd never get back . . .

Then – wham! – we were walking into the front yard with Grandpa between us. Mom was running up the hill from the warehouses.

'Thank heaven!' she said, panting. 'I went up the tracks as far as I dared, but I had to turn back because . . .' She gestured towards the 3:15 train as it roared by, blasting its whistle at the crossing. 'Where did you find him?'

'By the river,' said Colin. 'He was fine – just looking at the water.'

Mom gave Grandpa a hug. 'Come on into the house, Dad. You must be cold. I'll make you some tea.'

Grandpa smiled his beautiful, empty smile and followed her inside.

'Wow,' I said to Colin. 'As Grandpa would say, there's a grand future for you in lying.'

I expected him to be pleased (usually I don't bother to tell him he's done something right); but instead, he looked sore. 'What the heck do you mean by *that*!?'

'Come on! There we are with Grandpa, and no way to explain how the faeries got us to him, let alone into the front yard – and you make up that river story, smooth as glass.'

'Faeries!' he snorted. '*You're* the one who's got a grand future in lying!'

'Hey, you don't have to pretend to me, remember? I was there, too!'

'Sure you were,' he said, in a voice like lemonade without sugar. 'But finding Grandpa down by the river wasn't *interesting* enough for you, so you wanted to *embellish* it.'

'That's not so, and you know it!'

He shrugged. 'Have it your way, story-teller.'

I hit him – hard. He swung at me, but I caught his fist with my guard. That made him really angry, and he started punching so fast that I began to think how bad things would be ever after if I lost (which I never had) when Mom ran down the steps and pulled us apart.

'What on earth are you *doing*!?' she said, holding each of us by the shoulder.

Neither of us said anything, but not just because the answer was obvious. When we'd asked Grandpa to teach us to box, he'd said no. '*See, your mother's like her mother – it grieves her to*

61

see matters settled in the ordinary way. So we don't
want to be causing her tears; she's shed enough of those
already.' He finally gave in, but only if we
promised never, never to have fist-fights at home,
only in Pennsylvania. Up until then, we'd never
forgotten that promise. I was so ashamed that I
couldn't look anywhere but down.

'What brought this about?' asked Mom in a
quiet voice that was lots worse than yelling.

'Nothing, really,' I whispered.

'Right,' muttered Colin. 'We just . . . disagreed.'

'What about?'

I snuck a glance at Colin, then we both looked
up at Mom. She was almost crying, just like
Grandpa had said. 'Oh Mom!' I said.

'We're so sorry!' said Colin. 'We'll never,
never . . .'

'OK.' But she still stood there, blinking tears
away. Finally, she said, 'Look. It's hard on all of
us, having Grandpa like this. But the only thing
we can do about it is stick together.'

This wasn't the time to explain you could have
a fist-fight and still stick together, so I didn't.
Which was a good thing, because she looked at us
very closely and added: 'That doesn't just mean
no fighting. It means no secrets.'

'Absolutely,' said Colin, looking at her, not at
me. 'No secrets, from now on.'

Mom's face suddenly looked a lot better. 'Great,' she said. 'Let's have some tea.'

We did, and that was that, except after we went to bed, Colin snuck into my room.

'Just in case you think I've still got a grand future in lying—'

'It's OK,' I said. 'You said *no secrets from now on*; the old ones don't count, right?'

'Just wanted to be sure you got it,' he whispered, looking over his shoulder at the door. 'And look, Sarah. We *did* see Cathbad and Mongan, and we went to the Burkes' and . . .'

'Oh, for Pete's sake.'

'No, no! That's what I wanted to tell you! I don't know if you can believe this, but I . . . forgot. Honest. Like on a test, and everything goes blank, you know?'

'Really?'

'Yeah, really. And like after the test is over, when you suddenly remember the answer – bang, there it was: Cathbad and Mongan and the mission and everything else that happened before we got back and they told us Grandpa was down by the river.' He shivered. 'Spooky, right? I mean, you *know* the Sidhe are powerful and all, but if they can wipe out your memory like that—'

'Yeah,' I said, but then we heard Mom and Grandpa coming upstairs, and Colin whisked back into his room.

I lay there in the dark, thinking about what had happened after we left the laundromat, and wishing Colin hadn't left; it would have been nice if he'd been around when it all came back to me. But it was even spookier than I'd thought. Because it didn't come back. No matter how hard I tried, I couldn't remember finding Grandpa by the river.

4 Night-Elves and Dreams

The next Monday, the bus was late, which only happens when it's pouring. After we'd been standing at our stop for about ten minutes, the little white dog we'd seen with Jenny bounced out of one of the warehouses, and a moment later Jenny followed it. She didn't have an umbrella, so she was soaked by the time she got to us. 'You want to wait in our place?' she said.

'Oh . . . thanks,' I said, 'but we couldn't see the bus from there.'

Jenny glanced at the warehouse, and I knew she knew we could have seen the bus just fine, but all she said was, 'OK.' Then she asked us what our names were, and where we'd lived before, and I kept thinking we should make room for her under the umbrella, and Colin

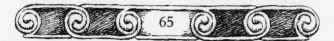

stood on one foot, then the other, and it seemed like forever until the bus finally came. As we climbed on, I looked back, wondering why she'd stand in the rain just to talk to us. She smiled, showing brown stumps where her teeth should have been. 'Have a good time,' she said.

A good time in Wheelock School – sure. Right after the Pledge of Allegiance, Miss Turner looked at Tiffany's math worksheets and found that she hadn't done any of the problems for the last week; so she said Tiffany would have to go 'Downstairs'. I'd learned by now that meant the Detention Room. I offered to help Tiffany with her math so she wouldn't have to go, but all that did was make Miss Turner look at my sheets, which meant she saw *My Friend Flicka* on my lap and took it away. Miss Turner went to the front of the room and wrote problems on the board, telling all of us we were falling behind the Russians because they knew more math (as if it was *our* fault that they'd just launched a second Sputnik). I was beginning to glaze over, when suddenly the piece of chalk she'd just put down disappeared. She stared at the tray, then at the floor, but it was totally missing, so she went to her desk and got another piece. Most of the kids didn't notice (I guess they were glazed over, too), but it cheered me up.

The next cheering-up thing that happened was that Tiffany sat next to me at lunch, instead of trying to sit at a table all by herself. It was so noisy we couldn't talk much until most of the kids had left, but then she gave me a Tiffany smile and said, 'You know Mr Crewes, that teacher I said was really nice? He was Downstairs today, and he told me he'd like to meet you. Would that be OK? He's over there.' She pointed across the lunch-room to a man who had one of those faces that would tell you he was a teacher in a line-up of a thousand people. He nodded in a friendly way when he saw us looking at him, but just as he got up, a short, square man teacher hurried up to him and started talking anxiously about something.

'Who's that?' I said.

'Mr Stegeth,' she said, looking surprised I didn't know. 'Your brother's teacher.'

'Oh!' I said. And right then, I stopped being worried that it was worry about Grandpa that was making Colin be 'disruptive' in class. After you've been in school awhile, you can tell when a teacher is the kind who teaches only the stuff in the textbook and feels threatened if kids want to know more. It doesn't always mean the teacher is stupid – but try, just try, to tell Colin that.

Mr Crewes took care of whatever was bothering Mr Stegeth in a few seconds and walked over to us. Most teachers would have started right in talking to me, but he let Tiffany introduce us, and he shook my hand. 'Glad to meet you, Sarah,' he said. 'Tiffany says you and your brother transferred from Maple Street School. How are you settling in here?'

'I'm settling in fine,' I said, 'but my brother—' Then I remembered that Tiffany had said Mr Crewes had been Downstairs, and I thought, *uh-oh*. 'Um . . . have you met him?'

'I met him this morning. Just briefly. We didn't have time to talk.'

So they'd sent Colin Downstairs, and Mom couldn't work things out because she didn't know. I gulped. 'Well, my brother is . . . like our dad – precocious. Is that the word?'

'That depends upon what you need a word for,' said Mr Crewes.

'Somebody whose mind grows up before the rest of him.'

He nodded, looking kind of interested.

'It was a problem, even at Maple Street School, because it means he gets bored easily, and then he gets fresh. So last year, they skipped him. He was still way ahead, but it worked, because the classes were small and the teachers were really good – but I guess nobody warned this school,

because they put him in Mr Stegeth's class.'
Suddenly, I realized what I'd said, and I blushed.

Mr Crewes didn't seem to notice. 'So it's a
matter of keeping him interested, is it? I thought
so. Let's see. Would your dad be willing to help
him at home if Mr Stegeth assigned him more
advanced work?'

I shook my head. 'Our dad was killed in
Korea.'

He gave me the kind of look grown-ups
always give after you say that. 'Oh, I'm sorry.'

'That's OK,' I said. 'It's not your fault. But,
about helping Colin at home, well, Mom used to
do stuff with him, but now she's pretty tired,
because . . .' I stopped. Telling him about
Grandpa might have made it sound as if it were
all Grandpa's fault Colin was Downstairs.

The bell rang, and Mr Crewes got up. 'I tell
you what. I'll look at Colin's transcript, and call
the principal of Maple Street School. Then we'll
see what we can do. OK?'

'That would be great,' I said, and I felt lots
better.

We started into the hall with Tiffany, who had
been listening the whole time. When he got to
his classroom, Mr Crewes smiled at us – not a
teacher's smile; a real one. 'Take care, girls,' he
said. 'I'll be in touch.'

*

Dinner was awful again. Colin had almost missed the bus home, though all the kids from his class made it in plenty of time. He knew I knew why he was late, but he didn't say anything about it, so I couldn't – so neither of us said much when Mom tried to make conversation. When she brought out a special cake for dessert, and still neither of us said anything, she looked hurt, and of course, that made things worse. Finally, after Grandpa had finished his piece and gone to pace around the living room, she put down her fork with a little clank.

'I thought there weren't going to be secrets.'

'There aren't!' said Colin, much too fast.

'Come on,' said Mom. 'I know something's wrong, and you know there's no way we can fix it if you don't tell me what it is. Is it school?'

Colin's face told me he'd die rather than make her worry about him, so I said, 'No, everything's fine at school; it just takes time to make friends.'

'Yeah,' said Colin. 'Really.'

Mom looked from one of us to the other, and I could see we hadn't fooled her. But she just said, 'Maybe we should read something aloud. We haven't done that for a long time.'

'That's a good—' Something crashed in the living room. We all jumped up, and there was

Grandpa, piling a chair on top of the coffee table. He'd started doing things like that after we moved; Mom said maybe he was trying to make the new house look the way the old house did. Anyway, it took us a long time to persuade him that the furniture was all right where it was, and by then, it was time for Colin and me to go to bed.

'I mean it about reading,' said Mom as she came in to kiss me good night. 'We'll start tomorrow, no matter what. Think of something exciting that we'll all enjoy.'

'OK,' I said. 'Mom . . .'

'Yes?'

I was all ready to talk to her about Colin, but when she leaned over to look at me, I saw how tired she was, and how she hadn't put on make-up or done her hair the pretty way she usually did. So I just said, 'Nothing, Mom. I love you.'

She started to give me a big hug, but there was a thump downstairs, so she hurried out the door, instead.

I went to sleep feeling bad – about Colin, about Grandpa, about Mom – but a dream came along and saved me. I'd had it so often that in the middle of it I always told myself I was dreaming, but it started with something that had happened once. I was in Pennsylvania, and I was riding Fay, the Smithes' pony, who was pretty big for me, then. It was my first lesson in riding a course, like they do in showjumping classes, instead of jumping one or two jumps at a time. Fay and I were trotting in circles; Grandpa was lowering huge jumps in the stadium jumping ring to two feet. That was the height I'd been jumping all week, but my hands were so sweaty I could hardly hold the reins.

Finally, Grandpa beckoned us over to where he was. 'Now, you're going to take the little poles first – see there? Then the bricks. Then the brush.' He went on through six jumps, and I sat there, feeling my heart bang-bang-bang and wondering how I'd ever manage Fay, who got pretty excited when we jumped just two little poles.

Grandpa looked at me. 'Sure and you're not frightened, a fine jumper like you?'

'Of course not!' I said. And to prove it, I set Fay off at a trot towards the first jump, without even making a circle first. We made it over fine, but then Fay realized there were going to be more jumps, and she took off. I tried to pull her down, but she shook her head back and forth and tore on to the bricks, which seemed to grow as we got closer . . .

'Hold it!' called Grandpa after we'd shot over it. 'That'll never do!'

Fay slowed down when she heard his voice, and I trotted her over to him.

Grandpa wiped my eyes with his red bandana. 'Tell me, what do I do when a horse goes too strong over jumps, not being able to hold him with only one good hand?'

'I don't know . . .' I sniffled. But then I realized I did. 'Oh. Is that when you sing?'

'That's m'girl. And how fast do I sing?'

I thought about it. 'Sort of slowly, like a collected canter.'

He thumped me on the shoulder. 'Now didn't I tell you,' he said to the air, 'that this is the smartest six-year-old gal that ever rode a horse? You've hit right on it – you sing at the speed you want the horse to go. And she will.'

I looked sideways at Fay's determined pony face. 'You sure?'

'Find out for yourself,' he said. 'I'll sing with you, to start. Get a canter, now.'

I made a circle at a trot, then asked for a canter. Behind me, Grandpa started up:

When Irish eyes are smilin'
Sure 'tis like a lark in spring . . .

There was no way you could NOT sing when Grandpa sang that, even when you were frozen solid with fear, so I joined in. My voice squeaked, but Fay must have heard it, because she settled into a nice canter, and we went over the first jump so smoothly I hardly felt it.

In the lilt of Irish laughter
You can hear the angels sing . . .

We took the second jump just right, and the third, and the fourth . . . and suddenly there was just the song, and Fay and me jumping fences in some green and wonderful place that went on and on, knowing we could jump for ever without getting hurt or scared.

When Irish eyes are happy,
All the world is bright and gay.
And when Irish eyes are smilin'
Sure they'll steal your heart away!

'Very nice,' said a dry voice from somewhere very near.

I opened my eyes and saw people standing by my bed, which meant I'd woken everybody up again by singing in my sleep. 'I'm sorry, Mom. Sorry, Colin. Didn't mean to—' Then I realized it wasn't Mom and Colin; there were three of them, one very tall, and two about my height.

They were wearing cloaks with hoods, and the stuff around their eyes lit the room with a strange orange glow. I dived back under my covers, hoping I was still dreaming.

'Are you afraid, Child of Lugh?' said Cathbad's voice. 'I have brought two minions to help you continue your mission, but if you have decided that the dangers—'

'—of course I'm not afraid!' I said, jumping up and groping for my glasses. 'Should I get dressed?'

'It will make no difference,' said Cathbad. 'You will be out with night-elves, so you will have to clothe yourself in many different shapes.'

I pulled on my sweatshirt and made a sloppy pony-tail with the first rubber band my hand fell on. 'I'll have to what?'

One of the night-elves laughed. 'You'll have to do what we do. Watch.' Suddenly, there wasn't an elf where he was standing, but a bush. Then the bush changed into a cow, which got halfway changed into an elephant . . . the floor started to creak, and Cathbad said something in a language I couldn't understand. The cow-elephant changed back into the elf.

'Let's go and find your brother,' said Cathbad, stretching out his hand.

When I took it, the room suddenly got larger,

and I was flying with three bugs, out my door and past the hall nightlight, which seemed much more beautiful and interesting than it ever had before. When we got to Colin's door, we landed and crawled underneath it; then I was standing by his bed between the elves. One of them took my hand in his left hand and touched Colin's shoulder with his right. All of a sudden, I could see Colin's dream – not the way you see things in a movie, but in my head, as if I were dreaming, too.

Colin and I were in our car, with me in the front passenger seat and him in the back, which meant I'd won the toss. We started down a steep hill, with a curve by a tree – and he suddenly realized he was supposed to be driving. He leaned over the front seat and turned the wheel so we missed the tree, but we kept going down, and his feet were still in the back, so he couldn't reach the brakes. He yanked on the hand-brake, but nothing happened, and we shot towards a brick wall, going faster and faster . . . the dream popped, and Colin turned over and hit out at the elf next to me.

'Easy there, m'lad,' said the elf, backing away.

Colin blinked at us in the light from the street lamp outside. 'Sarah, is that you?'

'I think so,' I said, looking down – and so far

as I could see, it was me, exactly as I'd been in my room. 'Cathbad is here with two night-elves.'

'Great,' he muttered sleepily, grabbing his sweatshirt. 'Where are we going?'

'To the world of visions, eventually,' said Cathbad. 'I will not be with you; I have a ceremony to attend to. But the elves will accompany you. This one is Hob, and this one is Lob.'

'Glad to meet you,' we said, shaking hands. As soon as our fingers touched theirs, all four of us slipped through the crack at the side of Colin's window and spun down into a pile of leaves. We lay there a moment, quivering; then a big puff of wind sent us whirling around the streetlight and spinning up over the warehouses. On the far side of the tracks, it dropped us, and we went scuttling through the used-car lots into a street filled with tumble-down houses, circled one of them a couple of times, and fluttered down lightly on its porch.

'All right, little ones,' said Hob's voice. 'Through the keyhole – here we go.'

Something pulled me up, and a tunnel whizzed by on all sides of me . . . then a long, strange-smelling hall tilted a few feet below me, then I zipped through another tunnel . . . and when I caught my breath, I was standing next to

Colin in the shadows of a room lit by a TV and nothing else. It was supposed to be a living room, I think, but it was so full of unsorted laundry, half-eaten TV dinners, soda cans, bottles, and other junk, that you could hardly tell.

'Sorry to be so quick,' said Hob, 'but I didn't want to run into him.'

'Her,' corrected Colin, pointing to a woman asleep on the couch.

Hob looked at Lob, and they both smiled – not very nicely. 'Oh, she's no problem,' he said. 'State she's in, she wouldn't see us even if we were visible. No, it's him that's the—'

The door to the living room slammed back against the wall. Colin and I shrank into the corner as a man stumbled through it. The woman woke up and gave him a dirty look.

'Shut it, can't you?'

The man slammed the door shut. 'The light's on upstairs. Where've you been?'

'Where've *you* been, is more like it?' she said. 'And where did you get the money to go drinking?'

'From a cash register.'

'Yeah? Whose?'

The man started up the creaking staircase without answering. That made her angry, and I thought she was going to run after him, but after she sat up, all she did was feel around the floor for the glass by the leg of the coffee table. When she found it, she pressed it against her forehead and shut her eyes.

Colin looked at me, and I knew what he was thinking, but Lob just laughed. 'Don't worry,' he said. 'We'd never show visions like hers to beginners. We're going upstairs. Slowly, now.'

He led the way, and we followed. About half-way up, we saw the man standing in an open doorway, huge and black against the light that came from inside.

'Now, look,' he said. 'We talked it over. We agreed. Supper, homework, bed. No reading on school nights – right?'

If there was an answer, we couldn't hear it.

'So what are you doing?' he demanded.

This time, I was sure there was no answer. How could there be? Questions like that aren't really questions; they're accusations with a question-mark at the end.

The man took a step further into the room and held out his hand. Somebody I couldn't see slowly held out a book and whispered, 'Don't tear it up. Please. It's from the library.'

The man looked at it foggily, then threw it on the floor and stumbled forward, grabbing for something. There was a yanking noise, and the light went out. A moment later, the man came out, carrying a bedside lamp.

'There,' he said. 'That takes care of it.' He stood there a minute longer with his free hand on the jamb and his head hanging down; then he shuffled through another door, and we heard the sort of muffled thump a bed makes when somebody lands on it hard.

Hob listened for a couple of minutes, then led the way up the rest of the stairs and into the little room. There wasn't much in it: a bed, a little table (probably for the lamp), and a desk and chair under the dirty window. I expected the kid in there to be under the covers, crying, but the bed was empty. A girl was sitting cross-legged on the desk, shivering. Something about the way she looked out at the clouds that were blowing across the half-moon — watching them, but not seeing them — seemed awfully familiar.

'Oh!' I whispered suddenly. 'It's Tiffany!' And I was just thinking, poor Tiffany — she lives *here*? when the elves each took our right hands in their right hands and touched Tiffany with their lefts. Suddenly there was light everywhere, as late afternoon sun shone on a deep green field with ancient trees standing here and there. The field was filled with horses — chestnuts, greys, blacks, bays — all with perfectly groomed, shining coats.

In the middle of the herd stood Tiffany, patting mares, stroking little foals, talking, talking, talking to them all in the kind of murmur Grandpa used to use. They nuzzled her dark, curly hair and rubbed their heads against her shoulder, looking perfectly happy. As Tiffany patted them, I caught a glimpse of her face, and I thought, that's funny, I never noticed Tiffany was so pretty . . . *Wham*. I was back in the room again, with lights blinking dizzily in my head the way they do when you stand up too fast. For a second, I couldn't figure out what had happened; then I felt cheated, because Tiffany was still in her wonderful daydream, and Colin was there, too, because Lob was still connecting him, but Hob had dropped me. I was just about to grab his hand – I really wanted to know where Tiffany was – when he raised it and shook his fist.

'Daydreams!' he hissed. 'Completely out of our area! And on top of it all – *us*, missing the ceremony!'

'Outrageous, that's what it is,' said Lob, dropping Colin's hand and raising both his fists. 'Treat us like dogs, They do.'

Next to me, Colin shook his head, and I steadied him as he staggered. 'Hey,' he muttered, 'it's that mousy girl in your class, isn't it? I didn't know she liked horses!'

'Sh!' I whispered, pointing to the elves. 'Something's up. Look zonked and listen.'

That wasn't hard; the elves were so excited it surprised me that Tiffany couldn't feel them.

'But the little ones?' said Hob. 'We can't *leave* them. And mortals at a ceremony—!'

'—They're under Protection. Doesn't that mean they're safe in Faerie, for as long as their mission lasts?'

'Surely. But remember what Cathbad said? Short journeys. A little way at a—'

'That's not *our* idea!' blurted Colin.

The elves whirled around, smiling elvish smiles I didn't like, but nothing stops Colin once he gets going. 'Listen,' he said. 'Don't think for a *minute* we wanted short journeys. We accepted them because that's all Cathbad would offer, but we want to go to Faerie!'

Lob cocked an eyebrow over his orange-glowing eye. 'Do you, now?'

He looked dangerous; but he also looked interested. Suddenly, I had an inspiration. 'It's not just that we *want* to go,' I said. 'It's the Rules. They're more powerful than Cathbad, aren't they?'

'To be sure,' said Hob, looking shocked that somebody would ask.

'Well then,' I said. 'Don't you see what that

means? The Rules say you faeries have to help us with our mission, and our mission is to go to Faerie! So if you take us there, you're obeying the Rules even if you're disobeying Cathbad.'

The elves' eyes glowed fiercely as they looked at each other – so fiercely that they lit the room. On the desk, Tiffany stirred a little and looked around.

'Ach!' muttered Lob. 'She'll be seeing us soon if we're not off.'

'Quickly, then,' said Lob. They pulled hand-kerchiefs out of their pockets and stepped towards us, leering. 'We'll have to take you by our route, so just for safety's sake—'

'Hey!' said Colin, hitting out at Hob. 'You don't have to tie us!'

But the elves grew half-way to the ceiling, and before we could argue or struggle any more, they'd blindfolded us. A moment later, we were whooshing through another tunnel, only this one felt much larger than a keyhole, and in spite of the cloth over my ears, I could hear it was filled with strange noises: the roar of trucks on a faraway road, the clickety-click of a night train, the barking of dogs, the echo of voices drifting in from the street. They were such sleepy sounds that I thought maybe I was dreaming after all . . . but then we landed with a thump that convinced me I was awake. I slipped the blind-fold off and straightened my glasses, looking around dizzily.

We were standing at the bottom of a hill ringed by a line of bonfires, and between the fires, there were shadows dancing to music that made the back of my neck prickle. They weren't human shadows. Some of them were tall and thin, wearing beautiful long dresses, or hats with long feathers, and capes fastened with clasps that shone in the firelight. Others were short and wiry, and had bells on their toes and ears. But most of them were animal shadows: dogs with horses' hooves, cats with gleaming eyes and tails that bristled three times their size, pigs that danced gracefully on legs much too long, sheep that pranced like horses, and cows with enormous shoulders and necks.

'Where on earth are we, do you think?' I shouted in Colin's ear.

'No place on earth,' he shouted back. 'This has got to be Faerie – and not just the Outskirts, either. You *did* it! You got them to bring us! That bit about the Rules was brilliant!'

'It was luck,' I said modestly.

'Yeah, but it worked!' he said. 'And now all we have to do is find Grandpa.'

I looked at the dancing shadows, wondering

where the elves had gone. 'How are we going to do that?'

'Just start hunting, I guess. You go that way, I'll go—'

'If we do that, when one of us finds Grandpa, the other one will . . .'

'OK, together, then,' he said. 'Which way do you want to go?'

I wasn't sure what difference it was going to make, but I pointed towards the top of the hill, and we started towards the fires. I had thought Faerie fires might not be hot, but as we got closer, I began to wish I hadn't put on my sweatshirt, and by the time we got to the outer circle, I wriggled out of its sleeves and pulled it over my head. As I came out from under it, a golden-cloaked shadow danced up to us. Suddenly, it stood still to look at us, and I saw it was Mongan.

'I'll be blessed – it's the Children of Lugh!' he said, and he didn't sound pleased. 'How did you get here?'

'I don't know,' I said. 'Cathbad told Hob and Lob to take us to the land of visions, but I heard them say they were missing something because of us, so we . . .' I looked at Colin for help, but fortunately, Mongan spoke before we had to say any more.

'Night-elves, eh?' he said, shaking his head. 'I

might have known. Totally unreliable, they are. Cathbad should have known better than to—'

'—Holy tomato!' interrupted Colin. 'Look at that!'

I looked – well, stared is more like it. Because even at the Smithes' farm, I'd never seen anything so magnificent. A huge grey horse was cantering towards the bonfires with a stride that made the ground tremble. As he came nearer, he snorted at the flames and began to change leads every few strides, slower and slower – until he broke into a high, springing trot, his mane rippling like sea foam over his crest and his tail held high behind him. I had only seen a horse trot like that without a rider, but he had one: a faery with long red hair that flowed from under a circlet of silver and over the shoulders of his sea-green cloak. He was the only person I'd ever seen who rode the way Grandpa did, as if he were part horse himself. As we watched, a pig blundered almost under the horse's feet, and he reared high, scattering animals and lesser faeries right and left. The faery rider brought him down, steadied him – and he trotted on up the hill, hesitating so long between each stride that it seemed he was floating.

'Wow!' I breathed. 'That's really something!'

Mongan grinned. 'Always puts on a show, my old man.'

'Your old man!' said Colin, staring. 'But you said your father was Manannan mac Lir!'

'And why would I lie?' said Mongan. 'It's nothing to be ashamed of, surely.'

'No, no,' said Colin, blushing. 'I meant that if that's really Manannan mac Lir, then the horse must be *his* horse . . . Enbharr[1].'

'Yes, more's the pity,' said Mongan. 'They've spoken to Dad about it, to be sure – schooled as he is, he's half wild still, and They're afraid he'll run amok one fine evening. But Dad's only part tame himself, having powers no other faery has; that makes it hard to reason with him.'

We nodded, but neither of us was really listening. All our lives, we'd known Enbharr – not the real one, of course, but the magical sea stallion in Grandpa's stories. Grandpa said he was what every horseman spent his life looking for but never found: the perfect horse, with the power, spirit and speed of a thousand horses combined. Sometimes, when he saw a really spectacular performance in the ring, he'd say, *'Sure and that'll be one of Enbharr's mortal children.'* I felt my eyes mist up as we watched Enbharr halt by the topmost fire, his muscles tensed to bolt, but standing absolutely still as the faery vaulted off.

[1]   Pronounced *En-var*.

Wherever Grandpa was in Faerie, I hoped he'd seen that horse . . . I blinked, then stared. The spot where Enbharr had been standing was empty.

'Hey!' said Colin. 'Where'd he go?'

'To the Fields,' said Mongan matter-of-factly. 'He'd never stand still for the whole ceremony, so Dad sends him there and calls him up when it's over. Hard on the horse, *I* say, being magicked about like that; but it does keep him from causing mischief.'

I was about to ask where the Fields were, when a trumpet sounded from the top of the hill. Mongan frowned; then taking each of us by the hand, he strode up the hill between the fires, so fast that we had to run to keep up.

'Where are we going?' puffed Colin.

'To the event the night-elves deserted you to watch,' said Mongan. 'I suppose they think of it as part of their specialty, since it's the ceremony in which the great Seer dreams of our next king, but of course, they are allowed no nearer than the fires; it's a matter only for the Sidhe.' He looked down at us sternly. 'That means that you have no right to be there; I'm bringing you only because I let you look at that foolish horse instead of sending you back to your world. So you must be absolutely quiet. If the Sidhe realize you are present, They will be very angry.'

I looked up the hill – and I'd have given up everything, even seeing Enbharr, to be back home. In front of us gaped the entrance to a cave, held up by huge stones that made it look as if the hill had been opened. On either side of the entrance stood the tall shadows we'd seen dancing by the fire. They weren't shadows, now, though: their clothes were made of gold and silver cloth, and they wore circlets in their hair. All of them had long, thin faces, and eyes that made me shiver, though they looked solemn, not cruel. Even if Mongan hadn't said they were in charge of the ceremony, I would have known who they were: the Sidhe – the most powerful and mysterious of the faeries. Mongan stepped among them, holding my hand so tightly that it hurt; but I didn't even think of pulling away.

The music stopped, and the dancing shadows stood still next to the fires below us. In the silence, Manannan and three other tall faeries came out of the cave and walked between the two lines of the Sidhe, carrying a wooden bed that was attached to two long poles. On the bed, leaning back against piles of furs, was the Seer, dressed in long robes that shone in the firelight. Behind him, so dark that all I could see was his white beard, came Cathbad, carrying a bowl of something that steamed. The four faeries put the bed down on four huge stones; Cathbad stepped to its side, raising the bowl high above his head and chanting in the language I couldn't understand. At the end of the chant, he lowered the bowl and gave it to the Seer. Slowly, slowly, the Seer lifted the bowl to his lips.

For what seemed a long time, everything was absolutely still; then the Seer lowered the bowl and gave it back to Cathbad. Somewhere, a harp started to play, and the four faeries picked up the bed and carried it into the hill. The Sidhe followed them, two by two. When the last pair disappeared, Mongan bent over us. 'Very quiet,' he whispered. 'And don't let go.'

We nodded, scared to death, and followed him through the cave entrance into a hall whose ceiling arched all the way to the top of the hill. It smelled like a garden after it rains, and everything was lit by torches. The faeries put the bed on four other stones, and the Sidhe stood around it in a circle. We stood on each side of Mongan, still clutching his hands. And although we didn't move, I felt us getting closer and closer to the Seer. Suddenly, though we were touching only Mongan, not the Seer, we saw – or maybe we had – the dream.

We were standing in a circle of tall thin stones at the top of a hill, looking down across a valley to the sea. There was an oak grove in the valley, and out of it came a procession of people in brightly coloured cloaks. Some of them were leading enormous white dogs with red ears, some were carrying birds on their wrists, and some were riding beautiful silver horses, and they must have had bells on their toes, because there were ringing sounds at every step. In the midst of the crowd was a chariot like the ones Grandpa had described in his stories. It was pulled by two prancing horses with silver manes, and it was decorated with gold and jewels that flashed in the sunlight. Driving the chariot was a long-haired man in a tunic, holding the reins and a pointed stick. Behind him, taller than he was, and much grander, stood a man in a red cloak, holding a huge spear in one hand and a golden shield in the other.

He looked up to the circle of stones where we were standing, and for a minute, he looked familiar, though I didn't know anybody who looked exactly like that. He spoke to the driver, and the driver steered the horses through the crowd. When they passed the last person, he touched the horses with a stick, and they came towards us at a gallop. The tall man laughed and looked up at us; then he put down his shield and waved. His hand glinted in the sun – not because he was wearing rings, but because his arm was made of silver. Suddenly I knew who he was.

'Grandpa,' I whispered — then I trembled all over for fear the Sidhe had heard me.

But there were no Sidhe, and there was no cave. I was sitting up in bed, blinking because someone had just switched on my bedroom light.

'Grandpa,' I said, frowning. 'Why did you turn my light on? It's the middle of the night.'

Grandpa gave me his lovely, empty smile. 'Breakfast?' he said hopefully.

I looked at my clock; it was a little past twelve. 'Grandpa, it's not time for breakfast yet. Would you like me to take you back to bed?'

'Breakfast,' he said stubbornly.

I got up and started to take him downstairs. Halfway down the hall, Colin slipped out his door, all lit up. 'Boy oh boy! You *got* him! Grandpa, we've been looking and looking . . . !'

'Breakfast time,' said Grandpa.

Colin stared . . . then he took Grandpa's hook gently and went downstairs with us. As we passed the living room, we saw Mom sitting at our father's old roll-top desk. She wasn't writing letters; she was asleep with her head pillowed on her arms. Grandpa started towards her, but we coaxed him into the kitchen and got him cold cereal and milk. Neither of us ate. Or talked.

When he was done, we led him up the back stairs. I was afraid he'd fuss about going to his room, but he went just fine; he even lay down on his bed when I asked him to. I covered him up, and we both kissed his forehead. 'Good night, Grandpa. Stay there until morning, OK?'

'OK,' he said. And he closed his eyes.

We waited to make sure he wouldn't go and wake Mom, then we tiptoed out into the hall.

'You saw him, right?' said Colin. 'In that chariot? That means he's really in Faerie.'

'You can't say "really" when it was a dream.'

'But it wasn't! We couldn't both dream the same thing!'

'Not *our* dream – when he was in the chariot, he was in someone *else's* dream.'

'Which means . . ?' His face fell. 'Oh, I see.' He turned to his door without a word.

I just *couldn't* let him go like that. So I said, 'They're faeries, remember? And They think if they keep confusing and scaring us, we won't go back to the Otherworld. But if we don't let being mixed up or scared stop us . . .'

'Right,' he said, setting his chin. 'We'll get to him. Next time, we'll bring him home.'

I gave him a thumbs-up and went to bed. And lay awake, wishing I believed he was right.

5 Captain Hook

I felt funny when I sat next to Tiffany on the bus the next morning. I mean, if I'd had a family like hers, I sure wouldn't have wanted anybody to know it – and there I'd been last night, spying on her. *If*, of course, I really had been at her house, or any of the other places we'd gone. But I didn't dare think about that, because next thing I knew, I'd start thinking I couldn't tell the difference between what was real and what I thought was real because I saw it in my mind, which was scary. So instead of thinking, I said, 'Tiffany, do you like horses?'

All of a sudden, she looked like a different person. 'Oh, yes! Do you?'

I nodded, feeling even funnier than I had before. 'I used to ride all summer; my grandfather trained showjumpers.'

'Your grandfather is a *trainer*?'

'Not any more. He's . . . retired. But all real horse people know who he is.'

'Wow!' she said, and her face was all lit up. 'Tell me about him.'

'Well, his father worked on a race-track in Ireland, and he came over here when Grandpa was a kid. First Grandpa worked racehorses, but he and his father didn't get along, I guess, and he ran away when he was fourteen. He got a job as an exercise boy for a man who trained showjumpers; after a while, he got so good that people paid him to ride their horses in important shows. He won so often that he got to try out for the Olympic team, even though he was too poor to own that kind of horse himself—'

'– You can *do* that?'

'Sure you can. If you're as good as Grandpa was, people with Olympic horses *want* you to compete on them. So they pay for all the expensive stuff, and you just ride.'

'Boy,' she murmured.

'Well, it's not as easy as it sounds,' I said. 'You don't just get to ride the Olympic horses. When Grandpa was eighteen, nineteen, twenty, he had to ride ten horses a day, sometimes more – and feed, groom, and muck out stalls as well. He says he never got enough sleep.'

'Yeah, but he made it to the Olympics, so it was worth it.'

'Actually, he *didn't* make it. In the try-outs, he was riding this really wonderful mare named Second Chance, and he and a big-name rider both had perfect rounds, so there was a jump-off for time. The other rider went clear in really good time, so the only way Grandpa could beat him was to do a perfect round extra fast. Second Chance could feel that Grandpa was nervous – that's what he says, anyway – and she got all excited. As they went around the course, Grandpa was having a harder and harder time holding her, and he was scared about the time, so when they came to the last triple bar, he let her go a little too fast, and she took off wrong, and . . .'

Tiffany hid her face in her hands. 'They fell,' she whispered. 'Disqualified.'

'More than that! It was a terrible fall. Second Chance got the last rail caught between her front feet, and she flipped over on top of Grandpa, landing sort of sideways so they banged into the side of the jump. Grandpa's right arm got crushed, but he didn't even notice, because he was so torn up about Second Chance.'

'Oh no! What happened to her?'

'She broke her back – and it was really awful.

She kept struggling to get up, in spite of everything Grandpa and the vets could do. Finally, she collapsed, and when Grandpa stroked her, she looked at him as if she were trying to say she was sorry they couldn't finish the course. He says he broke down and cried in front of everyone. And then . . .'

Tiffany looked out the window. 'Don't tell me what they did. I know.'

The bus pulled into school, and we got off, sort of quietly. As we started up the stairs to our classroom, Tiffany asked, 'What about your grandfather's arm?'

'It was so badly smashed that they had to take it off at the elbow,' I said. 'They made him an artificial arm – actually, it's a hook – and after a couple of months, he could do just about anything. But he couldn't ride any more.'

'Criminy,' she breathed. 'And he'd been good enough for the Olympics!'

'Well, he could ride; he just couldn't do showjumping. At first, he says he thought it was the end of him. But one day, his hook glinted in the sun, and he suddenly thought of Nuadu of the Silver Arm.'

Tiffany frowned. 'Of whom?'

'Nuadu. He was king of the Tuatha de Danaan, the Irish gods. He lost an arm in a battle

with the firbolg, and so had to give up his king-
ship because a king of the gods had to be perfect.
But after seven years, the great healer and smith
of all the gods made him a silver arm, and he
became king again. When Grandpa remembered
that story, he realized he *could* go on, just differently. If he couldn't go to the Olympics, he could
train horses that did. So he—'

The bell rang, and we hurried to our seats. But
when Tiffany went up to the front for her math
group, she slipped me a note and kind of waited.
I opened it quick: *There is a secret place on the playground. We could talk about horses there.* I nodded,
and she scooted up to the front.

Tiffany's secret place was a piece of storm
drain set between two of the scraggly trees that
lined the fence between the school and the apart-
ment houses that backed on it. Kids were
supposed to play on it, but there wasn't much
you could do with it, so nobody went over there.
When you sat inside it, it made your voice sound
funny, but it was a great place to talk. We talked
all through recess; and from the questions she
asked about Grandpa and the farm and the
horses, I knew she'd studied riding with a really
good teacher, and I kept waiting for her to tell
me about it. But she didn't, which was strange –
so strange that a little radar inside me told me

whatever she was keeping secret was connected to the way her parents were, and I should Keep Out. So the next recess, I asked her what horse books she'd read, which turned out to be just the thing, because we'd read different ones and it was library day. We both went home with a stack of new ones, and the next few days we talked about them, and pretty soon I felt so much better about school that I forgot Colin wasn't feeling better, too – at least, I forgot until the day after Veterans' Day when we got off the bus after school and I noticed his lip was swollen.

'Colin! Have you been . . . ?'

''Course not,' he mumbled, stuffing his hands in his pockets. We walked up the hill without another word, until we got to the side door and he looked at me. 'Don't tell Mom.'

'Of course not!' Then I remembered how big some of the boys in his class were. 'How'd it go?'

'Piece of cake, as Grandpa would say. No official winner – Mr Stegeth broke it up – but it took him a long time to get there, and I'd just about finished the job.'

'I'll say it took you a long time to get here,' said Mom, opening the door. 'I was beginning to wonder where you were.'

'You shouldn't worry,' said Colin. 'Sometimes the bus is late, that's all.'

We went in and made peanut butter sandwiches, and I was just thinking we had gotten pretty good at not telling Mom things that would upset her, when Grandpa wandered into the kitchen and patted Colin on the head.

'Hi,' he started – then he saw Colin's knuckles, and he raised his hand and his hook and punched the air. 'Watch eyes, think feet,' he muttered, shuffling the way he had when he'd practised with us in Pennsylvania.

Mom spun around from the refrigerator. 'Dad,' she said firmly. 'Colin does *not*— Colin! what happened to your hand?'

'Colin win?' asked Grandpa, smiling and hitting the air again.

Mom walked across the kitchen and yanked Colin's right hand from behind his back. After one look, she marched him up the back stairs.

Grandpa was still stepping around the kitchen like a boxer, which bugged me, so I pulled a horse magazine I'd been sharing with Tiffany out of my backpack and showed it to him. Pretty soon, he was looking at the pictures and eating my sandwich, so I was free.

Upstairs, Mom and Colin were in the bathroom, and as I tiptoed down the hall, I heard Mom say, 'It's absolutely *not necessary* for men to settle differences with their fists when they have brains.'

'You wouldn't say that if you'd been there,' said Colin sulkily.

'I certainly would have. You're old enough to walk away when somebody insults you.'

'I do, Mom – honest! But this time . . . well, look. One of the guys said this house was so slummy that for the last ten years, every single renter had left it after a week—'

'– It isn't slummy! It's run-down, but it's beauti—'

'– Sure, sure – but *listen*, OK? He said the *reason* we had to live in the house was that nobody else in town would rent to us, because my grandfather was just like the warehouses people, only worse, and all the real estate people knew the only way to keep him out of trouble was to chain him up in the back yard! You wouldn't want me to let somebody get away with saying things like that about Grandpa, would you?'

For a moment, there was no sound at all; then Mom sighed. 'It was a terrible thing to say, Colin,' she said, in a voice that shook a little. 'There's no denying that. Still, the best way to stop that kind of talk is not to let anybody know that it gets to you.' The first-aid kit clicked shut. 'You should have known better than to tell them Grandpa was—'

'– I never in the world told them!' said Colin. 'The guy who said it was Joe Butler. His dad rents a lot of places in town, and I guess our real estate lady told him about Grandpa when Joe was around.' He sniffed. 'Joe's big stuff Downstairs, and he's mad at me because I quit hanging around with him and the other boys who make trouble.'

'What's this about Downstairs?' asked Mom.

Uh-oh. I backed up a couple of steps, then hurried into the bathroom, making lots of noise. 'Mom, I have Grandpa settled with a magazine. Didn't you want to go shopping?'

Mom looked at her watch. 'I guess I'd better, if we're going to eat dinner. All right, we'll talk about this later.'

But we didn't, because she got caught in rush-hour traffic and didn't get home until after six, and then Grandpa spilled his plate all over the floor at dinner and started to cry about it, and by the time Mom and I got him calmed down, Colin had done the dishes and gone to bed.

The next day, as I was going back to my seat after reading group, I looked out the window, and I saw three boys who sat at the back of our bus step out of the four-square line and walk to the edge of the playground, where some man had stopped to watch the kids. A second later, I saw Colin running after them, waving his hands.

'Sit down, Sarah,' said Miss Turner, glaring at me.

I went to my seat, but the longer I sat, the more I thought about Colin's fight, and the more I wondered what he was up to right then. Finally, I couldn't stand it any more, and I got up to sharpen my pencil. When I looked out the window, I froze; the man who had been on the edge of the playground was close enough to recognize, now. It was Grandpa – and Colin was tugging on his good hand, trying to pull him away from a bunch of laughing boys.

I sat down quickly and raised my hand. Miss Turner looked up from her group. 'Yes?'

'May I go to the bathroom?'

She sighed. 'All right. But tomorrow, please try to wait until—'

I was out the door and half-way down the stairs before she finished. On the ground floor, I raced around the corner beyond the office – and smashed into somebody, so hard that he staggered backwards against the lockers. As I crashed to the floor, I thought, *oh no, it's Mr Beeker*! But for once I'd gotten lucky: it was Mr Crewes.

'Sarah Madison – human cannonball,' he said, helping me up. 'Don't you know you're not supposed to run in the . . . ?' Then he took a good look at me. 'Is something wrong?'

'It's my grandfather,' I said. 'He's on the play-ground, and I've got to go get him.' I tried to run, but he stepped in front of me.

'Walk, Sarah. It's nice for your grandfather to pay the school a visit, but it's hardly a national emergency.'

'No, no – it *is* an emergency!' I began to cry, which is a stupid thing to do in an emergency, but I couldn't make myself stop. 'He's not crazy, exactly, but he gets mixed up . . .'

Mr Crewes's eyebrows shot up, but not like he doubted me. 'You mean, he thinks school's out and he's come to meet you and your brother?'

'Uh-uh. He doesn't even know where the school is. It's that he esc— I mean, he goes for walks, sometimes, and then he can't find his way home, and this time he must have just wandered on and on and on.' I wiped my eyes with my wrist. 'Mom's probably looking all over for him, and maybe she's even called the police – she said she'd do that next time we couldn't find him, because he doesn't understand traffic any more – but she'd never think he'd come this far, and now the police won't know where *she* is, and the boys on the playground are teasing him, and Colin's all by himself . . . Please, please let me get out there!'

'You bet,' he said. 'Mr Stegeth is on play-ground duty; get him to help you and Colin bring your grandfather to the office. I'll call the police and tell them to look for your mom, then I'll come out.' He handed me his handkerchief. 'What does your mom look like?'

'She has reddish-brown-blond hair, like me, only she's pretty – her hair's short, so it curls, and she doesn't wear glasses, usually – and she's probably wearing her blue jacket.'

'Got that,' he said. 'Off you go, now.'

'Thanks a lot,' I said, and ran to the play-ground door. Mr Stegeth was standing in the foyer, talking to Miss Fitzgerald, the teacher in charge of the Detention Room. I jogged his elbow, but he told me (not very nicely) not to interrupt, so I ran outside. And it was a good thing I did; there were lots of boys around Grandpa now. As I raced across the playground, I found myself thinking of the picture in the Smithes' big entry hall, of a stag surrounded by dogs, only I think you were supposed to be rooting for the dogs when you looked at it, and I was definitely not rooting for these boys.

'Hey! He's got a hook!' shouted one of them as I got to the edge of the group.

'Captain Hook! Captain Hook!' yelled a boy on the far side. All the kids laughed and started making brilliant remarks like, 'Where's the crocodile?' or 'Where's Tinkerbell?'

Then a boy with a big shiner said, 'He doesn't need Tinkerbell. Colin's his little fairy.'

Everybody shut up, waiting to see what Colin would do. I edged to the centre to keep him from doing it, but before I got there, I heard him say, 'Joe, let me take him to the office, OK? He's sick.'

'He sure is!' said Joe, slicking back his hair. 'Sick in the head.'

They all laughed again, and just as I got to the middle, Joe walked up to Grandpa and touched his silver arm. 'Hey, Captain – why don't you talk to us?'

Grandpa whirled around and glared at him. 'Stupid boys!' he said. 'Go away.'

'Hey!' said Joe, grinning. 'Colin's old man talks baby talk! Let's find him a bottle!'

'Just leave him alone, will you?' said Colin, between his teeth. He turned to Grandpa. 'C'mon, Grandpa – don't pay any attention to him. Let's go inside the school, and I'll call Mom.'

He reached out to take Grandpa's hand, but Grandpa gave him a push that sent him spinning into the circle. 'Bad boy! Bad, bad, bad!'

Everyone stared, first at Grandpa, then at

Colin, who was trying not to cry. Finally, Joe laughed. 'Sure he's who you think he is, Tink? Take a good look, now. Old nuts all look the—'

'Stop it!' I shouted. 'Stop it, stop it, stop it!'

Joe whirled around, but when he saw it was me, he grinned. 'Looky here!' he said. 'It's big sister to the rescue! You're in luck, Tink.'

'Nobody's in luck when you're around!' I said. 'Any of you! Grandpa's sick, and it's really mean to tease him, because he can't fight back. Only jerks pick on somebody like that, and that's what you are – jerks, jerks, jerks!'

The boys around Joe just laughed, but a lot of the others looked ashamed of themselves, and the girls who had clustered around the outside of the circle started to go back to whatever they'd been doing. That was a good sign, so I held out a hand to Grandpa. 'Come on – let's go into the school. Wouldn't you like to see where Colin and I spend the day?'

'School,' he said, frowning. 'This school?'

'Sure,' said Joe, digging his elbow into the guy next to him. 'They teach kids to talk here – maybe you should come.'

'Bad kids,' said Grandpa. 'I teach you!' Raising his hand and hook, he took a couple of steps towards Joe. I grabbed his arm, but I knew I couldn't hold him long.

'Beat it!' I said to Joe. 'I mean it – get out of the way!'

'Oh no!' said Joe, rolling his eyes. 'The old crazy's mad at me. What'll I do?'

'Listen,' said Colin, 'you better stop clowning, or he'll—'

'Waste me?' said Joe, still pretending to look scared. 'Well, at least I got you to protect me, Tink.' And grabbing Colin by the shoulders, he shoved him between himself and Grandpa. 'There,' he said. 'Now, if he kills anybody, it'll be you.' He was laughing, but suddenly he stopped, because Grandpa jerked his arm out of my hand and started forward. And his face . . .

It wasn't just that he looked mad; it was that he changed completely. He was always a big man, but it almost seemed as if he was growing. As he grew, he got a lot younger, until finally he looked like the Grandpa we'd seen in the Seer's dream – except really, really dangerous. His eyes went deep black, and a weird kind of light started to glow all around him, making the rest of the playground seem dark. Suddenly, he raised both his arms and yelled. It was like nothing I'd ever heard before; there were no words, only a long howl that made me shake all over. Some of the kids began to run, but Joe and Colin just stood there, staring.

'Get out of the way!' I screamed – then something soft and black brushed by me, and the air filled with the most beautiful music I had ever heard. Everything stopped: the kids, Grandpa – even the wind. I turned my head very slowly, the way you do in dreams, and I saw someone in a black hooded cloak, holding a silver branch with golden apples hanging from it. I blinked and looked again, but all I saw was Mr Stegeth and Mr Crewes running across the playground.

Before I had time to decide if I was crazy or not, the two teachers were in the middle of the circle, and the kids were melting away. Mr Crewes looked at Mr Stegeth. 'Why don't you get some kickball going, while I see what I can do for Mr Madison.'

'It's not Mr Madison,' said Colin. 'It's Mr O'Brien.'

'Irish, huh?' said Mr Stegeth, smiling at Colin the way people do when they're ashamed of themselves but they don't want to admit it. 'So that's where you get your big mouth . . . Come on, you guys. Let's play ball.' He walked away, laughing with Joe and the others.

Colin doubled up his fists as he watched them go. 'Boy,' he said, 'if Grandpa hadn't been sick, he would have knocked his block off for saying that.'

'Nonsense,' said Mr Crewes, though he looked angry, too. 'He would have known Mr Stegeth was just trying to be funny.'

That showed how little he knew Grandpa; but of course we were too polite to say so.

'Grandpa,' I said, putting an arm around him, 'this is Mr Crewes. He's a teacher.'

Mr Crewes looked quick and held out his left hand to Grandpa. 'Hello, Mr O'Brien,' he said. 'I'm really pleased to meet you. One of my students has told me all about the horses you've trained, and I feel I know you.'

It was as if he had said something magic: Grandpa smiled. 'Horses,' he said, nodding.

A siren wailed on the street, and I was afraid it would distract Grandpa, but Mr Crewes just raised his voice. 'Why don't you come into the school? I could get you a cup of coffee, and you could tell me about your horses.'

The siren got closer; then a police car with all its lights going pulled into the school parking lot and Mom and two cops jumped out of it. Colin and I looked at each other and sighed: all we were going to hear for the next month was that our grandfather had been arrested.

Mom got to us a little before the cops did. 'Oh Dad!' she said, taking his hand. 'I've been so worried! How did you get all the way over here?'

Grandpa smiled at her. 'Home, OK? Tired.'

'Of course,' she said. 'In a police car – won't that be fun?' Then she turned to Colin and me. 'The police said you two saw Grandpa out here and told a teacher to look for me while you stayed with him. That was absolutely the right thing to do. I'm very proud of you.'

'You should be,' said Mr Crewes, and the way he looked at us let us know he'd never tell her there'd been trouble. 'They handled the situation beautifully.'

'Oh, are you the teacher who called?' said Mom, smiling.

He nodded and put out his hand. 'Jim Crewes,' he said; then he looked over his shoulder at the kids, who were beginning to hover around again. 'Let's get your father to the car.'

Mom nodded, and we started across the playground, with Colin, Grandpa and me in the lead, and Mr Crewes and Mom next, and the cops last, keeping everybody else from following. After we had taken a few steps, I saw I should have tried to get us into a different order, because Mom asked Mr Crewes if he knew how Colin was doing, and Mr Crewes told her the school had been trying to get in touch with her about him. There was nothing Colin or I could do, either, because Grandpa seemed to have understood he was going to ride in the police car, and he walked towards it so fast that we got there way ahead of them. When they caught up, I could see from Mom's face that Mr Crewes had told her a lot.

'So if it's OK with you and Colin,' he was saying, 'he and I will talk to Mr Beeker and Mr Stegeth today after school, and I think they'll let Colin work with me, on condition that there be no more . . . er, disruptions in the future.'

'Wow!' exploded Colin. 'You mean, I could be in your class instead of in that old—'

'– We'll have to see, Colin,' cut in Mr Crewes. 'And we'll have to have a chat about the conditions.' He turned to Mom again. 'He'll miss the bus, but don't worry. I'll drive him home.'

'Thank you,' said Mom. Then she turned to us. 'Why didn't you two tell me what was wrong? We could have had all this resolved two weeks ago.'

Colin nudged me, which wasn't fair, because it was his problem. 'Well,' I said, looking down, 'we thought you had enough to cope with at home.'

'Home?' said Grandpa, tapping Mom's arm. 'Now?'

'Take him home,' said Mr Crewes. 'He's had

112

a long morning, and it will take me a couple of days to work things out. Could I stop by Friday and tell you what we've arranged?'

'That would be wonderful,' said Mom. 'Come by around eight.'

'I'll look forward to it,' he said. Then he turned to Colin and me. 'We'd better get back inside, you guys, or somebody will give us a detention.'

Mom gave us both a big hug, so I knew everything was OK; then we hurried back across the empty playground with Mr Crewes. Inside, he gave us passes and hurried off to his class.

'Boy oh boy,' said Colin as we started up the steps together. 'Is he ever a prince!'

'I'll say,' I said. 'Colin, when Joe was clowning . . . did you, um, see anything funny?'

'Funny is the last word I'd use for a creep like Joe,' he said.

'No, I mean funny peculiar. Like fae—'

'Shhh!' he hissed. 'Not here. They might not like it.'

'It's not against the rules to talk in the halls...' I began, but then I realized what 'They' he meant. 'OK,' I said. 'Later.'

He nodded. 'Right after dinner. I was going to show you something connected with Them, anyway. Just you wait – you'll drop your teeth.'

6 A Glamorous Bus Ride

I spent the rest of the school day wondering what Colin had to show me, but when he got home, which he didn't until the 5:15 was long gone, he obviously had other things on his mind. Good things: he was so bouncy that he almost dropped the plates when he helped me set the table. After supper was finally all served and we'd said grace, Mom smiled.

'Well,' she said, 'aren't you going to tell us what happened?'

'Sure am!' said Colin enthusiastically. 'We went to see Mr Beeker and Mr Stegeth, and . . . well, see, ever since I got to Wheelock, Mr Stegeth's been giving me easy math problems. I *told* and *told* him he was wasting my time, but he never listened, so I quit doing them. Just a sec – I'm starved.' He cut his potato in half and stuffed one of the pieces into his mouth.

'I see,' said Mom dryly. 'And I don't suppose it occurred to you, Mr Einstein, that your intellectual objection to the easy problems made Mr Stegeth think you couldn't do them?'

'That's what Mr Crewes said,' mumbled Colin through the potato. 'Only nicely. Then he told Mr Stegeth and Mr Beeker he could "demonstrate my competence" – and he started giving me mental arithmetic problems. First they were pretty easy, but they got tougher, like counting backwards from a hundred by sevens, or multiplying four-digit numbers by twelve.'

'And they were wowed, right?' I said, trying not to sound jealous. Having a math whiz for a brother is a pain.

'You should have seen them!' he said, gulping down the second half of his potato and starting in on his sausage. 'Their eyes looked like saucers! Finally, Mr Beeker said he'd talk to Mr Crewes tomorrow. So I think I'll be able to switch, and that's *neat*, because Mr Crewes went to MIT, like Dad. I know, because he told me when I asked. That means he's a *real* scientist, not just a teacher—'

'Bad boy!' said Grandpa suddenly, thumping his hand on the table.

'Now, Dad,' said Mom soothingly, 'I know

115

Colin isn't minding his manners, but he's excited, and I think just this once—'

'Bad boy,' insisted Grandpa. 'I teach him!'

We all stared at each other; then something clicked in my mind. 'Oh!' I said. 'This morning, when Grandpa visited the school, some of the boys were teasing him, and when Colin tried to stop them, he got Colin mixed up with them, or something, and he—'

'– Right!' said Grandpa, glaring at Colin. 'Horsewhip.'

Mom put her hand on Grandpa's. 'Dad, Sarah's saying you got mixed up. Colin didn't *like* what the bad boys were saying, and he was telling them to stop. That's good, not bad.'

'But you're dead right about those boys, Grandpa,' said Colin. 'They're jerks, and—'

'Quiet!' shouted Grandpa.

Mom threw Colin a look that meant he had better do what Grandpa said, so he shut up and we finished dinner without talking at all. Mom tried to get Colin to talk about Mr Crewes while we did the dishes, but he wouldn't, and when we were done, he went up to his room and closed the door. So much for whatever he'd been going to tell me about Them.

'Oh, dear,' sighed Mom. 'And he was so happy.'

I nodded. 'I sure hope Grandpa doesn't keep *on* mixing him up with Joe and those guys.'

'Oh, no! He won't do that!' said Mom in the voice she used to make it seem as if everything were all right. Colin and I hated that voice, because of course we knew everything *wasn't* all right, but all of a sudden, I realized why she used it. She was scared.

After I went to bed, I lay in the dark a long time, wondering if that could possibly be true, because Mom just wasn't the sort of person who *got* scared. After Dad died, she'd run the family all by herself, including working; all our Maple Street friends' moms had thought that was very brave. Personally, I thought it was braver of her to give up her job when Grandpa couldn't be left alone any more; that scared Colin and me, because we knew her not being able to work made us poor, and we were afraid she'd run out of money altogether, like the warehouse people, before we got old enough to get jobs. But Mom was just as brave about not working as she'd been about working.

We also knew Mom was unscarable because of a trunk we'd found in Grandpa's attic when we were moving him out of his cottage. When we'd opened it to see if the stuff inside it was worth keeping, we'd practically fallen over,

117

because it was filled with big-time trophies and ribbons Mom had won, and pictures of her taking mammoth jumps at Madison Square Garden. We didn't dare mention it, though of course we were dying to know more, because there was this . . . space, I guess you could call it . . . between Mom and Grandpa, and we'd figured out long ago that it had something to do with the fact that Mom didn't ride any more – at all, ever – though you couldn't talk to either her or Grandpa long without realizing she'd been really good once. But that trunk just shouted how tough Mom was, because she couldn't possibly have been *that* good and then *quit* without running into Grandpa's Irish, and we'd never met anybody brave enough to stand up to that.

'You know what?' I said to Colin on the way to the bus stop the next morning. 'Mom's afraid Grandpa is going to get worse and worse.'

He stared at me. 'She *said* that?'

'Nope. But last night when I said I hoped Grandpa wouldn't keep on confusing you with Joe and his gang, she looked worried; and this morning, when you came down, she was watching the two of you every minute until he gave you his usual hug; then she looked better.'

'You mean, she thought he wasn't going to be able to recognize me ever again?'

'I think so.'

'He wouldn't do that! He just *couldn't*!'

'That's what I said to myself. But then I thought, he's forgotten just about everything else. Why not us?'

'Criminy!' He sat down on his binder, and I sat next to him, gathering my skirt around my knees. Neither of us said anything for quite a while.

'Think we could get to Faerie if we went to the Ring by ourselves?' he asked finally.

'I don't know. I sort of thought we could only get there with one of Them.' I pulled my knees a little closer; it was awfully cold. 'Besides, we don't really know he's *in* Faerie.'

'The heck we don't! Hob and Lob had instructions to take us somewhere *else* while that Seer was dreaming, right? That means They don't want us to go to Faerie; and Grandpa *has* to be the reason.'

'Well, maybe,' I said. 'But I wish we had more evidence about what's going on. What were you going to tell me last night?'

'Oh yeah.' He fished a milk penny out of his pocket. 'Watch this.' He flipped the penny, slapping it on the back of his left wrist after he caught it. Heads, heads, heads, heads . . .

'Hang on,' I said, 'let me see that penny.'

119

'Sure,' he said, handing it to me. I looked at it; it was a perfectly ordinary penny.

I took a penny out of my pencil-case. 'Try it with this one.'

He grinned and started to flip it. Heads, heads, heads, heads . . .

'All right,' I said. 'I'm impressed. Tell me how you do it.'

'I'm not doing it. They are.'

'How do you know?'

'Well, I don't, really, but the thing is, it only works on this side of the train tracks.'

'Come on!'

'No, let me show you. We've got time, if we do it fast enough.'

We raced across the tracks, and he started to flip. Heads, tails, tails, heads.

'That's unreal,' I said.

'It's more than that,' he said. 'It's proof.'

'Of what?'

'That They have special power in the area between the highway and the tracks, not just in the Ring. Remember the day Mom was bandaging my hand and you were listening? I only told her about renters leaving the house after a week, but there's more. Joe said the house was haunted and nobody had rented it for three years.'

I stared at him. 'Holy tomato! And you think it was Them?'

'Who else could it be?'

'But They haven't driven us out!'

'That's because of Grandpa, dumbbell! It's all connected, somehow.'

I thought it over. 'I guess it's got to be, but I don't see how.'

The bus came around the corner, and we ran to get our stuff.

'You know,' he said suddenly. 'We're never going to get those faeries to give us Grandpa back by ourselves. The whole thing is just too complicated. We need help.'

'Sure we do. But who would help us?'

'Mr Crewes.'

'Don't be a moron; he's a scientist.'

'So am I, and I believe in faeries. And look, when he was driving me home, he said even if I wasn't in his class, he was always around, and if things got tough, I should call on him for help.'

'That's really great of him,' I said, 'but he probably just meant—'

The bus stopped, and the door flopped open; Colin smiled at me as he swung in. 'I'll tell him tomorrow night when he comes over.'

I wasn't sure that was such a hot idea, but I was glad Colin had cheered up, so I didn't argue.

Not that I could have said much on the bus anyway.

When the doorbell rang the next night, Colin raced to answer it, and he brought Mr Crewes into the living room as if he were a king. Grandpa was pacing around in his usual circle; when he saw Mr Crewes, he looked puzzled.

'Don't live here,' he said.

'That's right,' said Mr Crewes, smiling. 'I don't live here. I'm just visiting. But I like your house.' He looked at the staircase. 'That's a magnificent stained-glass window.'

'Thanks,' I said, sidling up next to Grandpa. 'We like it, too. Won't you sit down? Mom will be right here. And I'll get you a cup of coffee if you want.'

He sat down on the sofa. 'That would be great.'

I took Grandpa's hand. 'Come on, let's go get some coffee and cookies.'

'Cookies,' he said. And he followed me, just the way I'd hoped.

When we got back to the living room, Mom was downstairs, looking very pretty in a dress she hadn't worn for a long time, and she and Colin were talking with Mr Crewes. Grandpa put the cookies on the coffee table, but when he and I sat down, he kept staring at Mr Crewes.

Suddenly, his face lit up. 'Boyfriend?' he asked Mom.

Mom turned bright red. 'No, no,' she said. 'He's a teacher, and he's here to talk about the kids' school.'

But Grandpa just chuckled, and he kept mumbling 'boyfriend . . . good, good' to himself, which made it hard to talk. Finally, Mr Crewes smiled at Mom and leaned forward.

'You know, Mr O'Brien,' he said, 'my dad used to take me to Madison Square Garden to watch the showjumping, and I was thrilled. Now I'm wondering if any of those horses were ones you'd trained.'

Grandpa looked confused, so I chipped in. 'Sure, you trained horses for the Garden, Grandpa. Remember Easy Does It?'

'Easy Does It,' he said, smiling. 'Good girl, good girl.'

'She certainly was,' said Mom, who was more or less the right colour by now. 'Don't you have a picture of her?'

'Picture,' said Grandpa, glancing at the stairs.

I saw what Mom wanted us to do. 'Come on, Grandpa, let's go find it,' I said.

'Yeah,' said Colin. 'We'll help you.'

Grandpa stared at Colin and started to frown.

I thought *Oh no! It's going to happen again!* but I said quickly, 'Easy Does It was a great horse! Let's go find her pictures.'

'Easy Does It,' said Grandpa. And he followed us up the stairs and into the room Mom had made into a kind of office for him.

Colin looked over the shelves of trophies, horse books, and albums. 'Which is the album with Easy Does It's pictures, Grandpa?'

Grandpa pulled out an album. It wasn't the right album, but neither of us said so; we just sat on either side of him on the old leather couch that had always been in his cottage and chatted with him about the horses in the pictures and newspaper clippings. After we got to the end, I took down another album and gave it to him; he began to look at it, humming the way he did when he was interested in something. We looked at each other and tiptoed out of the room.

When we got downstairs, Mr Crewes smiled at Colin. 'I've just been telling your mom that Mr Beeker has decided to put you in my class.'

'Wow!' said Colin. 'Can we do physics? Can we do algebra?'

'Well,' said Mr Crewes, 'there are thirty other students in the class who require my attention, but I think we can work something out. Miss Baker said you can spend time in the library on your own, if you want.' He smiled. 'She likes you; she worked hard on our collection of fairy tales, and you're the first person who has checked any of them out for a long time.'

'Fairy tales?' said Mom in a strange sort of voice.

'Yeah,' said Colin uncomfortably. 'I wanted to . . .'

'Mom,' I said, 'do you think maybe you should check on Grandpa?'

'I guess I'd better,' she said. 'I'll get us some more coffee while I'm up.'

Colin didn't even wait until she was all the way up the stairs; he plopped down next to Mr Crewes on the sofa and started in. 'About those fairy tales I checked out. It was research. See, Sarah and I know something about Grandpa that no-one else does. It's hard to explain, because . . . well . . . not everybody believes in what we know, but we thought you were the kind of person who would understand.'

'I'll certainly try,' said Mr Crewes. And you could tell he meant it.

'OK. Do you know what a changeling is?'

He blinked. 'Er . . . more or less.'

'Well, Sarah and I think that's what our grandfather is. Not our real Grandpa, of course. Just the man you met tonight and on the playground.'

Mr Crewes put down his coffee cup. 'That's an interesting hypothesis, Colin, but—'

'I know it sounds funny,' said Colin. 'But what if we could prove there was something strange about this house – something that let the faeries take Grandpa and leave somebody with us? Then would you believe us?'

I wanted to say, *hey, that's not right – he was sick before we came, so if he's a changeling, it's not the house that's done it*, but Mr Crewes gave me a look that told me to let Colin go on. And to Colin he said, 'It would have to be very convincing proof.'

'It is,' said Colin. He stuck his hand in his pocket and pulled out a penny. 'See, if I flip this anywhere between the railroad tracks and Route 495, it . . . well, watch.' He started flipping; Mr Crewes and I leaned forward. Heads, heads, heads, heads, tails . . . He stopped, staring. Then he flipped it once more. Tails.

He gulped and looked up at Mr Crewes. 'I've done it day after day ever since I first noticed something was weird, and it's been heads every time.'

Mr Crewes raised his eyebrows. 'That defies all the laws of probability.'

'It's true, though,' I said. 'Honest! We did it at the bus stop yesterday, and it came down heads over and over. We both saw it – he isn't just making it up.'

'I can see you're not making it up,' said Mr Crewes. 'But probability can act very strangely sometimes.'

'Not that strangely,' said Colin. 'At least, not without help. But I guess . . .' He swallowed hard. 'I guess They only mess around with it for people They know.'

Mr Crewes leaned back. 'Sometimes scientists have to believe things they can't prove are true, at least in the initial stages of their research. So I'm willing to listen to your hypothesis that your grandfather is a changeling, if you can tell me why you think so.'

'Well,' Colin began slowly, 'we . . . I mean, he . . . I mean . . .' All of a sudden he began to cry. 'He doesn't even know who I am, sometimes!' he sobbed. 'It almost happened tonight, before we took him upstairs! That only makes three times he's done it, I know – but our real Grandpa would *always* know who I was, and he wouldn't keep getting worse and worse, and I just can't stand it, and you've *got* to help us, or we'll never get him back!'

Mr Crewes slid over on the sofa and put his arm around Colin's shoulders. For quite a while, he didn't say anything at all, and I began to think maybe I should go away, but then he said, 'Sometimes, when terrible things happen it helps to understand *why* they happen.'

'Not with this,' sniffed Colin. 'There's no *reason* it should happen. They could make changelings out of a thousand usual people, and nobody would even miss them, but Grandpa's *famous*, like a king of riders, and he knows stories and songs and poetry, or at least, he did . . . it just isn't *fair*!'

Mr Crewes looked across the room very sadly. 'I'm sorry,' he said. 'I didn't mean to imply it was fair.'

There was an awful silence, and I had no idea how to break it. Fortunately, Mom came back with a pot of coffee, and Colin wiggled out from under Mr Crewes's arm. 'Have a cookie,' he said, picking up the cookie plate and passing it politely to Mr Crewes.

Mr Crewes gave Mom a funny look, but he took a cookie and started talking about Wheelock school, and I sat there, feeling bad for Colin and not really listening, until Colin gave me a 'wake up!' kick and I realized Mr Crewes and Mom had started talking about brain research.

'They say that by the end of the 1960s, we'll understand a lot more about connections within the brain than we do now,' Mr Crewes was saying. 'And even now, there's good research being done on the problem of recognition.' He looked at Colin. 'In the meantime, the important thing is to remember that even when he seems not to know you, somewhere in his mind, your grandfather still remembers you, and he still loves you. It's just that a loose connection in his brain keeps him from recognizing you consistently.'

'A lot of good *that* does,' muttered Colin.

Mom made a little noise, but Mr Crewes put up a hand. 'It does do good,' he said. 'It reminds you that the person you're dealing with is exactly what you said he was: a changeling.'

'A changeling!' said Mom. 'Colin, you should know better than—'

'– No, no,' interrupted Mr Crewes gently. 'It's a good metaphor. Changelings look just like the person who has been taken, and so do patients with diseases of the brain. The difference is on the inside, where nobody can see it.' He looked from Mom to Colin. 'That's what I meant earlier. Nobody can explain *why* your grandfather should lose his memory. But if you can understand *how* the brain works and what goes wrong with it, it at least gives you a way of dealing with what's happening. If you want, that's where we could start in science. I have some books about the brain. They're pretty technical, but I think if we did some groundwork first, you could handle them. Would you like to do that?'

Colin looked down at the floor. 'Sure.'

Mr Crewes nodded, and that was sort of it. He thanked Mom for coffee, and she thanked him for coming; then he left, and Mom hurried us off to bed.

Colin looked at me as we brushed our teeth. 'Boy, I really blew it! Now he thinks we just made up the changeling thing to make ourselves feel better, and we'll never be able to convince him that it's real.' He spat into the sink. 'I'm sorry. I should have let you do it.'

All my life I had been wanting him to say something like that, but the funny thing was, it made me feel just awful. 'It probably wouldn't have made any difference,' I said. 'If I'd told him what happened, he might have thought we were seeing things, and we'd be even worse off than we are now.' I stuck my toothbrush back in the rack. 'We'll just have take matters in our own hands again. Maybe if we go to the Ring, we can—'

'Shh!' he said, looking over his shoulder as Mom and Grandpa passed the bathroom door. When they were gone, he nodded. 'OK.'

So that's what we did. But it didn't work. We tried everything: circles on the ground, spells we remembered from Grandpa's stories, and even the Lord's prayer backwards (I spent all my time in Mass on Sunday writing it out, and Mom was so busy keeping Grandpa quiet that she didn't even notice). But nothing happened, and the only person we saw was Jenny, picking through the garbage next to the entrance ramp.

It rained on Monday, and it was so windy that our umbrella didn't do us any good while we waited for the bus. Colin turned up his collar and stuffed his hands into his pockets. 'This is it!' he grumbled. 'We spend the whole weekend freezing to death, and now—'

Suddenly, a giant puff of wind picked up a whole lot of oak leaves from between the warehouses and spun them all around us, slapping them in our faces. The umbrella jerked in my hand, and my glasses fell off. Colin grabbed them just in time, but the umbrella was a goner.

'Geez!' I said, rubbing my eyes. 'What was that?'

'A miniature tornado,' said Colin, rubbing his. 'With lots of grit in it.' He inspected the inside-out umbrella. 'Looks dead, doesn't it?'

'Sure does,' I said. 'Mom isn't going to be happy. Umbrellas cost money, and the other day she said we didn't have a nickel to spare.'

'That was for riding lessons, and we should've known not to ask.' He picked up his stuff as the bus turned the corner. 'Leave it here, or everybody will laugh at us when we get on.'

I put the umbrella corpse down, followed Colin up the bus stairs – and crashed into him, because he'd turned around. 'Get off!' he whispered, pushing me. 'Quick! It's the wrong bus!'

His face told me he was really scared, so even though I couldn't see beyond him, I turned around. But the door flopped shut in front of me, and the bus started moving. Colin pushed past me and yanked on the handle that said 'pull in emergencies'. He staggered as the door swung open, but then he gathered himself to jump. In the seats behind us, everybody was shouting, and in the back, two or three voices called 'Go, go, go!'

The bus screeched to a stop, and the driver leaped up and grabbed us. 'What the heck do you think you're doing?' he yelled.

I started to explain – then I realized why Colin was so scared. The bus driver wasn't our driver. He was a ghoul. 'You listen to me,' he said, shaking Colin (who was still struggling). 'Nobody opens that door when the bus is moving! Do I have to tell you why?'

He was so big and angry, neither of us pointed

out that it wouldn't have been dangerous to jump, because we hadn't been going very fast, and there were no cars on our street.

'You two are in *real* trouble,' he said. 'But for right now, you sit right here.' He picked us up and plonked us down on the first seat behind his. 'Not a single move, you hear?'

We nodded, and I guess he saw we'd do what we were told, because he slammed the door shut and started off again. For a while, everybody on the bus was buzzing and whispering, but pretty soon they were just talking again. If you didn't look, it sounded like a regular school bus, but if you did, it was very strange. Outside the windows, familiar things flashed past, but none of them were in their usual places. It was like we were driving through a wooden play village, and somebody had moved stuff around. Sometimes a house looked just the way it always did, but then there would be a block of stores that belonged a couple of streets down, then a gas station that should have been a few blocks back. I tried my best to keep track of where we were so we could get home again, but after a couple of minutes, I was so lost I realized I'd have to look for clues about what was up inside the bus.

That turned out not to be any better. It was obviously *some* kind of school bus, because everybody was a kid except the driver. But there was something wrong with all of them. The boy sitting behind Colin had a monkey's face, except saggy, as if it were made out of silly putty. The girl sitting across the aisle had a mask around her eyes – not a Halloween mask, but more like a raccoon. The girl across the aisle two rows in back of me had teeth that looked like a beaver's, and the girl she was giggling with had a cat's nose and whiskers. It was like looking at the strange creatures we'd seen dancing around the fire outside the Seer's cave.

Suddenly I went cold all over. Maybe they *were* the creatures. Everybody knew faeries spirited kids into the Otherworld, but since the kids never came back, *nobody knew what happened to them when they got there*. Maybe part of being spirited was turning into creatures, and what we were seeing was the change-over. I looked anxiously at Colin. He seemed OK – just scared, like me – but who knew how long the changes took?

When you got down to it, who knew what kind of journeys Cathbad had meant when he said we'd make them? If this was one of them, what would happen to us when we got to the Otherworld? Would the ghoul listen if we told him we were under Protection, and that made us different from the others? Or would he change

134

us into dancing creatures without telling Cathbad or Mongan? Or . . . I went even colder. Maybe Cathbad and Mongan had given the ghoul *instructions* to turn us into creatures. Cathbad was a stickler for the Rules, and the Rules said he had to help us. But all we'd asked was to be taken where Grandpa was. That meant They could do what their precious Rules required – and if we couldn't get back because Grandpa didn't recognize us inside the dancing creatures we'd become, well, that was our faults. Come to think of it, Mongan had hinted that Grandpa might not know who we were – but even though we'd heard hundreds of stories about stupid mortals who didn't make their wishes carefully enough, we hadn't realized what he'd meant. How dumb we'd been! And now . . . I looked out the window at the scrambled houses, and somewhere in my head I heard Mongan say: *the way home's the problem, surely.* He'd told us! And we hadn't listened.

I nudged Colin. 'Would we get creamed if we jumped out now?' I whispered.

'That's what I've been trying to figure,' he whispered back. 'I've forgotten the equation for how hard you fall at thirty miles an hour, but I don't think we could count on landing on our feet.'

135

Trust Colin to think in equations when he was being abducted by faeries. 'I meant the traffic.'

He looked at me scornfully. 'The traffic's *why* we need to land on our feet.'

The driver ghoul looked over his shoulder at us. 'All right, you two. That's enough. And when we get there, you sit tight, you hear? We're getting out last.' His huge hands crossed over each other as he turned the bus to the left, but we could see he was watching us in the mirror over his seat. I thought of Mom, looking and looking for us, the way she looked for Grandpa, calling the police . . . the tears that prickled my eyes joined up with some of the grit from the mini-tornado, and they really stung.

I was still wiping them with a kleenex when the bus pulled up next to a fortress with an asphalt moat, and all the funny-looking kids began to pile out. I'd expected a lot of faeries would be there to tell them which way to go, but they seemed to know. A little boy with yellow and purple bat's wings where his ears should be scuffled with a bunch of boys with gopher faces as they scuttled towards a side door. A group of girls with striped tails and shining black and white feet went that way, too. The cat girl and her friend walked straight to the front door, giggling and pointing back at us. A bunch of big boys with pig faces purposely pushed Colin as they went past, and laughed when he knocked his head against mine. At the end, a girl with a horse's mane and ears tried to stop next to us, but the ghoul waved her on.

'They're coming in with *me*,' he said. 'You hurry, now.'

She looked back over her shoulder as she trotted towards the front door, but the ghoul wouldn't let us out until she was all the way inside. Then he walked down the steps first (which was smart of him, because we would have run for it if he hadn't), and as we followed him out, he reached for our hands. For a second I thought there was hope, but nothing happened when his hands touched ours. He just held them tightly and hurried us in the main door, across a big entry hall, and into a big room with desks and file cabinets in it. At the back of it was a prison cell, guarded by two woman ghouls. As we came in, a jailer looked out the door of the cell. Not a faerie jailer. He was bald, which I couldn't imagine a faerie being, and the top of his head was painted luminous orange, to match his ears. It looked pretty funny with his purple beard and green uniform, but neither of us felt like laughing.

'Causing trouble already, are you?' he said.

Colin folded his hands across his chest. 'We're not *causing* trouble; we're *in* trouble!'

The jailer's purple eyebrows went way up. 'You sure as heck are – and being fresh won't get you out of it.' He stepped to the side of his door. 'Go in there and sit down. I'll be in as soon as I've heard what you've done.'

The bus driver gave us a little push, and the jailer shut the door behind us after we went in. There was a window on the far side of the cell; Colin raced to it and began to examine its bars. 'Think it's worth a try?'

'That will not be necessary,' said a voice behind us.

We both spun around. At first we didn't see anything but a wall, but it looked sort of wavy, as if we'd been looking at it through water; then Cathbad was standing in front it, huge and solemn in his robe. 'I have come to release you, Children of Lugh,' he said.

'Release us!' I said. 'Then you didn't . . . you hadn't . . .'

'I had not planned your journey to go exactly as it did,' he said, looking at me in a way that told me he knew what I'd been thinking. 'It performed its purpose, but the minions I sent to accompany you decided to amuse themselves along the way. The result is beyond their powers to repair.'

'Amuse themselves!' I said. 'You mean that after we'd asked to go to the Otherworld all weekend, you finally sent minions to take us – and they brought us *here*?'

'No,' he said. '"Here" was the appointed end of your journey. It was the change along the way that caused problems. The minions rubbed glamour in your eyes, so all that you saw looked new and strange. They were supposed to make you invisible, so your reactions to what you saw would not affect the people around you, but they could not resist the temptation to cause trouble. Playing upon mortal confusion is an old trick, I fear, but it provides a steady source of fun to those of vulgar wit.'

'Come *on*!' said Colin. 'You can't tell us what happened out there didn't happen!'

'No,' said Cathbad. 'It all happened. But what you saw as a bus of unrecognizable beings in a strange landscape, the others saw as your school bus, filled with its customary occupants and travelling its customary route. And unfortunately, they saw you.'

'You mean *we* were mixed up, not the kids or the bus route?' I asked.

'Indeed,' he said. 'As you will see when I remove the glamour.'

Before either of us could say anything, he cupped his hands over our eyes. When he took them away, the cell with the barred window was gone. We were standing in Mr Beeker's office.

'Holy cow!' I said. And suddenly it dawned on me. 'The jailer who was sore about our being in trouble – was that Mr Beeker?'

Cathbad nodded.

'Oh *no*!' gasped Colin. 'Yesterday, I *promised* him I wouldn't be any more trouble if I could be in Mr Crewes's class – and now everything's messed up! How *could* you?'

Cathbad gave him a long look. 'I thought I had explained.'

'Oh, you explained, all right!' said Colin bitterly. 'The minions decided to make our whole "little trip" a joke. Wonderful. What if we'd lost our heads and jumped off the bus and gotten hurt?'

'Then the minions would have been even more amused than they are now.'

'That's awful!' I said. 'I mean, it was really dangerous!'

'It is a great mistake to judge the Otherworld by the standards of your own,' said Cathbad. 'Faeries have little concern with the welfare of mortals – and of course, you are not in Our good graces. If it had been in your power, you would have told the man who came to your house last

140

Friday about Us. That's against the Rules.'

'Nobody told us that,' I said.

'No, but you knew that common mortals are not allowed to see the workings of Faerie,' he said. 'Did you not?'

We looked at each other; neither of us could deny it.

'So far as danger goes,' he continued, 'you were warned from the first that it existed. As your adventure this morning should have made it clear, the danger lies not only in the situations We lead you into, but in your reactions to them. Had you jumped from the bus into traffic, our Protection could not have saved you. In your trips towards your grandfather, you share his risks.' He looked at us, his eyes steely grey. 'That is why I have told you that you may discontinue your mission at any time.'

'Discontinue, phooey!' said Colin, before I could say anything. 'Of *course* we won't give up! What we want is *action*! Where is Grandpa? You *know*, and you won't tell us!'

'Sh!' I hissed, putting my finger on my lips, but he went right on.

'You *promised*!' he said, his voice getting louder and louder. 'You said you *had* to help us find him, and you would! And all we get is these crummy little trips that don't get any—'

'Colin!' I whispered, grabbing his elbow. 'Hush!'

He started to shake me off, but when he looked at Cathbad, he did hush. Because suddenly Cathbad towered over us, his eyes cold and wicked. 'Son of Lugh,' he said slowly, 'you have invaded the inner precincts of the Sidhe. You have tried to confide in a mortal about the secrets of Faerie. You have just accused Us of breaking Our word. Because of your youth and ignorance, We have not inflicted the punishments upon you that would normally be meted out to mortals who break the Rules. But it would be unwise to push Us further. There are far more powerful faeries in the Otherworld than the ones who played with you today; do not anger them.'

We both looked away, and Colin mumbled, 'Yes, sir.'

'As for the journeys you have taken,' he went on coldly, 'if you give them sufficient consideration, you will see that they have filled their appointed purpose.' He paused, then glanced at the door. 'Your principal is coming back. We must leave.'

'Won't he be awfully upset if we aren't here when he comes in?' I said.

'He has already lost all memory of seeing you this morning,' said Cathbad. 'As have the rest.

Close your eyes until the world settles around you.'

I closed my eyes, and everything began to spin. When it stopped, and I opened them, I was sitting in Miss Turner's room, staring at my spelling list. Nobody seemed to notice I'd just turned up. Most of the kids were turning their lists into sentences; across the aisle, Tiffany was staring out the window with a dreamy smile.

I looked back down at my spelling list, but all I could think about was what Cathbad had said about our journeys. *If you give them sufficient consideration . . .* Darn it, we'd *been* considering! And I was considering even harder, now. Talking with Cathbad had made me see how wrong I'd been on the bus. Whatever the minions might do, the Sidhe weren't trying to keep us from going to Faerie and finding Grandpa. They were doing something different. I chewed on my pencil, trying to think what it was, but all I could come up with was something I'd sort of known already: that Colin's changeling theory didn't explain what was wrong with Grandpa. It wasn't just that what he wanted to call evidence wasn't the kind of evidence that allowed you to prove anything. And it wasn't just that we couldn't blame the house for making Grandpa worse, because he'd been getting worse before we got there. There was something else. One of those things that, when you saw it, made you say 'Oh! Of course!'

I quit chewing the pencil, but what I wrote, instead of a sentence with 'expostulate' in it, was A LOT OF GOOD **THAT** DOES. Because the only people who knew what was wrong with our theory – and thus, the only people who knew what was wrong with Grandpa – were the Sidhe. And Cathbad had just made it very clear that They did not appreciate the way we'd been trying to make things go faster. All we could do was what Grandpa said you had to do with faeries: be very polite, and let Them help you in Their own way, on Their own terms.

7 Dream Horse

I was afraid Colin would get feisty when I told him about waiting for the Sidhe to do things their way, but he just gave me a look that said he'd already figured that out. We hoped our reward for figuring it out was going to be another trip to Faerie, but it wasn't. Miss Turner's chalk disappeared almost every day, and the pennies Colin flipped at home came down heads every single time, so we knew They were around, but we stayed put. After a few days, we started to the Ring, just to see what was up, not to push Them or anything, but Mom stopped us. She'd heard that it was a place where burglars met the people they sold stolen stuff to (she called them 'fences', but she couldn't tell us why). Colin pointed out that our statistical chances of being there at the same time as a robber or a fence were very low, but with things like that, mothers just don't listen to statistics. So we didn't go.

It was frustrating, because Grandpa was having more and more trouble knowing who people were. Like, a few days before Thanksgiving, he got Colin mixed up with a stable boy at the Smithes', and he kept telling him he should be in the barn cleaning tack, not in the house. Then at Thanksgiving dinner, he got *both* of us mixed up with the Smithes' kids, who've been grown up forever, and he got so upset when we tried to explain who we were that he left the table and stomped upstairs. Mom tried to fetch him back, but he wouldn't come, so we had to go on without him. It sort of scotched the holiday atmosphere.

After that it seemed like something went wrong every day. Grandpa started calling me Deirdre, which is Mom's name – though he still knew who Mom was now, which logically he shouldn't have. Anyway, he'd start talking to me (thinking I was Mom long ago) about shows she'd ridden in, and of course, that was our chance to learn about the side of Mom we'd found in the trunk – but it usually didn't work, because we couldn't figure out what he meant, and then he'd get angry. One time when Mom was out shopping, and Colin, Grandpa, and I were sitting in the kitchen, waiting for the soda bread we'd made to be done, he said 'White horse – dressage' over and over, until I got it and asked if he meant the Spanish Riding Academy in Vienna. He did, and bit by bit, it came out that he wanted me (meaning Mom) to go study there, and to pack right now. We knew better than to frustrate him, so we got a suitcase out of the cellar, playing for time until the soda bread came out and distracted him, but he got more and more upset, and we were really glad to hear the old Ford stutter up the driveway. When Mom came in, I told her quickly what was wrong. I thought she'd help us play along with Grandpa, but instead, she told him – lots more sharply than she usually told him anything – that nobody was going to Vienna, and he should stop bugging me.

He stared at her for nearly ten seconds (which is forever if nobody's talking); then he jumped to his feet and roared 'Don't live here! Call police!' He did call, too, even though Colin and I hung on him and begged him not to. Of course he didn't get the police, because the phone was unplugged, but he thought he had, and he paced around, waiting for them, until eventually he forgot who he was waiting for. When I went to tell Mom everything was OK, her face was all red and swollen. And if *Mom* had been crying . . . well, all I could think was, it would be nice if the faeries quit punishing us for pushing Them (if that was what They were doing) and took us to where Grandpa was.

It would also have been nice if it hadn't been Christmas, which had been the best part of winter when we lived on Maple Street. We'd always decorated the house the first day of Advent, and when we'd come home from school, it had smelled of Christmas tree, cookies, and spiced cider in a way that made you feel all tingly when you came in the door. Then there'd been our Christmas vacation visit to our Madison grandparents at their big house on the Cape. It was the only time they saw us all year, so they and their servants always made it a big deal, with lots of presents and fussing, and it had been a magical week, even though Grandmother and Grandfather Madison weren't very magical themselves.

This year, though, Mom said we couldn't afford to decorate the house. We were upset (we'd been talking for a month about winding a chain of hemlock boughs and red ribbon up the banisters under the stained-glass window), but maybe it was just as well; even the little tree we got made everything seem sad instead of Christmassy. As for the visit to Grandmother and Grandfather Madison, I wasn't really looking forward to it. You think more when you grow up; ever since last Christmas I'd wondered why Mom never got to go with us, and why they never wrote to her, only to Colin and me. And this Christmas, it hit me that we didn't even have enough money for hemlock boughs, and Grandmother and Grandfather had a huge house and a limousine, and . . . I don't mean I was greedy, or anything; it just seemed strange. I didn't say anything about that to Colin, though. He was counting the days 'til we left, and I didn't want to wreck it for him.

Anyway, with one thing and another, I spent most of Advent wishing someone would cheer me up. Tiffany would have been the obvious someone, but after Thanksgiving, she looked out the classroom window more and more, so I guessed Christmas at her house was even sadder than at ours. She'd cheer up a bit if we could meet at recess in our storm drain, but there was a lot of freezing rain, which meant spending recess in the gym playing dodgeball. When that happened, she just stood still until she got hit, then went to the sidelines and dreamed off again. Sometimes I let myself get hit so I could join her, but it was so noisy neither of us could talk.

Then, two days before Christmas vacation, she gave me a big smile when I got on the bus. I sat down beside her and waited, but she didn't say anything. Tiffany was like that, so I didn't push, but it was a nice day for a change, and when we crawled into our storm drain at recess and she *still* didn't say why she was all lit up, I forgot to be patient. 'For Pete's sake, Tiffany – tell me what it is!'

'It's nothing. I mean, it might not work out. Sometimes things don't, with horses—'

'– With horses! You're going to keep a secret from *me* about *horses*!?'

'Well . . .' she drew a deep breath. 'OK. Near where I live there's these really nice people who have a stable, and for the last couple of years, I've groomed for them, and cleaned tack and mucked out stalls, and they've . . .' Her voice was so quiet I could hardly hear it now. ' . . . they've been giving me lessons.'

'Oh, Tiffany!' I thought of that stable, which had to be near our house if it was near hers, and how if she'd just been willing to share, we could have . . .

'I've been wanting to tell you,' she said. 'Honest! But I spend a lot of time at the Gordons' (that's their name) when my parents are . . . I mean, when my parents aren't home. And they don't like people to know that, so I just haven't told anybody that I ride. Not even you.'

I looked at her red face, and I thought how awful it would be to have parents like hers, and I quit feeling sore. 'That's OK,' I said. 'I won't even tell Colin, if you don't want. But if you've been riding all this time, that can't be what you're excited about.'

'No, it's not,' she said. 'It's . . . well, the Gordons don't have any students except me, so they don't have a school horse. They started me on a pony they borrowed, and then when I was ready for something more advanced, a couple lent them a gymkhana pony that their kid had wrecked, and I rode him. After a year, I got him going really well, but this fall his owners came by and saw me jumping him, and they said "Hey, this pony is worth a lot of money!" and they told the Gordons to put him up for sale. So they did, and at Thanksgiving, he went to a really nice girl. Of course I was glad he'd found a good home, but . . .'

'You don't have to explain,' I said. 'I cried and cried when I said goodbye to my pony in Pennsylvania, and she didn't even belong to me.'

'Yeah,' said Tiffany. 'But then—' She looked up, and her eyes were shining. 'Last night, just before I left, Mrs Gordon got a call about a really good horse. He's four, and he belongs to a girl who's just been offered a working student job in England, and she's looking for somebody who'll take him on a free lease. She's having trouble finding someone, because everybody wants to start him over big jumps right away, and she says he's too young.'

'She's right,' I said. 'Grandpa says there's a special corner in Hell for people who jump four-year-olds, because it wrecks their knees.'

'That's what Mrs Gordon said,' said Tiffany. 'And she promised that if the girl (her name's Gwen) leased the horse to me, I wouldn't do anything more than cavelettis and one-foot gymnastic jumps with him.' She smiled all over. 'So Gwen said she'd trailer him to the Gordons' Saturday afternoon, so I could try him out.'

'Wow! And if you like him, he'll be yours for a whole year?'

'Not until April,' said Tiffany. 'You have to apply for working student jobs way in advance. But the Gordons don't have an indoor ring, so I can't ride much until April anyway.'

'That's true,' I said. 'And besides, it's only four months. Boy, are you ever lucky!'

'Yeah,' said Tiffany, but she looked worried. 'What if I'm not good enough? Mrs Gordon lets me ride her horse once in a while, but mostly I've just ridden ponies, and Gwen's going to see that.'

'Horsefeathers! If she wanted a fancy rider to school him, she could have one, right? It sounds like she'd rather find somebody who'll ride him carefully and give him lots of love.'

Tiffany gave me a faraway smile. 'I could do that, all right.'

'No kidding,' I said. 'Look, we'd better head back – they're lining up.'

'OK.' But she didn't move. 'Sarah . . . the Gordons' street is only two school bus stops after yours. Could you . . . I mean, would you like to come when I try out the horse?'

'Wow! That would be . . . Oh wait, I can't. We promised that we'd stay home with Grandpa when Mom went Christmas shopping with a friend. And we just *can't* let her down.'

'Your grandpa! Listen, when you told me he was Angus O'Brien, I told the Gordons, and you should have seen them. He's their hero. So if I ask them if he can come with you (and Colin, too, if he wants) they'll say yes for sure.'

I looked away. 'Um, Tiffany, about my grandpa. He isn't like he used to be.'

'I know,' she said. 'Mr Gordon told me; I guess he'd heard about it. But, well . . . you know how when you have a headache, and then you get

153

interested in something, it goes away? Maybe if your grandpa saw horses again, he'd forget he was sick for a while.'

Suddenly I remembered how much happier Grandpa was when he looked at pictures of horses than he was the rest of the time. And I thought, *hey, maybe that's it — maybe he's been getting worse and worse because there aren't any horses to remind him of who he is.* 'OK,' I said. 'Ask the Gordons, and if they say it's all right, we'll come.'

The Gordons did say it was all right, and Colin thought I really had something about Grandpa's needing horses to be Grandpa. So we were all set, but we agreed not to ask Mom if we could take him; she might have said no, and it would have made us feel bad to disobey her.

It took a long time for Saturday afternoon to come, and when it came, Mom took for ever deciding what to wear, and we were sure we'd be too late to see Tiffany ride. But she finally left, and the moment the car bumped over the railroad tracks, we asked Grandpa if he'd like to go look at a horse. He jumped up right away, looking so happy that I forgot about feeling guilty.

When we were halfway to the tracks, Jenny's little dog ran out of the warehouses and barked at us, and she came out to hush him. It took me a moment to recognize her, though; her hair was clean, and she was wearing a decent skirt and a pea coat instead of her usual ratty clothes.

'Going for a walk?' she said. 'Lots of traffic that way.'

Colin and I nodded and started to go on, but Grandpa stopped and smiled at her. 'Horse,' he said. 'Going look over horse.'

'That's nice,' she said, giving him a smile that made me feel funny. 'I like horses. Can I come, if I leave Bran behind?' She pointed to the dog.

'Well, um,' I said, 'we don't really know these people . . .'

But Grandpa interrupted me. 'Come,' he said, smiling. 'See horse.'

That did it; Colin and I couldn't argue with two grown-ups, even if they were both a little crazy. So we waited while Jenny put the dog inside, and then she came with us. I was embarrassed at first, because I didn't know how we could explain her to the Gordons, but pretty soon, I was glad she was there, because walking along the road was a lot different from driving down it. There were pick-ups turning in and out of gas stations and hardware stores, and big trucks backing out of lumberyards, and cars making U-turns in parking lots of supermarkets

155

– and none of the drivers were looking for people, so we had to stop and run and dodge all the time. I was really scared for Grandpa, but Jenny took his arm and steered him through everything as if she'd walked in craziness like that all her life.

'Thanks a lot,' I said to her, when we finally turned off on the Gordons' quiet street. 'We really shouldn't have . . .'

'It's all right, hon,' she said. 'I owe you a favour, remember?'

A favour? Then I remembered the oatmeal, but too late to make some witty remark. Grandpa saved me by taking my hand and pointing around us with his hook. 'Horse here?'

'Close,' I said. And it was pretty close. We passed five houses that looked like ours only not run-down, then three smaller, newer houses hidden by trees; then, just like Tiffany had said, we came to a sign with *Gordon* written on it. And there, at the bottom of the driveway, were Tiffany and two grown-ups watching a girl in chaps ride a liver-chestnut horse in a ring beside a beautiful little barn. The horse pulled up when he saw us, with his ears pointed forward and his nostrils wide open. I reached for Grandpa's hand, but it was OK; he waited until the horse decided we were all right, then he walked quietly to the fence and settled down to watch.

Colin gave me a poke. 'Look at him,' he whispered. 'It's working.'

It was true. Grandpa really looked like Grandpa, with the expression that meant he'd blotted out everything but the horse he was watching. I stared at him, hardly able to believe it . . . then gradually he stopped looking like Grandpa, and started looking like the warrior in the Seer's dream. I blinked, and when I looked again, Grandpa was just Grandpa, of course – but Jenny was looking at me with a funny kind of smile. I turned to watch the horse, feeling my cheeks get hot and wondering why Jenny, of all people, always made me feel so dumb.

The horse was one of those Quarter Horses that are built like Thoroughbreds and make great jumpers. He was young, all right, but you could see Gwen had spent a lot of time with him, because he did everything she told him to, even though he was looking all around. After a few minutes, when she halted him in the middle of the ring, he stood without fidgeting, and I was impressed, because most young horses won't do that in a new place.

'You've done a great job with him, Gwen,' said the man who had to be Mr Gordon. On

157

our side of the ring, Grandpa nodded.

Gwen smiled. 'Thank you. I'm afraid his mind is everywhere but here, but I think he'll be OK for Tiffany now.' She dismounted and patted the horse. 'What do you think, Dandy?'

Dandy gave her a little bump with his nose. Mr Gordon and Tiffany ducked through the fence, and he shortened the stirrups while Tiffany stroked Dandy's neck. After a minute, Mr Gordon gave Tiffany a leg up, and Gwen gave her the reins. 'Just walk at first, Tiffany,' she said anxiously. 'Hardly anyone's ridden him but me.'

Tiffany nodded, and her face was very serious. When they started off, her back looked like someone had shoved a riding crop down it, and Dandy walked as if he were on eggs, but you could see they both knew what they were doing. I glanced at Grandpa; he was nodding.

After they'd walked around the ring a few times, Mr Gordon called, 'Try a trot.'

Dandy swished his tail and looked at Gwen as Tiffany closed her legs, but he went into it. Tiffany's serious look turned into a smile, and I knew why: it looked like Dandy was floating.

Gwen smiled, too. 'Isn't that nice?' she called to Tiffany. And then, turning to Mrs Gordon, she said, 'She's good.'

'She's very good,' agreed Mrs Gordon. 'She's

one of those kids whose whole heart is in her horse, but it's more than sentiment. She works.'

I gave Tiffany a thumbs-up as she rode by, but I wasn't sure she saw it. She'd stopped smiling, and her face looked just like Grandpa's; her whole mind was wrapped up in getting Dandy to go just exactly right. Walk, trot, halt. Walk, trot, circle, halt. Gradually, Dandy stopped looking around; his head came down, his strides got evener, and he looked really good.

'OK,' said Mr Gordon finally. 'You've both done great. Let's give him a break.'

Tiffany looked sad, but she halted him in the centre and slid off. The Gordons and Gwen ducked through the fence and strolled towards her; before I could stop him, Grandpa had ducked through the fence, too, so we had to go with him. I was afraid he might go straight for Dandy, but he just nodded at everybody and stayed out of the way.

'Well, what do you think, Tiffany?' said Gwen. 'Do you like him?'

Tiffany nodded so hard I thought her helmet was going to fall off, but she didn't say anything; she just stroked Dandy's neck.

'It looks like a good combination to me,' said Mrs Gordon. 'But of course, the decision is yours.'

Gwen swallowed and looked over Dandy's back. 'You wouldn't just ride him, would you, Tiffany? I mean, you'd talk to him?'

'Oh yes!' said Tiffany. 'I've got lots of time, and I'd spend it all with him!'

Gwen looked at her, and I saw tears in her eyes. 'OK, then,' she said. 'It's a deal.'

'Thank you,' whispered Tiffany. And she put both her arms around Dandy's neck.

Mr Gordon cleared his throat. 'Well,' he said, 'that's that. Dandy can go in the extra stall while we do the paperwork, but first . . .' He put his hand on Tiffany's shoulder. 'I think we should meet Tiffany's friends.'

Tiffany turned around, looking embarrassed. 'I'm sorry,' she said. 'This is Sarah Madison, and her brother Colin, and her grandfather, Angus O'Brien, and . . .' Gwen made a little noise and stared when Tiffany said Grandpa's name, so I thought that's why she stopped. But when I looked at her, I could see that wasn't so. She was staring at Jenny.

I opened my mouth to explain who Jenny was, but Mr Gordon had already stepped forward. 'Tom Gordon,' he said. 'And this is my wife, Judy.' He held out his left hand to Grandpa. 'We're very pleased to have you here.'

Grandpa smiled and shook hands, and when I introduced Jenny as our neighbour, everyone shook hands with her, too. Tiffany was looking OK then, so I figured she'd just been surprised to see us with a stranger.

After all the introductions were over, Grandpa got down to business, just the way he always had. 'Good girl, good horse,' he said, laying his good hand on Tiffany's shoulder and nodding at Dandy. 'Good.'

I bit my lip, because I wasn't sure what everyone would think when they found out Grandpa couldn't speak a whole sentence, but Tiffany and Gwen looked as if he'd just given them a trophy, and both the Gordons looked pleased, so it was OK.

'Let's go back to the tack room and have some cocoa,' said Mrs Gordon.

'Good idea,' said Mr Gordon. 'Would you like to see our horses, Mr O'Brien? They're Thoroughbred crosses that we've raised from weanlings.'

Grandpa nodded happily, and he followed Mr Gordon, Tiffany, and Gwen to the barn. Mrs Gordon looked after him, shaking her head. But before she could say anything, Jenny spoke up. 'It's great that Tiffany's going to get that nice horse.'

'I'll say,' said Mrs Gordon. 'There's *some* justice in the world at least, and she deserves all she can get. Her parents are . . .' She glanced at Colin and me and broke off.

Jenny watched Tiffany stop Dandy at the barn door. 'She spend a lot of time here?'

'A fair amount,' said Mrs Gordon. 'But it's always touch and go. Most of the time, her parents are glad to have her off their hands, but sometimes they get defensive, or something – I can't figure out exactly what it is. When that happens, they don't let her come for a while. Fortunately, they slip back into their old ways pretty fast, but it's very hard on her.' She sighed. 'I wish there were more we could do, but her social worker says there isn't, since it's not a matter of physical abuse—'

'Cocoa's ready!' called Mr Gordon.

We went in, and there was Grandpa, nodding while Gwen told him how she'd trained Dandy, and looking happier than I'd seen him look since he'd left Pennsylvania. I gave him half a cup of cocoa (so he wouldn't spill it), and then listened to the horse talk until Tiffany edged over to me and said, 'Let's go look at Dandy.'

I nodded, and we slipped out. As we walked down the aisle, I thought she was going to talk

162

about how great Dandy was, but instead she said, 'Is Jenny really your neighbour?'

'Well,' I said, looking over my shoulder to be sure the tack room door was shut, 'she lives in one of the warehouses, with those . . . er, poor people. But she's really nice.'

'Oh, sure,' said Tiffany, looking embarrassed. 'I didn't mean that. It's just . . . never mind.' She dug two carrots out of her pocket and handed one to me. 'Let's give him these.'

Dandy stuck his head over the stall door and bopped her with his nose. She giggled and gave him his carrot. 'Isn't he cute?' she said.

'He sure is,' I said, and I felt a little sad as I watched him rub his head on Tiffany's shoulder. He'd never go to the Olympics – he just wasn't that sort of horse – but he was well-trained, and sweet, and if I'd had a horse like that, I'd have been the happiest kid in the world.

Tiffany looked out the barn door. 'Look, it's starting to snow! Isn't it pretty?' She sighed happily and leaned against the stall door. 'Oh, Sarah – I never even dreamed things could be this perfect. Not for me.'

Something about the way she said it made me ashamed of feeling jealous. 'You deserve things to be perfect,' I said. And I meant it.

★

We didn't have to walk back; Mrs Gordon gave us a ride as far as our road. She wanted to take us all the way to our house, so she could tell Mom we could come and visit the horses whenever we wanted – but I said we hadn't been sure Grandpa could walk that far, so we hadn't told Mom where we were going, and it would be better, all in all, if we explained what had happened and got her to call. Mrs Gordon gave Jenny a funny look and said it sure was a good thing she'd come along with us, but she smiled when she dropped us off by the tracks, so we knew she wouldn't squeal.

We were going to tell Mom right away – both about the Gordons and about how much better Grandpa was when there were horses around – but when we got home, there was a three-coloured Chevy with fins behind our old humpbacked Ford in the driveway, and there was smoke coming out of the chimney. I looked at Colin. 'Should we go in the front door and say hi to Mom's friend?'

'Uh-uh,' he said quickly. 'It'll take a lot of horse visits before Grandpa's comfortable with guests. It'd be better to go in the side door and up the back stairs.'

We did, and it worked, which showed us Grandpa really was better. Usually when we came home, he looked around for Mom, but this time, he settled right down in his study. I brushed my hair and put it back in the clasp Mom was always trying to get me to wear; then I went to Colin's room to persuade him to come be polite, but he'd put his No Trespassing sign on his door. I couldn't figure that out – he'd been so happy all the way home because of Grandpa – but I knew better than to barge in when that sign was up, so I left him be.

When I got downstairs, the sliding double doors to the living room were closed, which was unusual. Of course, in a drafty old house like that, it didn't do much good to light a fire unless you closed the doors, but . . . I tiptoed up to them and peeked through the little crack. And I saw Mr Crewes and Mom sitting on the sofa.

I thought of going to fetch Colin; then I thought some more. Mr Crewes had driven him home the afternoon Grandpa went to the playground, so he must have recognized the new Chevy. Maybe that was what had upset him. I peeked through the crack again. There wasn't much to be upset about; there was a whole cushion between them, and they were both drinking coffee. But Mom wasn't looking very happy, so I decided I'd better listen a little before I went in.

Mr Crewes was talking. 'And you think he's getting worse?'

'Define "worse",' said Mom. 'He's been wandering less, but doesn't always recognize Sarah and Colin any more. And if you knew how much they meant to him . . .'

Mr Crewes frowned. 'Did the specialist you saw expect the disease to stabilize?'

'I thought so,' said Mom, 'but maybe that's just what I wanted to believe. Recently – well, one of the big maples in the front yard is rotting from the centre. And every time I pass it, I look at the rot and think, what is there to stop it?'

What is there to stop it? Of course, she wasn't really talking about a tree; she was talking about Grandpa. I swallowed hard, wondering if it was wrong to pray to faeries.

'It's always possible that the process can be retarded.'

'By whom?' she said. 'All the specialist could tell me was that nobody understood the brain well enough to help Dad, let alone to cure him.'

'There are other specialists,' he said. 'My college roommate is a doctor now. If I wrote to him, he might be able to recommend somebody.'

'Suppose he did,' she said bitterly, 'and suppose I took Dad to see the specialist, and the specialist told me what I already know in my heart – that the deterioration will go on and on until Dad loses everything that gives a man *self*. Would we be any better off than we are now?'

Mr Crewes got up to put down his coffee cup; when he sat down again, it was on the cushion that had been between him and Mom. 'If a specialist knew that, he could at least give you sympathetic and reliable advice. And that would be valuable, if not now, at least later. Eventually, for both the children's sake and your own, you'd have to send him to—'

'– an old folks' prison?' She looked into the fire; then she said, in a tight sort of voice, 'You don't know who he was.'

'Not directly,' he said. 'But I've gotten to know Colin pretty well. And every time I talk to him, I run into a hero. Sometimes it's Einstein, sometimes it's a warrior with an unspellable Gaelic name, but they're always grand and wonderful, from a world altogether different from the TV and comic-book facsimiles the other boys idolize. That kind of consciousness can only come from personal experience.'

Mom nodded. 'Oh yes – and it wasn't just the way he survived losing his arm, or his genius in the ring. He had a . . . bardic gift, I guess you could call it. He lived and breathed stories as he

167 ·

lived and breathed horses. And they interacted, somehow. One foot in the Otherworld, the other in the barn.' She smiled, but her face looked sad. 'And I lost him. Not now – long ago.'

'Lost him?' Mr Crewes sounded surprised.

Mom sighed. 'We had a major falling out over my marriage.'

I edged closer to the door.

'You see,' she went on, 'Peter's family was of the same . . . class, I guess you could say . . . as the Smithes. That's why we met, as a matter of fact – he roomed with the Smithes' oldest son at Harvard, and they came to the farm for Easter. But Dad was the runaway son of an Irish drunk, self-educated, prone to settle matters with his fists – proud as a king, but no gentleman.'

Mr Crewes nodded.

'You're going to laugh,' Mom went on, 'but I didn't understand what that meant. I went to school with children like the Smithes', and because I was Dad's daughter, and in the paper a lot because I'd won horse show championships, most of the other kids looked up to me. So, although the Smithes never even invited us into the living room when we went there to talk about strategies for the next show, I always thought we were their equals.'

Suddenly, in my mind, I was running over

to the Big House at the Smithes' to ask Mrs Smithe if she wanted me to ride one of the young hunter-jumpers in the next show instead of Fay ('my' pony). I was all excited, because Grandpa had said Mrs Smithe would probably say yes. I burst in the front door and dashed past the picture of the stag and the dogs into the living room – and stopped short, because the Smithes were sitting there with some of the people whose horses Grandpa trained. They were all in riding clothes; it wasn't a party or anything. But when Mrs Smithe turned and saw me, I could tell I'd broken the rules, and I backed out, saying I was sorry I'd interrupted, which was what I thought I'd done wrong. But now I saw that what I'd done wrong was *be* there, in the living room. And I saw why, all those years, though the Smithes had been nice to us kids, I'd never really liked them.

I came back to the real world with a bump, and realized I'd missed something. ' . . . no differ-ence to two eighteen-year-olds in love,' Mom was saying. 'But both families exploded. Peter's parents said I was a fortune-hunter; and Dad said a man like Peter never married an Irish girl – he just made promises until she was in a family way, then left her.'

Mr Crewes shook his head, but he didn't say

anything. Maybe he was knocked speechless, like I was, that anybody – let alone Grandpa or Grandfather and Grandmother Madison – would say things like that. Mom glanced at him and went on.

'Dad was especially bitter because the minute the War ended, he'd started making plans for me to study dressage at the Spanish Riding Academy. With that behind me, he figured I could qualify for the 1948 Olympics.'

'You were *that* good?' Mr Crewes's voice said he was as impressed as I was.

'That was part of the problem,' said Mom. 'I wasn't. I was beautifully taught, and I worked hard, but I never had that extra ounce of genius that makes a truly great rider like Dad. He never admitted that, but I knew.' She shook her head. 'So there I was, between Peter – bright, polished, subtle in all the ways Dad wasn't – and Dad, with his prejudices, his left fist, his hopes ...'

'And you chose Peter,' said Mr Crewes with a sad smile. 'Throwing over years of training for a school boy.'

'A *Harvard* boy, to make things worse. When Dad realized I was really going to do it, he said terrible things. I'd heard them before, plenty of times, but they'd never been directed at me. This time, though, they were, and finally I got angry back, and I said . . .' Her voice lowered. 'I said I wanted my own life, because I was sick of living out his Olympic dreams.'

'Oh, Deirdre!'

'Don't say it. The moment it was out of my mouth, I was sorry.' She sighed. 'But the rift never healed. Peter and I got married – his parents relented at the last minute and came, but Dad didn't. I wrote sometimes, but he didn't write back until Sarah was born. After that, he called on her birthday, and later, on Colin's; and when I wrote that Peter's reserve unit had been sent to Korea, he offered to take the kids for the summer. And so they became . . . ambassadors. Bearers of the regret I wasn't allowed to offer in person.' She dropped her head into her hands. 'It was so unnecessary. And now – what can I say? It's too late.'

Mr Crewes put an arm around her shoulder. 'It's not too late,' he said. 'You said yourself how much the children mean to him. And look how much you've given him since he's been ill.'

'I couldn't just turn him out in the streets, could I?' she said, in a voice that didn't sound like Mom's at all.

I couldn't believe she'd said that, but Mr Crewes didn't seem to be upset about it. 'That's what I was saying earlier,' he said quietly. 'There are hospitals, as well as old folks' homes.'

'What?' she said, turning on him. 'Send him off to strangers? Leave him to lose his sanity and his dignity with nobody to grieve for him? How could I do that? He was the king of trainers, a poet, a hero! And even if he hadn't been, he's my father, and I love him with all my heart!' Her voice choked off, and she cried and cried, and Mr Crewes put both arms around her and stroked her hair.

I went upstairs and checked on Grandpa. He was asleep on his office sofa, so I could have gone and told Colin about Mom and Dad and all the rest. But I didn't; I wasn't sure how he'd feel about it.

I wasn't sure how I felt about it myself.

8 The Grey Land

I never did tell Colin about Mr Crewes and Mom; after all, it might not have been what it looked like, and I didn't want to upset him, especially since he spent every supper telling us about the nifty things he and Mr Crewes were doing at school. I didn't tell him about the hospital stuff, either, because he was impatient enough about not being able to get back to Faerie as it was. But I did tell him about Mom and Grandpa, and he thought it was just as sad as I did. We agreed it meant we had to be extra nice to Mom, and we started cleaning the house and doing all the dishes without being asked; she was really pleased. So everything was fine, except the way I felt about her not telling us that Mr Crewes had been the friend she'd gone shopping with, or that he'd come to visit. There was

nothing wrong with those things, of course; it was just . . . well, she was the one who'd said 'no secrets'.

Christmas morning was sad. Mom had said there weren't going to be many presents, and we'd said that was fine, but we both gulped when we saw there were only two things for each of us and one of them was clothes; we hadn't known things were *that* bad. Mom liked the books we got for her, and she made a super Christmas breakfast, but Grandpa didn't understand what was going on, and he was upset because things weren't the way they usually were. All in all, even though I'd been feeling funnier and funnier about seeing Grandmother and Grandfather, by the time Paddy came with their limousine, I was as ready as Colin for some Christmas cheer.

We got it. All the way down to the Cape, we sang with Paddy – Christmas carols until we ran out of those, then Grandpa songs like *Wearin' o' the Green* and *Macushla* – until our voices went fuzzy. Then we hung over the front seat, listening to Paddy's stories about the things his brother's children had done to free Ireland from the Brits since last Christmas – and it seemed hardly any time at all before we turned in the big gate to Grandfather and Grandmother's driveway. It was like coming to a crystal castle; all forty of the windows were lit up with electric candles. Inside, the front hall was filled with pine boughs and silver ribbon, and we were welcomed in with Christmas hugs from Maureen and Jack (Paddy's wife and son), who were waiting at the door, and another from Molly, who scooted in from the kitchen, smelling of roast beef and garlic and fresh-baked rolls. Then Maureen and Paddy took our stuff upstairs, and Jack took us into the living room, where Grandmother and Grandfather were sitting by the fire. They said how much we'd grown, and we kissed them, and then we admired the tree, which was huge, with real glass ornaments and white lights (Grandmother thought coloured lights were vulgar). Under the tree there were lots of boxes, all perfectly gift-wrapped by people at expensive stores. We were allowed to look at them, but we couldn't open them until after supper.

Supper was an old-fashioned Christmas dinner, and it was a big deal. Grandfather and Colin wore dinner jackets (Colin's had been our dad's when he was a kid), and Grandmother wore lots of diamonds and an evening gown that had been made especially for her. I wore my best dress, and I took my hair out of its pony-tail and brushed it smooth, and though I knew I wasn't as splendid as Grandmother would have liked, I looked pretty good for me. Dinner started out with fruit cocktail (not the stuff in cans) served in crystal bowls that sat in silver dishes of crushed ice; then there was roast beef with Yorkshire pudding and roast potatoes and Molly's rolls with lots of butter, and glazed carrots, and at the end, baked Alaska, which Molly had made into a Christmas tradition two years ago when Colin told her it was his favourite food. It was wonderful, just the way it always was, but this year a part of me kept worrying about what would happen if Grandpa spilled his food on the tablecloth, and the first time Grandfather Madison picked up his wine glass, I almost told him to be careful.

Colin obviously didn't feel the way I did; he ate and ate, and after he'd polished off his baked Alaska (which he did before the rest of us had taken five bites), he began to talk just as cheerfully as he did at home. 'I'm learning about the brain at school,' he said. 'And it's—'

'Oh please, dear,' said Grandmother Madison. 'Not at the table.'

Grandfather looked pained, but he just said, 'Do you have a good teacher?'

'Boy, do I ever!' said Colin. 'His name is Mr Crewes, and he went to MIT—'

'– Did he know your father?' said Grand-mother.

'He couldn't have,' said Colin. 'He was there when Dad was at Harvard, and by the time Dad went to graduate school, he was already in the army. While he was overseas, he married a Korean girl . . .'

I looked up from my plate, surprised that Colin knew that (not to mention, surprised that Mr Crewes was married) – and when I saw Grandmother and Grandfather's faces, I tried to kick Colin so he'd stop, but the table was too wide.

' . . . but something went wrong when she had a baby, and both she and the baby died. When he got back home, he went to graduate school in Physics – right, Grandmother, just like Dad – but his family had money problems, so he became a teacher to help them out instead of finishing his thesis.' Colin smiled at Grandfather. 'Which means I'm studying with somebody who could have been a college professor, like Dad wanted to be.'

'That's good to hear,' said Grandfather. 'I was disappointed when your mother said she couldn't manage the drive to the private school I'd picked out for you. But we'll try again, after your . . . er, later.'

'And later, of course, you'll go to Andover, dear,' said Grandmother. 'We have to keep up the family tradition.' She turned to me. 'And I was thinking of Abbot Academy for you – though it's very intense and intellectual.'

'That's very nice of you,' I said. But when I glanced at Colin, I saw we were thinking the same thing: if Grandmother and Grandfather sent us to boarding schools, Mom would be all alone with Grandpa, and if Grandpa got worse, how could she possibly manage?

Grandfather put down his demi-tasse with a little rattle. 'I think it's time to open presents,' he said into the silence. Jack appeared out of nowhere (we always wondered how he did it), helped him out of his chair, and handed him his gold-headed cane; then we all trooped into the living room.

Colin got the expensive science books he had asked for, and a lot of things he hadn't asked for, including his 'big present': a little television that was supposed to go in his bedroom. He was really excited – we were the only kids in Wheelock School who didn't know what was going on in *Rin-Tin-Tin* or *Zorro*, and that made us outcasts. I got the books I'd asked for: a new series of books by a man called C.S. Lewis and all the *Anne of Green Gables* stories. Then there were some beautiful, soft sweaters that weren't the sort of thing I wore at all – and my 'big present': an envelope. I could hardly believe it; I'd asked for riding lessons, but after I'd heard Mom talk to Mr Crewes, I'd almost given up hope of getting them.

'Go ahead,' said Grandmother, smiling. 'Open it.'

I lifted the flap carefully and slid out the card. Inside, under the gold Christmas poem, it said 'To Sarah at Christmas – a permanent wave and contact lenses. With love from Grandmother and Grandfather Madison.'

I gulped and looked up. 'Thank you,' I whispered.

'Do you know what contact lenses are?' asked Grandmother eagerly. 'They're the latest thing – glasses so small they go in your eyes. It sounds terrible, but they say you get used to them very fast. The eye appointment is tomorrow – think of that! I can't wait to see how lovely you'll look when you stop hiding behind your hair and glasses.'

Colin looked up from his TV instructions. 'She looks just OK to me.'

'Ah, but just you wait,' said Grandmother.

Then they opened their presents from us – Colin had carved them little figurines (Grandpa had taught him how to do it the summer before he got sick), and I'd made them a book of the poems and stories I had written that year — and they kissed us good night and sent us upstairs with Jack and Maureen, who carried our presents. In my room, Maureen smiled a secret smile and slipped a beautiful flannel nightgown out of the top dresser drawer; she'd made it herself, even the lace around its square neck. I hugged her and gave her the little presents Colin and I had bought for her and Paddy and Jack and Molly with what had been left over from our Christmas money from the Smithes after we got presents for Mom and Grandpa (it wasn't as goody-goody as it sounds; we always got $50 apiece from Grandmother and Grandfather, and Mom only made us put $35 of that into our savings accounts). She looked at me carefully and asked if anything was wrong, and I said no, I was fine — and she should hurry downstairs for her Christmas with Paddy and the others. So she left, and I stared into the fancy mirror on my dressing-table for a while, then lay down on my bed.

A bit later, I heard my door open, and I looked up guiltily, wiping off my face, because I thought it might be Grandmother. But it was only Colin, so I went on with what I'd been doing. There was silence for a second; then I heard him cross the room, and I could feel him standing next to the bed. 'I wish *I* could give you riding lessons,' he said finally.

'It's not . . . well, it is, but . . . get me a kleenex, will you?'

He brought me the whole box from the dressing-table. Sometimes Colin was all right.

'Maybe it won't be too bad,' he said as I mopped up. 'I read somewhere that people actually see better with contact lenses, especially if their glasses are coke bottles like yours.' He jumped back as I punched at him. 'Tell you what! I'm going to get into the nifty bathrobe Jack and the others gave me; then I'm going to set up my TV. Sneak to my room in half an hour, and we'll watch some show.'

I said I would; he'd tried to cheer me up, and I knew he was burning to show off the TV. After he left, I changed into my new nightgown and washed my face in the bathroom that was all mine, then went back into my room. It was very nice – Grandmother had had it redone just for me, with a canopied bed and the dressing-table and lace curtains and paintings of beautiful women in long white dresses – but I didn't feel like spending a whole half hour in it, so I wandered down the long hall towards Colin's room, looking at the ghosts of myself that followed me along the oiled wood panelling, and wondering what Mom and Grandpa were doing at home.

Just before I got to the door of Grandfather's den, the light in it went on. I froze, because we weren't supposed to be up, but there was no sound of footsteps or sitting down or opening a paper, so after a few minutes I peeked around the corner. The room was full of Grandfather – rows of matching books, a glass-doored cabinet filled with trophies, piles of *Wall Street Journals*, a leather easy chair a bit cracked on the arms, a desk covered with typed papers in manila folders, the smell of pipe smoke – but there was nobody in it. Which meant that, though you'd never, never expect faeries in this house . . . I waited for some other sign, but there was only the light, burning away invitingly. Finally, I tiptoed in, holding my breath. It was against the rules for anyone to go in but Grandfather; he'd never said so, but we knew.

I looked over the books, which were mostly about law, then edged down to the trophy case, listening nervously to the silence and wondering what could possibly interest faeries in this room. It was kind of neat; the trophies turned out to be for golf, which I hadn't known Grandfather played, and behind them were framed diplomas from Andover, Harvard and Yale Law School, which I hadn't known about either . . . but what did faeries care about those sorts of things? I was about to tiptoe back into the hall when I saw two pictures on the desk. One of them was of Grandfather and Dad, at what must have been Dad's Andover graduation, because Dad's face was lots younger and more awkward than it was in the pictures we had at home. The other was Grandmother and Grandfather's wedding picture, and it gave me a real jolt. For one thing, I'd always thought of them as being the same age, because they were both old, but in the picture, Grandfather's hair was already a bit grey, and Grandmother couldn't have been twenty yet. For another, though Grandmother was still pretty good-looking and I knew she'd been a debutante, I hadn't realized she'd been *that* beautiful – I mean Marilyn Monroe and Audrey Hepburn and Grace Kelly all rolled into one, except 1920s. What really hit me, though, was the way Grandfather was looking at her, which, when I glanced back at the picture of him and Dad, was the same way he was looking at Dad. I stood there, trying to think what it was about that look that made me feel sad . . . and the light went out.

183

I scurried out into the hall and ducked into the empty room next door, my heart thumping wildly as Grandmother gave some sort of orders to Maureen and Jack downstairs. Nobody came up the steps, though, so I snuck down the hall to Colin's room, which it was about time I should do anyway. But that expression of Grandfather's went with me – and suddenly part of my mind was not in his house, but in the too-bright sunshine of a big show, and Grandpa was talking to the owner of Go For Broke, this great Thoroughbred that had just won a big hunter championship. The owner shook Grandpa's hand and the rider's hand and patted the horse; then he walked away, and everybody he passed tipped their hats and said congratulations until he reached his car and drove off alone. Grandpa looked after him, then down at me. 'Funny, you meet quite a few like him in this business,' he said. 'Every man tips his cap to him, and they mean it, surely – but there's no-one that likes him.' I nodded, because I could see exactly what he meant. But it hadn't occurred to me until just now, when I saw those pictures, that that sort of man might *want* people to like him.

I went into Colin's room, thinking so hard that I forgot I was going to ask him if he thought it was possible They'd followed us from home. But probably I would have forgotten anyway, because he was curled up on his window-seat, looking out into the dark.

'What about that show?' I asked, wondering what was wrong.

'Sorry,' he said. 'I can't find it.'

'Well, turn the dial, for Pete's sake! Isn't that what you do?'

'It's not the show I can't find,' he said. 'It's the TV. It seems to be in television limbo.'

I stared at him. 'You mean—?'

He nodded.

'Holy cow! What'll we tell Grandfather when we have to take it home?'

'It won't be a problem. Here, come stand in the hall with me.'

I did, of course, and when we looked back into the bedroom, there was the TV, sitting on his desk, packed and ready to go. As soon as we stepped over the door sill, it disappeared.

'And there you have it,' said Colin, sighing. 'Too bad. I was looking forward to having a normal childhood.'

'I wonder what They think of perms,' I muttered. 'That's as normal as you can get.'

'Omigosh!' Colin sat on the bed. 'Look, we've got to talk Grandmother out of it. It's a dumb idea anyway – your hair curls all by itself, or at least it would if it was shorter.'

'You're going to talk *Grandmother* out of doing something fashionable?'

'That's a problem, all right,' admitted Colin. He thought for a minute, then grinned. 'I got it – I can say the boys in my class think permed hair is uncool, and the older guys only date girls with the new, stylish cuts.'

'But that's not true!'

'So? We're not talking about truth,' said Colin. 'We're talking about something Grandmother will listen to. And you know she'll listen to that.'

I did know, but I was surprised that Colin did. 'OK,' I said. 'It's worth a try, anyway.'

'You bet it is,' said Colin. 'If we let Grandmother turn you into a poodle, and They don't like it, They might not let you back in Faerie. And I don't think I could manage to get Grandpa back without you.'

He really was an all right brother.

It worked. The moment Grandmother heard that popular girls didn't have permed hair, she said we'd get me a really good cut. So that's what I got. Nobody wanted me to get it but Grandmother – the hairdressers all said what a shame it was to cut off all that beautiful thick hair, and the poor woman who did the job was practically crying when she finished, because her thinning scissors and clamps and things kept disappearing when she reached for them – but Grandmother was firm, and what I had left when it was all over was the most conservative cut I could get her to agree to, and a two-foot braid of what had been cut off. It looked awful with glasses, but on the way home, we stopped at the contact lens place (it was one of those fancy places where you can get your lenses the next day, if you pay enough), and I practised putting them in and taking them out, and finally, I wore them back to Grandmother and Grandfather's house. I'd planned on going upstairs and hiding my head under a pillow, but Grandfather and Colin had just gotten home from the Boston Museum of Science, and they were in the front hall when we came in.

'Here she is!' said Grandmother proudly. 'Isn't she beautiful?'

They both turned around and stared.

'Jiminy Christmas,' said Colin. 'They really did a job on you.'

'Oh hush, Colin!' said Grandmother.

Grandfather gave me a long look, and he almost smiled, which was something he didn't do very often. 'Your brother certainly got all the Madison genes,' he said.

'I'll say,' said Colin. 'You look just like Mom, except with Grandpa's green eyes.'

All of a sudden, I thought of what Mom had told Mr Crewes about what Grandfather and Grandmother had said she was, and how they must still think so, because she was all alone at home with Grandpa instead of here with all of us. And something – maybe it was Them – made me look Grandfather straight in the eye. 'That's OK with me,' I said. 'Mom's really pretty.'

Grandfather shifted from one foot to the other, the way Colin does when he's embarrassed. 'Yes, of course she is,' he said.

There was a funny sort of silence; then Colin said, 'Would it be OK if Sarah and I went down to the beach?'

'Good heavens!' said Grandmother. 'What are you thinking of? It's much too windy!'

'Not if we stay between those two dunes at the end of the boardwalk.'

'You've found that place, have you?' said Grandfather. 'That was your father's favourite haunt. Yes, go ahead.'

Grandmother fussed, but we both knew whose word really went, so we zipped upstairs to put on real clothes. I got dressed really fast, but it took me a long time to get the contact lenses out, and when I finally ran down the hall to meet Colin, Grandfather was just going into his den.

'Sarah . . .' he said.

I stopped. 'Yes?'

'Come in a minute. I'd like to talk to you.'

He walked to his desk and eased himself stiffly into the big chair behind it; I stood on the other side of it, looking at the pattern on the rug and missing my hair.

For maybe a whole minute, he didn't say anything; downstairs, I could hear Colin fidgeting around in the hall. Then he cleared his throat. 'About your mother and your grandfather.' He picked up his pen, not paying attention to it. 'Er . . . how are things at home?'

All sorts of thoughts crowded into my head – Mom crying as she paid the bills, the way Grandfather smiled at Grandmother in the picture, Grandpa getting worse and worse and nobody knowing what to do, Grandfather and Colin at the Museum of Science, Mr Crewes, boarding schools – but they were so jumbled that all I could do was stare at the law books and the trophies and the desk, and his fingers, clumsily screwing and unscrewing the top of the pen. Finally I realized he'd think I was an idiot if I didn't answer, so I shook myself and said

'Everything's fine, thank you.'

He looked up, and for a second I was afraid he saw I'd lied – but he gave me an awkward smile and said, 'That's good to hear.' Then he nodded the way he nodded at Jack when he wanted him to go, and I escaped.

'Criminy,' said Colin as soon as we were outside. 'The hair and stuff isn't *that* awful – just different. You don't have to look so—'

'– Shut up,' I said. 'Race you to the end of the boardwalk.'

His red jacket flashed as he took off down the lawn, but I passed him just before we got to the edge of the beach, and he knew better than to try to push past me on the boardwalk, because it was narrow and half-covered with ice and drifted snow. When we got to the end of it, we jumped off and plopped down in the snowy sand, panting and shivering. The wind had died down, but the sky was wild and grey, and the waves were dark and fierce and wonderful.

Colin looked at me. 'Something's still bugging you,' he said. 'Is it Them? Grandfather kept losing things all day. At first I thought it was funny, but then—'

'– It's *not* funny!' I picked up a piece of driftwood and started scratching angry circles in the sand. 'All They do is play around!'

'That's what I've been saying all along!' he said, looking sore. 'And every time I've said it, you've said we have to be patient, or that there's nothing to the changeling theory—'

'OK, OK – I was wrong!' I said, breaking the stick over my knee. 'You've been right all along! There *has* to be something to it – nobody else understands, and nobody will help but us, and I really, really goofed just now, because Grandfather asked how things were, and maybe he *would* have helped if I'd told him – but I said the wrong thing, so now we have to depend on Them and Their little journeys, and Their own sweet time! It's so dumb!' I threw the three pieces of stick over the dune, one by one, as hard as I could. 'You stupid Faeries!' I shouted, trying not to cry. 'Take us where he is!'

There was a strange sound, and I turned around to see what on earth Colin was doing. But Colin wasn't there. *Hey, come on!* I said. But it was like the words I wanted had got stuck in my head; all that came out was gibberish. I tried again. *Colin?* No words; only a silence like cotton in my ears. *Colin! Colin!* I started towards the dunes to look for him . . . but there were no dunes. Instead, there were dark cliffs, so steep and so high I couldn't see their tops. And in front of them was a beach. Not Grandfather's beach,

191

which was perfectly smooth except for driftwood and seaweed; some other beach, with rocks jutting out of the sand, and towers of stone looming like castles out of waves that smashed against them in fountains of spray. Faerie, then. Only it wasn't at all like the other parts of Faerie we'd been to, which were green and beautiful. Here there was no colour. No wind. Just pounding waves and suddenly, a huge bank of fog, smothering the stone castles, the rocks, the cliffs, me . . . *Colin! Colin!*

Somewhere in front of me, I heard voices, half-wailing, half-singing. I stared as hard as I could, but there was nothing but grey. Stretching out my hands, I inched forward, sensing the rocks all around me, but somehow not running into any of them. The roar of surf got louder, and I knew I must be close to the water. My fingers touched something. One of the rocks, probably. I slid my hands along it to see how big it was — then I snatched them back, because it didn't feel the way a wet rock should. It was soft, and it shuddered.

Above me, a harp played a strange rippling chord, and the sound swirled around me in a breeze that melted the fog into scraps of clouds. I looked up and down the beach . . . and where there had been rocks, there were people, all silent and still. An old woman encrusted with barnacles, shaking as the waves broke against her. A man half-buried in wet sand that made channels on each side of him where the surf swept back out. A woman sunk up to her waist in sand that swept around her and buried the man behind her up to his shoulders. And more, and more, as far as I could see, all part in and part out of the sand, hardly even seeming alive until you looked at their eyes, which blinked from time to time. But they didn't seem to see anything; they just stared out to sea, singing a moaning sort of lullaby. I looked out at the sea myself, groggily wondering what was there.

A wave crashed onto the beach and wooshed around my knees, winding long brown ropes of kelp around my legs and leaving my feet half-buried in sand as it slid back. Stooping down, I picked up a couple of pieces of the kelp, so I could pop little nodules when I got back to my bucket and pail . . . wait, it was winter, so no bucket and pail. Just people. But when I looked down the beach again, there were no people. They'd turned back into stones, or at least most of them had. One was left, and it was strange, because the others had all been grey, and he was wearing a red jacket. He looked lonely, so I wrenched my feet out of the sand and staggered towards him, holding out a piece of kelp. He smiled a faraway smile, and we stood amongst the rocks, popping nodules and watching the fog settle around us again. The tide was coming in; the waves sneaked up and swirled around the rocks . . . and around us . . . a little deeper each time. Somewhere inside me, a voice said I should move back and take the red jacket person with me, but I couldn't think why; the sandy water around my legs was a lot warmer than the air.

I heard a harp again, much further away this time, but it sort of woke me up, though I hadn't been sleeping. I dropped the rope of kelp I'd been holding and took the red jacket person's hand, whispering *home*, *home*! But the word wouldn't come out, and even in my head, it didn't mean anything. I pulled him with me as I turned around and started towards the cliffs, hoping I'd remember what *home* was if I stopped looking at the sea − but after we'd staggered a couple of steps, the red jacket person stopped dead, tightening his grip so hard it hurt. In front of us, a tall rock was moving in the fog . . . leaning, pulling, struggling out of the sand as the white bubbles of a wave washed against it. The faraway harp played again − and then its music was drowned out by a terrible sucking sound as the rock broke out of the sand. Only it wasn't a rock. It was a man in leather armour, and the sword in his left hand was as long as I was tall. Over his right shoulder, he carried a huge shield that shone bronze-gold. *A hero*, buzzed my mind.

He stared at the waves, brushing away the fog that swirled around him with his sword. Then he turned his head and saw us. In a terrible flash of silver, his right arm swung his shield into position, and he raised his sword, striding towards us. We backed away – right into a rock. He could have cut us apart a thousand times, but instead, he stood still, staring at us until he blurred around the edges. A harp played chords and chords and chords, and I struggled to make my mind work. A hero. Cuchulain. Finn . . . no, Cuchulain's hair was two colours, and Finn's was really blond, not grey, and both of them were young. This hero was old, and he looked like someone I'd seen in a dream.

The hero's green eyes clouded over, and he walked slowly towards the grey sea, then into it. *Be careful!* I shouted. But no words came, and he waded in further and further, until he reached the place where the waves curled over and broke. Then in a huge burst of foam, he slashed at the waves with his sword, staggering as they smashed over his shield.

The person in the red jacket jerked my hand,

and his face told me he wanted to help the hero. Something about that didn't make sense, but I nodded, and we splashed into the grey waves, kicking them, shoving them back with our hands. Behind us, the rocks moaned louder and louder, until the air all around was filled with howls and screams and crashing surf. A big wave swept me onto a rock, and I stood up, looking for the hero, but there were breakers so high, all I could see was the flash, flash, flash of his silver sword. Then something bumped me – it was the person in the red jacket, sweeping out to sea. I grabbed him, and we struggled towards the beach through waves that tried to suck us back and rocks that shrugged us off as we tried to hold on to them. As we staggered onto the beach, we both stumbled over something, and as we fell I saw what looked like an arm reaching plead-ingly towards us out of the sand. When we got up, though, I realized it was just a long, thin edge of a buried rock. The red jacket person reached for a long piece of kelp that had wound around it, and popped a few pieces. Neither of us moved; standing still felt too good. The moans were turning back to a lullaby, softer and softer as the waves grew higher and the rocks disappeared.

Somewhere quite close, a horse whinnied. I straightened up and listened; there shouldn't be horses on the beach in winter. Maybe it had gotten loose. Or maybe it had thrown its rider. I took a few steps, and so did the person in the red jacket, which meant he knew something about horses. Together, we looked up and down the thin strip of beach. There was nothing there.

Then suddenly there was something there. A huge breaker rolled in; just before it crashed, it became a horse's crest with a shimmering silver mane, and a gigantic grey horse burst out of the dark water that smashed onto the sand. On its back, riding as if he were a part of it, was a red-haired man in a sea-green cloak that billowed out behind him. The horse tossed its head and reared, neighing as the next wave rolled in behind it, but its rider brought it down with a tremendous splash, and trotted it towards us through the surf. It moved as if it were on springs, with its tail high and its nostrils flaring, and when it got near us, it sidled away. The rider put a hand on its knotted neck. 'Steady there.'

I *heard* him, and understood. But that wasn't all. Something stirred in my mind, like when you first wake up in a strange place and you suddenly know where you are. I looked at the person in the red jacket, hoping he'd give me some clue . . .

'Colin!' I shouted. And this time, the shout didn't stay in my head. 'Oh, Colin!'

'Sarah!' he whooped. 'Boy, am I ever glad to see *you*! I've been looking all—'

The horse half-reared, and we both quieted right down. 'I'm sorry,' I said to the rider. 'It's just that it was so foggy, and we lost each other, and . . . oh.' I stopped, because his sea-green eyes had fastened on to mine. They were full of wild and mysterious things – the centres of hurricanes, the beginnings of winds, sea trenches so deep that light never reached them – and they were as powerful as his horse, except in a different and much scarier way. As I looked into them, a fog cleared in my mind, and I saw flickering, dancing faerie silhouettes . . . and that cloak, that red hair and beard, that half-tamed horse cantering through rings of bonfires to a cave where a Seer waited.

'Manannan Mac Lir,' I whispered.

'Enbharr,' whispered Colin, almost at the same time. For a moment, we just stared – not stupidly, the way we'd been staring before, but in a kind of wonder that there could be something so magnificent, even in the Otherworld. Then I nudged Colin, and we bowed.

A seagull flapped close over our heads, and all at once, there were hundreds of them, wheeling and diving and squabbling, the way they always do . . . except there had been no seagulls here before. Manannan glanced at them with a grim sort of smile; then looked down at us. 'You are a long way from your world, Children of Lugh,' he said.

I nodded and looked at Colin, but he shook his head and gave me a 'you-say-it' look. So I swallowed a couple of times and said 'Um . . . could you send us back? We've been gone an awfully long time, and I'm afraid Grandmother and Grandfather Madison will worry.'

'If you could be sent back,' he said, 'you would be there now. The harp called and called, but you were too far away to be sent for.'

Colin grabbed my hand, and I held his tight. 'You mean, we're stuck here?'

'No, no,' said Manannan quickly. 'I mean only that I cannot *send* you back. I was not sure, when I first saw you, that I would even be able to *take* you back, for like the stones, you knew neither me nor each other.'

'But we do now!' said Colin. 'For sure! Absolutely! Isn't that enough?'

'It is enough,' said Manannan. 'I – we – can restore you to your world.'

We breathed a tremendous sigh of relief. Colin looked up and down the beach and shivered. 'I've never even *dreamed* there were places like this.'

'I'm sure you have not,' said Manannan. 'This is no land for children, waking or dreaming. Even the Sidhe shun it; of all the Faer Folk, only I have the power to be sure of leaving it, once come. If, indeed . . .' He glanced at the stones, and when he looked back at us, I saw something I'd never seen in faery eyes before.

Enbharr struck out at a gull that landed nearby, then began to dig a furious hole in the sand with his front right hoof. He stopped when Manannan tapped his shoulder, but Colin and I took one look at his bobbing head and flat-back ears and stepped away.

Manannan nodded. 'As you see, I cannot keep him here – he fights the danger, though he neither sees nor understands it. Up behind me, Son of Lugh; the lady will go in front.'

There was no time to be afraid; the ringed hand was already flashing down. A minute later, Colin was behind him, I was in front, and Enbharr was walking towards the open beach. He was perfectly collected, and the wild look had left his eyes; but muscles underneath me coiled at every stride.

'Oh, please,' I said, looking up over my shoulder, 'let him out, just a little.'

Manannan's eyes met mine, and suddenly he smiled. 'Ah,' he said, 'I see they left you your courage, though they took your hair.' He spoke to the horse in the language Cathbad used, and in an instant, we were cantering, sending up flocks of shore birds in front of us. Enbharr felt like a bird himself; his strides grew longer and longer, but he moved so smoothly his feet hardly seemed to touch the sand. Faster, faster, nearer and nearer the water . . . sea-foam whirled around us, and the sound of hoofbeats was drowned in the splash of surf – then Manannan laughed, and we turned straight into the waves. I gasped and put my arm in front of my face, but it wasn't at all what I'd thought it would be. Enbharr didn't swim; he galloped over the waves, and through them, as if he were part of the sea. Whitecaps flashed around us, and swells rolled under us, but somehow we never got wet, just thundered on and on, until finally land rose up in front of us where no land had been before, all surrounded by mist.

We burst onto the shore in a splash of foam and came to a prancing halt. 'Your way lies there,' said Manannan, pointing. 'You will have no trouble finding it.'

He was right: there was a blaze of furry light behind the dunes, which meant somebody had turned on the floodlights at Grandfather's house. Even if we missed the boardwalk, we could get back easily. Yet, for some reason, I was so shivery when he lifted us down onto the sand that I began to wonder if they *had* taken my courage when they cut my hair. I reached out to stroke Enbharr. My hand slid down the sweaty neck – and touched Colin's.

'Your people are looking for you,' said Manannan. 'We must be off.'

But neither of us could speak; we just stroked Enbharr again and again, wanting him to stay – not only because he was beautiful, but because he was alive and animal and warm.

Manannan looked down in the gathering darkness. 'The horror of the land to which you journeyed lingers long after one has left it . . . but your fear will fade, in time.' A light flashed very near us, and we jumped back as Enbharr reared. Manannan rose with him, lifting one hand to us as he urged him forward. 'Farewell, loyal Children of Lugh.'

'Goodbye,' I said. 'Thank you.'

In three long strides they were in the surf; then they plunged into the breakers and disappeared. As we looked after them, a beam of light swept by us, then switched directions and stopped, making huge shadows in front of us on the sand.

'Colin! Sarah!'

We turned around, half blinded; the light-beam dropped, and we saw Grandfather Madison limping towards us with an expression I'd never seen on his face before. We both ran to him, and he put his arms around us as well as he could, holding a flashlight and his cane.

'I should never have let you come down here at this time of year,' he said. 'As soon as I saw the fog over the ocean, I came out, but by the time I got here, it was so thick I could hardly find my way.' He pulled the perfectly folded handkerchief out of the breast pocket of his suit and wiped Colin's face; then we started back. It felt like it took us for ever, but eventually, we got to the house, and there was Grandmother, frantic because we hadn't come back, and Paddy and Jack, frantic because they'd realized Grandfather had gone out alone to look for us. They lit a huge fire, and Maureen and Molly brought in sandwiches and gallons of cocoa with whipped cream and marshmallows, and everything was all right again, except I sort of thought Grandmother should have been worried about Grandfather instead of fussing over the way my new haircut had gotten sand and salt-spray in it. He'd had a lot of trouble walking in the deep sand, and when we'd gotten to the boardwalk, he'd slipped so much because of his street shoes and his cane, he'd had to let go of Colin's hand.

He didn't complain, of course, but he let Jack help him sit down in his big chair, which he usually didn't, and something about the way he stared into the fire after we'd eaten made me give him a real hug when we were sent up to bed, instead of my usual kiss.

I expected Colin to sneak down to my room, but he didn't, and I was glad, because I didn't want to talk. Part of me was still on that beach, between the terrible cliffs and the grey sea, listening to the rocks . . . keening. That was the word for that terrible lullaby. In the silence of the house, I half-heard it again, rising and falling in long, low moans. I crawled under the covers, shivering. The cocoa and everything made it feel as if everything had come out all right for a while, but now . . . now I realized that if we'd stayed on that terrible grey beach a little longer, we never would have gotten back, even though Manannan had ridden all that way to save us. If we hadn't recognized each other . . . *and we hadn't, all that time* . . . or known who he was . . . *and we hadn't, not at first* . . .

I shuddered and looked quickly around the room, to be sure I'd really gotten all the way back. I had, of course. I was lying under a pink quilt on my canopied bed, as far from Faerie as I could possibly get. But when I half-closed my eyes, the white dresses on the beautiful ladies in Grandmother's pictures looked like sea-foam on the edges of waves that slithered towards me across grey sand, higher and higher. *The horror of the land to which you journeyed lingers long after one has left it.* I buried my face in my pillow and closed my eyes. It didn't help; the sea-foam slid away, but I could still see the expression in Manannan's eyes after he'd glanced at the stones, and in some kind of double image, the hero with the bronze shield, swinging his sword helplessly at the enormous grey waves.

I could never have admitted to Colin that I was afraid to go back to Faerie. But I was.

9 Humpty Dumpty

We didn't talk about it for a long, long time. At first, I thought Colin was waiting until we left Grandfather and Grandmother Madison's, but he didn't say anything after we got home, either, so finally I just let it go. Not talking about it made a space between us, but there was a lot else going on, and it was easy to think we could patch things up when there was time. At least, that's what I thought, and I was pretty sure Colin was thinking the same thing.

Anyway, we got home. And Grandpa didn't recognize us. For a while, I didn't think much of it, because nobody else recognized me, either. Mom did this amazing double-take when she first saw me, and it was days before she stopped staring whenever I came into the room. As for school, the first time I got on the bus, everyone whistled, and at recess, all the girls clustered around, asking about the cut and the contacts and the sweater. But pretty soon, they saw I hadn't really changed, so they went back to ignoring me, and things were just like they'd been – except Grandpa never did quite figure out who Colin and I were. Finally, I realized that though Grandmother Madison hadn't been able to change me, something had changed him.

It kept on changing him. By Valentine's Day, he'd forgotten how to use a knife and fork; we had to teach him all over again at every meal, and finally it got so hopeless that we just let him eat with his fingers. Sometime around St Patrick's Day, he started having trouble putting one leg in each side of his pants; Colin and I thought that was pretty funny at first, but one day he got both legs stuck in one pant-leg and hit his head when he fell. After that, Mom helped him dress – and take a bath, because he couldn't do that by himself any more. Baths were awful; he seemed to think he was going to drown or something, and he yelled and struggled the whole time. Mom tried all sorts of ways of coaxing him, and some of them worked sometimes, but it got so we all dreaded Monday and Thursday nights.

The clincher came the last day of the Easter vacation. Mr Crewes and Mom were at the movies (that happened once a week; I felt funny about it, but it was the only time Mom got out of the house except when she went shopping, so I didn't dare tell her I wished she wouldn't go), and Colin and I were home with Grandpa. Colin came running downstairs to show me something he'd read about, but before I could look at it, Grandpa started pacing around, looking very unhappy.

'What's wrong, Grandpa?' I asked.

'Come *on*,' said Colin (he'd been really excited about whatever it was). 'You know he doesn't know what's wrong any more. Maybe he's hungry; I sure am – want a sandwich, Grandpa?'

Grandpa nodded, so we took him into the kitchen, but when I turned to give him his sandwich, he was standing in a puddle. It only took one sniff to tell what kind of puddle it was.

'Oh, Grandpa!' I began reproachfully. 'Why didn't you . . . ?' But then I saw how embarrassed he was, and I stopped.

Colin looked at me. 'What do we do now?'

'Clean up, I guess,' I said. 'I'll mop if you take him upstairs and—'

'– change him?' Colin stared at me. 'You know how he is about baths.'

'So don't give him a bath. Just use a wash-cloth.'

He gulped. 'I think you'd better do it.'

'But Colin . . .' I couldn't finish, but I turned red, and he saw what was bugging me.

'Oh,' he said, turning red too. 'Yeah. Well, come on, Grandpa.'

He took Grandpa's hand, and they went up the back stairs together. I got out the mop and the disinfectant, and I took care of the puddle and the drips that had followed them upstairs. Colin and Grandpa were in the bathroom; as I started back down with the bucket, Grandpa came out, wearing his pyjama bottoms. Colin has a lot of sense, sometimes.

When Mom got home, she said we'd handled everything beautifully (she was especially happy about the way we'd run Grandpa's pants through the washing machine, as if that had been the hard part). Still, I was really shaken, and I had a feeling Colin was too. I was right; ten minutes after Mom had kissed us goodnight, my door opened a crack and a light shone in.

'You awake?' whispered Colin's voice.

I sat up. 'Yeah.'

He made his way slowly across the floor. 'Geez,' he muttered, 'what a pig-sty. OK if I sit on the bed, to avoid contamination?'

I let that pass, partly because he was right; in the last couple of months, my room had started getting messy, and I'd sort of given in to it. 'What's up?'

'I'm not sure,' he said. 'But I've been doing research. Look what I found.' He handed me a book and his flashlight. 'It's what I came to show you just before . . .'

I opened the book to the place he'd put a marker and began to read. *Once upon a time, at the very edge of a village in Ireland, there was a cottage that always stood empty. Every year, it looked more and more forlorn, but nobody would go near it. One day, an old woman hobbled into the village. When the villagers greeted her, she said she had come because she had no place to live, and she had heard that there was a cottage there that nobody wanted.*

'That's true,' said the villagers, 'but there is a reason nobody wants the cottage: everybody who has lived in it has disappeared, even the dogs and cats that lay before the fire. It's death to go in it; do not try.'

'I am very poor,' said the old woman. 'And I am so old that if I die today, I will lose only a few months of life. So I will live in the cottage.'

All the villagers tried to persuade her she shouldn't, but she just thanked them for their warning, bought a little oatmeal for herself to eat, and moved into the cottage. The first day, nothing unusual happened, so the second day, she swept out the cottage and set up house-keeping very comfortably. But the third evening, there came a knock on the door. The old woman opened it and saw a tall, beautiful lady.

'Excuse me,' said the lady, 'may I borrow some oatmeal?'

I looked up at Colin. 'Criminy!'

He nodded. 'Keep reading.'

The old woman hurried to her shelf and gave the lady all that was left of the oatmeal she had bought from the villagers. The next morning, there came another knock on her door; it was the lady again, and she was holding a bag of oatmeal.

'I have come to pay my debt,' she said.

'There's no need for that,' said the old woman. 'The oats have gone to good use, I'm sure, and I am happy I could help you.'

'Thank you,' said the lady, 'you have been very kind, and the Faer Folk thank you. Just beyond the back garden of this cottage is a Faery Ring, and we know what harm foolish mortals can do to paths to the Otherworld. But you are a woman to be trusted, and so long as you stay away from the back garden on moonlit nights, you may live here as long as you like.'

The old woman thanked the faery, and on moonlit nights she was careful to stay in the front of her cottage. True to their word, the faeries never bothered her, and she lived happily in the cottage for the rest of her life.

I shut the book. 'Wow. So Jenny . . . I mean, that *is* what you think you found, right?'

'Right.'

I shivered. 'What do you suppose it's all about? I mean, why would They bother to disguise one of Them as a mortal when the rest of Them hover around the way They do?'

'So They can make sure Grandpa is OK,' said Colin. 'Like that day she went to the Gordons' with us.'

'Um, look,' I said (very carefully; I didn't want to hurt his feelings), 'that could only be true if Grandpa's a changeling. And I don't . . . well . . .'

'Don't hum around like that! I'm a scientist, not a baby! The changeling idea was just an early hypothesis – it was way too simple. But that doesn't invalidate it entirely.'

'Oh, come on! If you're wrong, you're wrong!'

'Not so. What I've learned studying science with Mr Crewes is that you can be wrong, but on the right track. Like that guy who thought giraffes grew long necks because they had to reach up into trees for food. It's silly, right? But he had the right *idea* about evolution; he just didn't have enough facts to let him figure out how it worked. Then Darwin came along and—'

'– Ahem!' I said. 'We were talking about changelings.'

'We weren't either! We were talking about hypotheses that are wrong but right. Like, our research shows that Grandpa isn't a changeling, except in the way Mr Crewes said he was—'

'– Would you please leave Mr Godalmighty Crewes out of it?'

He sighed. 'What I was *trying* to *say* was, research – this story – shows that Jenny is one of Them, and . . .' He shifted uncomfortably. 'Well, she *did* go to the Gordons'. And she'd never protect him like that if They didn't have some kind of interest in him, right?'

'OK, OK,' I said. 'But what kind of interest can They have?'

'Beats me. That's what I came to talk about. We need more research. Which means . . .'

' . . . Faerie.'

He nodded, and we both sat still, listening to the rain outside.

'There might be another way,' I said, finally. 'This rain should melt all those disgusting drifts by the entrance ramp, so we can get to the Ring again. Maybe we can talk to Cathbad or some-body and . . . er . . . well, we've never actually *asked* Them what's going on.'

'What if They get sore, or send us to Faerie instead of answering?'

'We could start by telling Them — extra politely — that we'd rather stay here.'

'OK.' He drew a deep breath. 'I suppose we could try it Saturday.'

'Not Saturday,' I said. 'Dandy's coming on Thursday, remember? And we promised Tiffany we'd watch her ride him on Saturday.'

'Oh, sure,' he said quickly. 'Maybe Sunday, then.'

'Yeah.'

He sat there a little longer, clicking his flash-light on and off. When he went away, I had a feeling we weren't going to do it on Sunday, either.

Tiffany didn't say much on the bus the next day, but I would have known Dandy was coming even if I hadn't been counting the days with her. Ever since Christmas, she'd been losing that timid look, and her smile had started being a real one. She was doing better in school, too; just before the holidays, she'd gotten an A on a math test, and Miss Turner had moved her up a group. I heard her tell one of the other teachers it was a miracle, but I knew better.

Anyway, with three days still to go, Tiffany

was looking happier than I'd ever seen her, and on Wednesday when we got out to the storm drain, she could hardly sit still. 'Gwen called the Gordons to make last-minute arrangements last night,' she said, smiling all over. 'He's coming tomorrow morning at ten. I can't believe it! I can't believe it!'

'You'll believe it soon enough,' I said, trying not to smile back. 'Starting tomorrow night, you'll have three horses to shovel for, not two.'

'Oh, that's OK,' she said. 'I'll shovel, and I'll brush him for a whole hour every day, and I'll clean his tack, and I'll pick out his hooves, and I'll pull his mane once a week, and . . .' She went on and on, all bubbly and not like Tiffany at all.

The next day, she wasn't on the bus, which didn't surprise me a bit; if I'd been getting a horse at ten, there's no way I would have gone to school. Even as it was, I might as well have been at the Gordons' as in class; I kept looking at the clock and thinking of Dandy leaving his old stable with Gwen, or unloading at the Gordons', or settling in his new stall while Tiffany watched. On the bus, Colin and I talked about getting off at the stop two after ours and nipping down to the barn, but we decided Mom would have a heart attack between the time we didn't show up at home and the time we called from the Gordons', so we just went home.

'It's all right,' said Colin. 'She'll tell us all about it tomorrow.'

But when tomorrow came and we raced up the bus steps, Tiffany didn't even look up. Colin and I blinked at each other; then he took the seat in front of her and turned around, and I sat next to her, but even though she must have known we were there, she didn't say a word.

'What do you suppose happened?' whispered Colin as we got off.

'I don't know,' I said. 'I'll try to find out at recess.'

But at recess, Tiffany dawdled all the way to the storm drain, and after we crawled in, she just sat there. Finally, I couldn't stand it any more. 'Tiffany, what's the matter?'

She didn't say anything.

'Gwen didn't decide to sell Dandy or something, did she?'

She shook her head.

'Then he's at the Gordons'? And he's OK?'

'I think so,' she said, so low I could hardly hear her.

'You think so! You mean, you weren't there?'

She shook her head. 'My parents don't want me to go to the Gordons' any more.'

I stared at her. 'Not ever?'

'That's what they said.'

I could hardly believe it. 'But . . . but don't they know about Dandy?'

'That's why. Because of Dandy. I told them about him Wednesday night. And they said I couldn't go any more.'

'You mean, they were angry because you hadn't told them before?'

'I'd told them before. So had Mrs Gordon.'

'Then what were they angry about?'

'They said I was their kid, and the Gordons didn't have any right to get a good horse for me, so I couldn't go back.'

I tried to make sense of that, but I couldn't. Finally I said, 'Well, you said they didn't like your going to the Gordons' before, but they let you go after a while. They'll probably change their minds this time, too.'

'No, they won't.' She looked up with the smile I hadn't seen since Christmas. 'Don't look so upset,' she said. 'It doesn't matter.'

'It does, too, matter!'

She shook her head. 'It really doesn't matter what happens to me.'

And that was all she'd say.

After recess Mrs Turner sent my reading group to the library to work on reports, and as I finished checking out my books, Mr Crewes came in. I started out the door, trying to act as if I hadn't seen him, the way I always did, but he caught my elbow.

'Sarah, come into the conference room. I want to talk to you.'

Of course I couldn't say no, so I followed him. He closed the door carefully. 'Tiffany looks very unhappy,' he said. 'Do you know if something's wrong?'

'I . . . I don't think she wants anybody to know.'

'But you know?'

I thought of saying I didn't, but that seemed wrong, so I nodded.

'Sarah,' he said, 'I don't want to make you tell me something you promised not to, but you need to understand. Some children's parents don't treat them the way parents ought to—'

'— Sure. It's called child abuse.'

It didn't sound very polite the way I said it, but he just raised his eyebrows and went on. 'OK. If a teacher suspects one of his students has been abused, he can report it to authorities, and they'll check up on it. Sometimes it makes a big difference to a kid who has had a terrible time and not dared to tell anyone. So if you think not telling me what happened to Tiffany will help her in the long run, think about it once more.'

I did think about it, and all of a sudden, I remembered how he'd helped us with Grandpa on the playground that day, and how he'd gotten Colin into his class, and . . . well, whatever else you might think of him, he was good at solving problems. So I told him all about Tiffany's riding, and how she'd finally gotten a good horse, and what her parents had done. When I got to the end, I swallowed hard and I said I'd appreciate it if he could do something.

He gave me a funny look. 'I'll sure try,' he said. 'I'll talk to Tiffany at lunch, and if I find out anything that makes me a candidate for your appreciation, I'll let you know when I come over this evening.'

I felt a little better as I went back to class, even though I wished he'd been angrier at Tiffany's parents – and Mom hadn't told us he was planning to come over. As it turned out, he didn't stay very long; Grandpa decided he didn't belong there, and when Grandpa decided that sort of thing, it was hard to talk him out of it. This time, he made such a fuss that Mr Crewes finally said he'd come back another time. But before he left, he took Colin and me out on the porch. 'I talked to Tiffany,' he said, 'and I hate to say it, but I'm afraid there's nothing I can do.'

'There's got to be!' said Colin. 'She couldn't

even talk on the way home! She just stared out the window, like she was in some sort of trance.'

'I know,' he said. 'But unfortunately, you can't get a kid away from her parents because they've made her unhappy. You've got to be able to prove they've hurt her physically.'

'Oh,' I said, suddenly remembering. 'Mrs Gordon said something about that, the first time we went over there. Does that mean nobody can help her? Not you or the Gordons or us or anyone who cares about her?'

Mr Crewes looked out at the streetlight. 'I'm afraid it does,' he said finally. 'At least it means nobody can make the law work for her, but—'

'– That's crummy!' Colin exploded. 'For Pete's sake, why do we have laws if they don't help people out?'

Mr Crewes looked at him. 'What I was going to say was, there are ways we can help that don't have anything to do with law. Counselling, for instance.'

'A lot of good that'll do!' muttered Colin. 'Social workers don't have craniums.'

Mr Crewes tried not to smile. 'They've helped a lot of kids, Colin.'

'OK, OK.'

'And you two and I will just have to try to get her out of herself. I know it doesn't sound like much, but it's important.' He looked at us both carefully. 'Do you understand?'

We nodded.

'You're good kids,' he said, and I was afraid he was going to put an arm around us. But he didn't. 'Good night,' he said. 'See you Monday.'

We went to the Gordons' on Saturday – without Grandpa, though Mom had usually driven him there with us before, because he'd caught a cold, and she was worried about him. It was probably just as well; the Gordons were really upset. Mrs Gordon was one of those women you see a lot of if you know horse people; she had this strict, determined face, and I'd always been a little afraid of her. But that weekend, she cried and cried, and it hit me for the first time that they didn't have any kids, and it was more than the riding that made Tiffany important to them. Then, of course, there was Dandy in his stall, beautiful and friendly and wanting attention. Colin and I padded around as quietly as we could, mucking out, cleaning tack, and brushing horses; the Gordons said that helped a lot, but none of us smiled the whole time we were there.

The next week, it was even worse. Tiffany didn't look up when we got on the bus, and she didn't answer when we tried to talk to her.

Some of the kids started to tease her, and we shut them up, but that was about all we could do. In class, she dreamed off all day, looking out the window and smiling. She still went out to the storm drain with me, but all she'd do was sit there, smiling that terrible sweet smile, and looking out the opening. I tried everything I could think of – talking, not talking, suggesting we play tether-ball, telling jokes – but nothing worked.

'Tell you what,' said Colin when I told him. 'Let's ask her over, and when she comes, we can go to the Gordons'. Her parents will think she's at our house, and—'

'– What if they find out and beat her up?'

'Then Mr Crewes can get her out of there,' he said, half-meaning it.

That's where we left the idea, but by Friday I was so desperate I decided to try it. 'Tiffany,' I said, 'would you like to come over to our house tomorrow?'

She looked out the bus window. 'My parents won't let me go anywhere. They say I'll sneak off to the Gordons'.'

I glanced over my shoulder at Colin, wondering if he felt as cheap as I did. 'What if our mom called your parents and said we were just going to be around the house all afternoon?'

Tiffany didn't answer, but just before we got to our stop, she scribbled a number on a scrap of paper and gave it to me. That evening, Mom made the call; and when she came back downstairs, she looked sore.

'Well,' she said. 'Tiffany's parents have said she can come tomorrow afternoon *if* she comes on her bike (not our car) and *if* they can call her here every half hour.' She shook her head. 'And I thought you were exaggerating when you told me how they were. Poor Tiffany.'

Poor Tiffany was about it. It was rainy on Saturday, and her jeans and sneakers were soaked when she got to our house. Luckily, she was the same size I was, so we could fix that fast enough, but that wasn't the real problem. It wasn't exactly that she didn't want to do anything – she said of course she'd love to put on a play, and of course she'd like to see the costume closet in the attic – it was that when we started doing it, she drifted off. The costumes were great (we'd been collecting them for years), and I was sure we could have gotten her involved in them if we'd had her to ourselves, but with her parents calling every half hour, it was impossible – especially since the phone upset Grandpa, and we had to dash down from the attic to get to it before he did. The last time it rang, we were too late; just as we got there, he yanked the phone out of the wall by the roots, and stomped down the back stairs with its cord trailing behind him. Tiffany jumped back with her hands over her mouth, and her eyes made me wonder if maybe her parents didn't hit her, but Mom put an arm around her.

'It's OK, dear,' she said sadly. 'He wants to stop the phone from ringing, and he's forgotten how to answer it. There's another phone downstairs. I'll call your parents right away.'

She hurried down the front stairs, and we heard her dialling. But we also heard the side door slam, and when we ran to the window, we saw Grandpa striding up the little hill between us and the Ring, still carrying the phone.

'Criminy!' said Colin. 'We've got to catch him!' And we all dashed downstairs.

'Sure you want to come?' I asked Tiffany as we ran up the hill. 'You'll get wet again.'

'That's all right,' she said, 'it's my fault he went out.'

I was just going to say it wasn't, when we got to the top of the rise, and she peered ahead through the drizzle. 'Oh!' she said. 'I know this place! My dad stops off here to give stuff to a friend of his. Gosh! Your grandfather's almost at the entrance ramp! Suppose he—'

And she took off, jumping over old tyres and piles of junk. You'd never have thought Tiffany could run like that, but she was over the second guard rail by the time we got to the first. Grandpa ducked behind a refrigerator when he saw her; she stopped the way she would have if he had been a horse, and held out one hand coaxingly. Right in the middle of the Ring.

'Tiffany!' I yelled.

'Back up!' yelled Colin. We raced up and grabbed her, but the minute our hands touched hers, there was music and spinning and colours, and when it stopped, the sun was out, and we were standing in an enormous green field with groves of trees and rolling hills.

'Oh no!' whispered Colin. 'They've got us.'

'Maybe it won't be so bad,' I said. 'I mean, it's pretty here.'

Tiffany looked all around, and her face slowly changed from the way it had looked all week to the way it had looked when she first saw Dandy. 'Where are we?' she breathed.

'Er . . . it's hard to explain.'

'Never mind then,' she said. 'It doesn't matter. It's just . . . I think I've been here before. Not really, of course. But . . . you know those places you always go in dreams?'

'Oh!' I said. And Colin and I looked at each

225

other – because we'd both realized it was the place we'd seen her daydreaming about when we'd gone to her house with Hob and Lob.

'If it's the place,' she said, looking more and more excited, 'there should be horses . . . oh, here they come!'

She pointed to the left, and I saw a couple of horses at the top of the hill behind us. Tiffany whistled, and one of them nickered and started down to visit; a few others followed him, and in a minute, the whole herd of horses we'd seen in Tiffany's daydream was walking towards us, snatching up mouthfuls of grass as they came.

'Aren't they beautiful?' said Tiffany happily. 'I'd never want to be out in the open with a herd this big anywhere else. But here, they seem to know they're safe, so they never spook, and they're very careful.'

She was right. As the horses circled around us, there was no pushing or nipping or jostling at all. Tiffany walked between them, stroking faces, patting necks, straightening manes, and talking, always talking, the way Grandpa had in the barn. By the time we caught up with her, she was on the far edge of the herd, patting a mare that stood between her and a foal.

'Look!' she called softly. 'A new filly.'

We helped Tiffany convince the mare that we

wouldn't think of taking her baby away from her, and after a minute, she let it step around her and sniff us. It was covered with dark brown fur, but you could see it was going to be black, and it had an adorable white star. Tiffany leaned over and kissed it, and the little thing rubbed its head against her.

Colin patted the mare, looking at her appraisingly. 'If Grandpa *is* here, he's going nuts,' he said. 'I've never seen so many terrific horses. I wonder who they belong to.'

'They belong to all of us,' called a beautiful golden voice. 'But they're in my care.'

We looked around, and there, coming out of a grove of oak trees, were three stocky brown mares with glorious manes and tails, their coats shining in the sun. One of the mares walked half a length in front of the other two, and on her back was a lady in a dark brown dress and long red-gold hair with a lot of grey in it. She wasn't beautiful the way women are supposed to be beautiful, but she had the most wonderful face I'd ever seen, and something in it told me that we were as safe as the horses were, even though we were in Faerie.

'Welcome, Children of Lugh,' she began; then she saw Tiffany, and something changed – just a little – about the way she looked.

'This is our friend Tiffany,' I said. 'She's here because . . . well, we didn't mean to come ourselves, and it was totally an accident . . . but she's been here before in dreams . . .'

'Indeed she has,' said the faerie rider, looking at Tiffany with a smile that seemed sad.

Tiffany slid one arm around the filly's neck, staring. 'Who are you?' she whispered.

'I am Epona,' said the lady, 'and I have charge of all the horses in Faerie.'

'Even Enbharr?' said Colin, forgetting his manners.

'Even Enbharr,' said Epona, and her smile wasn't sad at all, now. She slipped off her mare and walked towards us. 'He is the sire of this little one.'

Tiffany stepped away from the filly as if she were afraid she shouldn't have touched it, but Epona shook her head. 'There is nothing to fear,' she said. And then, in exactly the same tone of voice, 'Come here, child.'

We looked at each other, wondering which one of us she'd meant, but then the filly started towards her with a funny baby prance, and we realized she'd been talking to it. She stroked its neck, then ran her hands down its legs, and Colin and I glanced at each other; she really knew what she was doing. When she was finished, she put her arm over its withers.

'She's perfect,' she said affectionately to the mare.

Tiffany nodded, but Colin nudged me and drew me back a little way. 'Should we tell her about Jenny and Grandpa?' he whispered.

I glanced over my shoulder and I found myself looking straight into Epona's deep brown eyes. They didn't scare me, the way Jenny's eyes had when I'd met them at the Gordons', but they told me that she already knew that we knew about Jenny and Grandpa – and much, much more. I shook my head at Colin, feeling very young and stupid.

Epona turned away, looking thoughtful; then she said, 'I have to take a young horse to the new palace of Faerie; would you three like to ride there with us?'

'Oh yes!' we said, all together.

'Very well, then.' I didn't see any signal, but the two brown mares that had been on each side of her stepped forward to Tiffany and me, and a dappled grey pony trotted out of the herd and stopped in front of Colin. I vaulted on my mare (thanking Grandpa in my mind for teaching us how), and in a minute we were following Epona's mare and a pretty black three-year-old through the fields. Our horses were . . . well,

Grandpa had always told us (and anyone else who would listen) that a good trainer wanted to make his horses move as beautifully when they had someone on them as they did when they were free. I'd understood, of course, but I'd never *felt* what he was talking about until right then. There were no reins or stirrups, but the horses were so perfectly collected that we could trot along without bouncing at all – and when we came to an oak grove and Epona started to canter, Tiffany laughed for the first time since I'd met her.

I brought my mare up next to hers. 'Isn't it great?' I said. 'We should sing something!'

Her face changed a little. 'I don't know any songs. My parents don't like me to—'

'– All it has to be is something cantery,' said Colin quickly. 'Like a nursery rhyme.'

Tiffany frowned, and I thought, *gee, she doesn't even . . .* but then she smiled. 'What about *Humpty Dumpty sat on a wall . . .* ?' she said, right in time to the horse's feet.

'Perfect!' I said. And we joined in.

Humpty Dumpty had a great fall.
All the king's horses and all the king's men
Couldn't put Humpty together again.

It *was* perfect – so perfect that we said it over and over, until Epona looked back at us, and we realized how stupid nonsense must sound to a faery. I suppose that should have shut us up, but it made us silly instead, and we laughed so hard that the hills around us began to echo.

Epona led us on, shaking her head; we quieted down and began to look around, because it was very pretty. We were riding towards a range of misty mountains, and the grass on the hills was filled with delicate spring flowers – and I thought of home, where the melting snow was uncovering weeds, rusty cans and broken bottles. The hills around us got steeper, and at last, we stopped at the top of one of them to rest the horses. Epona circled her right hand three times, but I was too busy staring at the view to ask why. Below us was a lake, deep, still and almost black. Marble cliffs of a craggy mountain rose out of its far shore, so perfectly mirrored by the lake that if it hadn't been for the ripples of swans swimming in the water, it would have been hard to tell which cliffs were real and which were reflections. At the top of the cliffs, just below a peak half-covered by clouds, stood a palace. It wasn't finished yet – two of its four towers still had scaffolding all around them – but the finished towers were tall and gold, and the walls glistened white and silver between arched windows that shone like diamonds. As we gazed at it, two swans rose out of the lake and flew majestically in our direction.

'Oh,' breathed Tiffany. 'I've never seen anything so beautiful.'

'Me neither,' I whispered – then suddenly the swans circled us, banked, and landed a few feet away. The three-year-old shied at the great pounding of wings, and even my mare kept me busy. When I looked again, the swans were gone; Mongan and Cathbad stood next to Epona.

'Welcome, Children of Lugh,' said Cathbad, bowing to us.

'And to you too, Fay Child,' said Mongan, bowing to Tiffany.

All three of us bowed as well as we could, being on horseback; when we straightened up, something about the way the faeries were looking at Tiffany made me uncomfortable.

'Um,' I said, 'we were admiring your palace. It's . . . wonderful.'

Cathbad nodded. 'It's being built by the greatest craftsmen in the Otherworld for the king we will soon crown.'

'And nothing but grief we've had in the building of it, with the rush and all,' muttered

Mongan. 'It's a good thing kings only happen once a century or so.'

'The rush?' I said, frowning.

Epona nodded. 'It must be ready for the king's coronation. That's the greatest occasion in the Otherworld: everyone comes to honour him.'

She smiled at us. '*All the king's horses and all the king's men*, as your rhyme says.'

'Wow!' said Colin. 'Would *that* ever be a sight!'

Tiffany had been looking more and more excited. Now she urged her mare towards Cathbad. 'Sir – if Sarah and Colin come to the king's coronation, could I come, too?'

The faeries looked at each other; Cathbad cleared his throat. 'Fay Child,' he said slowly, 'Sarah and Colin have unusual privileges. No other mortals can travel back and forth between the Otherworld and their own.'

'I see,' whispered Tiffany, looking down. Suddenly she looked up, her eyes wide open. 'No mortals can travel *back and forth*! Does that mean I . . . can't go back? Now?'

I looked at Cathbad's inflexible face and suddenly went cold all over. 'That's . . . that's not true, is it? I mean . . . you'll let her . . . just this once . . . ?'

We all stared at the faeries; they were absolutely silent.

'Please . . .' I begged.

'Shh,' whispered Tiffany. 'You don't understand; I don't *want* to go back.'

'No, no, *no*!' we both said together.

'Yes, yes, yes!' said Tiffany. 'I want to stay here – always.' She looked shyly at Epona. 'I could help you with the horses.'

Cathbad laid his hand on the neck of Tiffany's mare. 'Fay Child,' he said, 'Mortals must live in their world, and faeries in the Otherworld. If a mortal child stumbles into the Otherworld, as you have, the Rules which permit her to return exact a concession, lest that child be damaged by eternal longing to return. Thus, you must go back to your world. And when you do, you can never visit this one again – in person or in any other way.'

'Any other way?' said Tiffany, staring at him. 'You mean, in dreams?'

'Yes. You will never dream of the Otherworld again.'

Mongan turned away and looked over the lake.

'Not even . . . even in daydreams?' whispered Tiffany.

'Especially not in daydreams,' said Cathbad.

'For those carry you here most frequently.' Tiffany looked at Epona, but the beautiful, sad face was just as firm as Cathbad's. 'It will be painful at first,' she said, 'but you won't lose the Otherworld entirely. In fact, you will lose less of it than you would have if you had continued with your daydreams. If mortals dream of Faerie too often, gradually it slips away from them, and only the dreams remain. When that happens, they drift into the Grey Land, and no-one, faery or mortal, can save them.'

'Then let me stay here!' begged Tiffany. 'Here where everything is beautiful, and all the horses are trained right, and nobody is ever hurt!'

The three faeries exchanged glances; but Epona shook her head. 'The price of staying is too high, Fay Child,' she said gently. 'Go back to your own world.'

Tiffany put her head down on her horse's mane. 'No, no,' she sobbed, 'please . . .'

But even while she was speaking, the mountain and the lake and the palace began to spin, and when they stopped, we were back in the cloverleaf, with the junk all around us and the traffic roaring by in the rain. Grandpa was sitting on the side of a fallen-over stove, dialling the telephone. Tiffany was sitting on a wrecked car, crying and crying.

Colin cleared his throat as he looked at her. 'Geez.'

I nodded, wondering what we should do; I'd never seen anyone cry like that before. 'You collect Grandpa and start home,' I said finally. 'We'll catch up.'

They started off, but as soon as she heard the junk shifting around, Tiffany raised her head and slid off the car. I walked beside her, and if it hadn't been so uneven, I would have put my arm around her. 'Listen,' I said. 'I know this is going to sound really strange after what you saw today, but Epona's right. If you have to stay in one place or another, it's much better here.'

'No, it isn't,' she whispered. 'Not for me.'

'Yes, it is,' I said stubbornly. 'The Otherworld is beautiful, but . . . look, we accidentally got to the Grey Land she talked about – at least, I think we did – and you can't even *imagine* how awful it is. And . . . I can't explain it exactly, but even when the Sidhe are being nice, like today, they're sort of scary. And I don't think it's just them – except maybe Cathbad and one called Manannan, who wasn't there today. It's the Otherworld, even when it's all horses and mountains and lakes and flowers, because you always *feel* the Grey Land, sort of hovering . . .' I gulped. 'What I mean is, it's *dangerous* there – like downtown, only worse, because you aren't ready for it – and if you stayed there for long, you'd be finished.'

'So what?' she said, and slowly her face settled into the look she'd worn all week. 'It doesn't matter what happens to me.'

'It does, too!' I said. 'Think of all the people it matters to: Colin and me, the Gordons—'

'Hush!' Colin looked over his shoulder as we came into the yard. 'Somebody's here.'

I looked at the beat-up car in the driveway, and at the two people who were talking to Mom at the side door. I knew who they had to be even before I recognized them.

'Here they come,' said Mom's voice, getting louder as we got closer. 'See? They went out to bring my father back after he ran outside to throw the telephone away, and now they've got him. There's no need to take Tiffany home now; they've only been gone for as long as it took you to get here.' She turned and started to introduce us, but Tiffany's father cut her off.

'OK, Tiff,' he said. 'Thank Mrs Madison for having you over, then into the car. We made a deal and you didn't keep it, so that's it.'

Tiffany smiled her terrible smile at Mom. 'Thank you very much for having me over, Mrs

Madison,' she whispered. And she started for the car.

'Wait!' said Tiffany's mother. 'You didn't apologize for the trouble you caused.'

'Oh, she was no trouble at all . . .' began Mom.

'I'm afraid Tiffany's lots of trouble,' said her mother – and it was strange the way she said it, as if everybody could see she was right. 'That's why we have to be so sure she does what she's told. I'm very sorry you had to see that, but I'm sure you know all families have problems.' She glanced at Grandpa, then dropped her hand on Tiffany's shoulder. 'OK, Tiff – say it.'

Tiffany looked down. 'I'm very sorry I was so much trouble,' she said.

'There,' said Tiffany's father. 'That does it. We'll leave you to yourselves.' He put his hand on Tiffany's other shoulder, and they walked her to the car. The four of us watched as they backed out of the driveway and drove past the warehouses.

'You know,' said Mom finally, 'all my life I've said the age of heroes was over, and people should solve problems with their heads, not their fists. But this time . . .' She looked at Grandpa almost pleadingly, and Colin and I did, too. But what we were looking for wasn't there; all we saw was an old man standing in the rain, tired and confused.

Mom swallowed hard and pushed a lock of wet hair off his forehead. 'Come on, Dad,' she said in a sort of scratchy voice. 'Let's go inside. I'll help you get into dry clothes.'

10 Beltane

When Colin and I got on the bus on Monday, I knew we'd been right to worry about Tiffany all day Sunday. She smiled at us, which at least meant she wasn't spaced out, but . . . well, Grandpa used to say you could see a horse's spirit had been broken, because its eyes told you it had given up hope of living without pain. Tiffany's eyes looked like that, and we knew it wasn't just because of her parents. They'd taken Dandy from her, but before Saturday, she'd at least had Faerie. Now she didn't even have that – and it was all our fault.

She moved over to make room for me on the seat. 'I'm going to have to get off at your stop on the way home and pick up my bike,' she said in a flat sort of voice. 'I hope that's OK.'

'Sure,' I said. 'I'll ride home with you.'

She shook her head. 'They wouldn't like that.'

I offered to ride to the end of her street and then turn around, but she just looked out the window. That was all she did in class, too; at least until Miss Turner got a really good look at her and sent her somewhere. She was gone a long time, even at recess, but I never found out where, because when I went to lunch, she was talking to Mr Crewes, and of course I didn't join them. None of it seemed to help, anyway; she looked out the window all afternoon, too, and somehow her face got thinner and thinner.

Colin felt just as bad as I did, and on the way up the hill after the bus let us off, he tried to cheer Tiffany up by doing his Mr Stegeth imitation. It was great, but Tiffany just smiled politely and looked off at one of the warehouses, where Jenny was hanging up some tattered laundry. She hardly even talked when Mom came out to say hello; she just got on her bike, thanked Mom for letting it stay in the shed, and coasted slowly down the hill.

Mom looked at me. 'Has she been like that all day?'

'Yeah,' I said, 'no matter what anybody did.'

Mom frowned. 'Boy. I wish I knew of a good counsellor to call.'

'Mrs Gordon said Tiffany has a social worker,' I said. 'Maybe she knows his number.'

'That's a good idea,' she said, starting inside. 'I'll slip upstairs to see if Grandpa is still asleep; then I'll get on the phone.'

'This is a funny time for Grandpa to be asleep,' said Colin.

'He's got a terrible cough,' said Mom, 'and he's pretty groggy. I wanted to take him to Dr Greenstone, but he didn't have an opening until tomorrow, so it'll have to wait.'

We looked at each other, because we both knew Mom would never take Grandpa to Dr Greenstone unless she was really worried about him. The last time they'd gone, Grandpa had yelled and screamed the whole time, and she'd been a wreck when she got home. 'You want us to help?' I asked. 'You could pick us up at school, and—'

'— Thanks,' said Mom. 'I'll take you up on it if I have to, but I think I can get someone else to go with us.' She gave us a smile that didn't look quite right. 'Meanwhile, I made cookies; help yourselves while I call Judy about Tiffany's social worker.'

Colin and I grabbed some cookies and wandered into the living room. 'You have to wonder if that social worker can do any good,' I said. 'After all, he's been seeing Tiffany's family all this time.'

'Yeah,' said Colin, checking his watch as the 2:45 roared by. 'Holy cow! Look!'

I looked – then stared. Tiffany was leaning on the handlebars of her bike, waiting for the train to pass and talking to Jenny. Actually, it seemed more like Jenny was talking, because her hands were moving; but Tiffany was certainly listening. After a moment or two, she turned her head slowly towards the train . . . and something about the way she nodded made me remember the way she'd stared when I introduced Jenny at the Gordons'.

'Geez,' I breathed. 'Do you suppose she knows Jenny's one of . . . ?'

We looked at each other; then without another word, we dashed back into the kitchen to get our jackets and raced out the side door.

Outside, the 2:45 was gone. So were Jenny and Tiffany.

'That's funny,' I said.

'No, it isn't,' said Colin. 'She was waiting for the train to pass, and Jenny came out, the way she does – and when the caboose went by, Tiffany went home.' He turned around, looking disgusted. '*We're* the ones who are funny. The house must be getting to us.'

243

I looked up past the huge, dirty windows at the peeling tower; but what I saw, instead of the mossy slates on the roof, was the faerie palace, glistening just below silver clouds of mist. When I blinked, it was gone. 'OK,' I said. 'You've got a point.' And I followed him inside.

The next day, Tiffany wasn't at school. Miss Turner asked me if I knew where she was, and though I said I didn't, I had a pretty good idea. Mrs Gordon had probably gotten the social worker to talk to Tiffany's parents, and they'd been so angry because someone was trying to help her that they'd kept her out of school. Which meant she was trapped in that horrible, messy house with nothing to dream about. Thinking about that made me pretty miserable.

Things were pretty miserable when we got home, too, because Mom and Grandpa were at Dr Greenstone's. We'd been planning to make soda bread, so it would be ready when they got home, but instead, we just sat at the kitchen table and listened to the empty house. We had gotten used to the way it felt when everybody was around, but now . . . I got up and fetched the flour, wishing I hadn't read the oatmeal story. Colin got out a mixing bowl, but I could see he was antsy – and when somebody knocked at the side door, we both jumped out of our skins.

Colin gulped. 'Who do you suppose it is?'

'I guess we'd better go and see,' I said. My feet dragged all the way to the door, and I slipped the chain into the slot before I opened it – which made me feel pretty silly when I saw it was Mrs Gordon. 'Oh, hi,' I said, undoing the chain. 'Mom has taken Grandpa to the doctor's, but they should be home soon. Come on in! Would you like a cup of tea?'

Mrs Gordon took off her boots and came in. 'Thanks. And I think I'll take you up on that tea. It's been . . .' Her voice choked up.

I pushed Colin towards the tea kettle and got out the tea-ball so she'd have a moment to put herself together; then I asked, 'Is everything OK at the barn?'

'Oh, the barn's fine,' she said – and she actually said it as if the barn didn't matter. 'I'm here about Tiffany. She's gone.'

'Gone!'

'That's what her parents say. They came to our place about an hour ago, accusing us of kidnapping her – and, boy, I thought they were going to turn the whole place upside down. They finally left when Tom threatened to call the police, but after they steamed off, it occurred to me that she might be here, and if she was, there

245

might be trouble. So I jumped in the truck and came over.' She picked up the mug of tea Colin had put on the table and took a sip, looking at us very carefully over the rim. 'You'd tell me if she were here, wouldn't you?'

'Of course we would,' I said. 'But she's not. Cross our hearts.'

Mrs Gordon looked down into the tea. 'Then she really is gone,' she said, very softly. 'I would have thought she'd come to us.'

'Well,' said Colin, 'she may not have had time yet. When did her parents see her last?'

Mrs Gordon made a face. 'They *said* it had only been a couple of hours, but I don't believe them. They . . . heck, you're old enough to understand. Tiffany's parents are just about at the end of the alcoholic road; half the time they're so drunk they don't know whether she's home or not. Then when they come to, they get really possessive – or maybe vindictive is more like it. I suppose it makes them feel they're acting responsibly about her, but all it really means is they've suddenly remembered she exists.' She wiped her eyes. 'I'm sorry,' she said. 'It just makes me so darn mad. But let's get down to business. When was the last time *you* saw Tiffany?'

'Yesterday,' I said. 'She got off the bus with us and picked up her bike, and . . .' I looked at

Colin, and I saw he was thinking what I was.

'Yesterday,' muttered Mrs Gordon. 'That's what I was afraid of. Well, at least that gives us something concrete to tell them.'

'Tell who?' squeaked Colin.

'The police, of course,' said Mrs Gordon. 'If Tiffany's been gone a whole day and hasn't come to you or to us, it's a matter for professionals – and you can be sure her parents won't tell them. When a social worker has been seeing your family, and then your kid clears out, it looks bad, especially if the Dad has had a few brushes with the law.' She got up and started to the door; we followed, watching numbly as she shoved her feet into her boots. 'I'll go to the police station and get things moving. And listen, if Tiffany shows up, you call us right away, OK? One of us is going to be sitting by the phone until we find her.' She gave us both a kind of hug at the same time as she hurried out the door.

Colin took a deep breath as the truck started up outside. 'I wish she hadn't said that. About sitting by the phone, I mean.'

'Tiffany may have just run away,' I said. 'She sure had a reason to.'

'Oh, come on! When we went out, they were just . . . gone.' He looked at me defensively. 'And don't say what you're thinking.'

I hadn't been going to, anyway. 'The thing is, They said she couldn't go back.'

'Sure — on her own, or with us. But she *really* wanted to go, and if Jenny got her to say something about that . . . well, did you ever hear of a faery who could kidnap a kid and didn't?'

'Jenny doesn't seem like the kidnapping sort,' I objected.

'I know. But there are plenty of others hanging around, like the ones who put glamour in our eyes that day. They'd do it. If she let them — Jenny, I mean. Do you suppose it would help if . . . Well, Jenny's right down the road, and we could sort of . . . mention that Tiffany's . . .'

I thought of Jenny's eyes, and Epona's eyes, and of all I didn't know. Then I thought of having to live with myself (not to mention, having to live with Colin), if I chickened out now. 'OK,' I said. 'Let's go and talk to Jenny.' And I put on my jacket.

It was a perfectly beautiful afternoon, and the daffodils and forsythia in the yard were beginning to bloom, but the nearer we got to Jenny's warehouse, the less I noticed. Colin knocked at the door, which was three times the size of a normal door, with *Patrick Rogan & Co.* stencilled on it in faded gold letters. Nothing happened, so he turned the handle with both hands and gave it a push. It swung open into a hall that stretched the whole length of the warehouse, with a high ceiling held together with wood beams as thick through as Colin and me together. There were bare electric light bulbs strung across the beams; half of them had burned out, so it was pretty dark (the windows were mostly covered with cardboard), but we could see wheelbarrows and laundry carts lined up along the walls, filled with clothes and other stuff. Some of the people who lived in the warehouse were lying next to the carts, sleeping in their winter coats under dirty blankets. The others were sitting at scroungy tables, playing cards or eating. They were wearing coats, too, because the air was cold and damp. We walked forward slowly, sniffing the smells of canned tomato soup, and bathrooms, and dirt, and maybe beer – and I wondered what it had been like living there all winter.

After we were about halfway into the hall, one of the card players looked up and saw us. 'It's the kids,' he said. In a minute, everybody was staring at us, but nobody got up.

'Hello,' I said, and my voice sounded very small in all that quiet. 'We're looking for Jenny. Can you tell us where she is?'

The man at the card table looked around the hall. Everyone who looked back at him shook his head, and finally he looked back at us. 'Jenny's gone.'

Colin stared at him. 'Gone? But we saw her yesterday!'

He grinned. 'Then you saw her before she left.'

'But . . . but where did she go to?'

He shrugged. 'Couldn't tell you.'

I looked around the big hall, and lots of pairs of eyes looked back at me; but no-one said anything. 'Um, OK,' I said. 'Thank you very much.'

'Don't mention it,' said the man. As we turned to go, he asked, 'How's your grandpa?'

'He's fine. Actually, he has a cold now, but . . .'

The man coughed – it was the most awful cough I'd ever heard. 'Well,' he said when he was done, 'you two take care of him.'

All of them watched us go; there wasn't a sound but our footsteps. By the time I shut the big door behind us, my hands were shaking.

'Oh boy,' said Colin as we started up the hill, 'I guess we know where Tiffany is.'

I nodded, and I felt just sick.

As we started up the driveway, we heard a car and the whistle of the 4:15. We turned around just in time to see Mom's car before it disappeared behind the flash-flash-flash of the train. As a line of flat-cars went by, we saw Mr Crewes's new car pull up behind ours.

I kicked a stone out of the driveway. 'So *that*'s who she got to help her!'

'Of course it is! Who else would do it?'

'Us,' I said, and started inside.

He grabbed my arm. 'Look,' he said. 'Ease off, will you?'

'Ease off what?'

'Mom and Mr Crewes.'

I stared at him. 'I thought you hadn't noticed.'

'You think I'm blind? He takes her to the movies "to get her out of the house". He comes over in the evenings with some excuse about an assignment for me. It's pathetic.'

'It sure is!' I pulled away. 'And if *you* don't care if Mom makes a fool of herself—'

'– Cut it out! Think. He could be old, or nasty, or stupid . . . or have kids.'

'Geeeeeeeez.'

'Right. So maybe you should try – just try, mind you; I know what a strain these things are for you – to be polite to him. It would make things a lot easier; they wouldn't have to lie.'

I gulped. 'They're lying because of *me*?'

'Sure they are. You don't see *me* snarling whenever he comes up – or over.'

251

I wanted to run up to my room, but the 4:15 was out of the way, and the cars were almost at the driveway. When they pulled up, Mr Crewes jumped out of his car and helped Grandpa out of the far side of Mom's. 'Come on, Angus,' he said cheerfully. 'We're home now.'

Grandpa nodded and started towards the side door, looking old and sick, and shuffling a little, the way he'd begun to lately. I followed him, walking very close to Mom. 'How was he?'

'He was . . . well, it was better than last time,' she said. 'But the doctor says he has bronchitis. We got some medicine for it, but we'll have to be very careful to keep him warm and dry.'

'Sure,' said Colin. He hurried ahead of us and slipped his hand into Grandpa's. 'Come on, Grandpa,' he said. 'We didn't have time for soda bread, but we'll make you pancakes.'

So we all went in, and Colin and I made our very best pancakes. Mr Crewes was impressed, and he joked around about Colin's having a great future in chemistry. That made Mom and Grandpa laugh, and it was almost fun; but when we gave Grandpa his pancakes, he only took one bite, then wandered away upstairs. After that, nobody felt like talking much.

★

Two cops came and talked to us about Tiffany. We told them the truth, of course, which was that we hadn't seen Tiffany since the 2:45 went by on Tuesday. But we didn't tell them about Jenny, because we didn't want to get the warehouse people in trouble – and besides, what could we have said? I think they suspected we were leaving something out, because they talked to Mom after she sent us upstairs, but she said she'd backed us up, and that everything was fine.

It wasn't fine; there were still the kids at school to deal with. They were all excited because Tiffany's picture was in the paper and even on TV, and of course, everybody asked us about her. That meant we had to tell our half-truth story over and over, which we hated – plus, it made us angry because none of the kids had paid any attention to Tiffany before.

Then there were the Gordons. We were free to go to the barn every day, because Grandpa was really sick, and Mom didn't feel she could leave us alone with him. It seemed to cheer the Gordons up to have us there, and brushing and feeding and mucking out cheered us up, the way it always does. But after about a week, Mrs Gordon told us to ask Mom to call her. Mom did, and after they were through, she came down to the kitchen.

253

'Judy and Tom want to know if you'd like to exercise Dandy,' she said. 'They called a couple of days ago, asking how experienced you were, and of course I told them about the young horses you worked with Dad. Now they've gotten in touch with the girl who owns him – they phoned all the way to England, can you imagine? – and she said it would be fine if you worked him.'

We looked at each other over the dishes we were washing; neither of us said anything.

'Of course, it would just be until they find Tiffany,' Mom went on. 'But I told Judy you'd understand that, and since I've heard nothing but horses, horses, horses, since you left Pennsylvania, I said I thought you'd be thrilled. I was right, wasn't I? Sarah?'

'Sure,' I said, watching a soap bubble pop in the dishpan.

I felt her look at me. 'You don't *seem* thrilled.'

'I am. It's wonderful. It's just . . .'

'I understand,' she said, patting my shoulder. 'All right, I'll tell them you'll do it.'

We listened to her climb the back stairs.

'Geez,' said Colin. 'I feel like a criminal.'

'Me, too – except criminals can confess, and we can't.'

He dried the frying pan fiercely. 'There's nothing *to* confess. It's not like we planned it.'

I nodded, but I couldn't say anything, because Mom was coming back down.

'All set,' she said. 'Tom will work him tomorrow and Saturday, to get the kinks out of him, and you can start Sunday.' She picked up a pencil to write it on the calendar, then smiled for the first time all day. 'That's the first of May. Just think – you can celebrate Beltane by going riding.'

'Great!' I said. And I really tried to smile back.

It was sort of rainy on Friday, but the Gordons' ring had really good drainage, like the ones in Pennsylvania, so Mr Gordon could longe Dandy anyway. Dandy bucked a lot at first, but he never pulled on the line, and pretty soon he settled down. Saturday afternoon, Mr Gordon rode him, and we hung on the fence and watched through the fog and drizzle, and he was so beautiful that I stopped feeling guilty, except about not feeling guilty, if you see what I mean. We were both really excited, even though it started to pour when we were riding our bikes home; and as soon as I'd changed, I went into Grandpa's office. There was a horse magazine on his lap, but he wasn't looking at it; he was watching the drops slide down the windowpane.

'Hi, Grandpa,' I said, sitting next to him.

255

'We're going to ride a horse tomorrow.'

'Horse?' he said, looking at me eagerly.

I heard Mom and Colin stop in the hall outside the door, and I knew why; Grandpa hadn't said anything for days. 'That's right,' I said, smiling at them as they came into the room. 'Horse. Colin and I have a horse to work. Isn't that great?'

Grandpa smiled. 'Horse,' he said again. 'Work horse. Great!'

'I'll say,' said Colin. 'Hey! Mom, do you suppose Grandpa could come watch us?'

'Dr Greenstone said not to take him out, but . . .' She looked at Grandpa's lit-up face. 'Well, tomorrow is supposed to be sunny and warm. If it is, I'll bring him over for a little while – would you like to see the kids ride, Dad?'

'Great! Great!' said Grandpa, smiling all over, and we all left him with his magazine, feeling good because he was so alert.

'Maybe he's getting better,' said Colin as he poured milk into a pan for cocoa – then he stopped and looked up. 'Was that the front door?'

It had been, which probably meant Mr Crewes had come. This time, I went with Colin to say hello, making myself smile. But Mr

Crewes wasn't there. Just Mom, looking frantic.

'In his shirt-sleeves!' she said, pulling on a sweater. 'And he's been so sick!'

'You mean, Grandpa went out?' I gasped. 'In *this*?'

She nodded and ran out on the porch, looking down the road. It was raining so hard that the warehouses looked like ghosts. 'Where could he have gone?'

To the Ring, said Colin's pale face; but for once I shook my head. 'We were talking about horses, and he sort of knows the way to the Gordons' by now. I bet—'

'For Pete's sake! Of course!' Colin tossed me my poncho and slipped his own over his head. Mom grabbed Grandpa's as well as her own, so we beat her to the tracks, but she caught up with us as we stopped to see if he'd gone one way or another on them. There was no sign of him, so we all started to jog towards the Gordons'. The edge of the road was ankle deep in water, but it was either that or the shoulder, which was all mud and broken bottles, so we stayed on the pavement. Every time a car passed us, we got splashed up to our ears, and lots of the drivers honked because there wasn't room for them and us too. Finally, we got to the supermarket, which was closed, of course, because it was after five, and I was thinking the traffic would be less scary, now – when Colin yelled: 'There he is!'

I shook the rain out of my eyes and saw Grandpa in the middle of all the empty parking spaces, shuffling between the yellow lines, stopping, turning, and shuffling up to the next set.

Mom stopped dead. 'Dear God!' she whispered. 'He's pacing out a course.'

For a moment, all three of us just stood there, watching. Then Mom reached a hand out to each of us, which she hadn't done since we were really little, but neither of us fussed about it. Slowly, we sloshed through the parking lot and stopped in front of Grandpa.

'Dad,' said Mom. 'Let's finish the jumps tomorrow. It's raining now.'

He shoved his dripping hair out of his face and looked up. 'Wet.'

'Right,' she said. 'So the footing is terrible. Let's wait, huh?'

Grandpa coughed a terrible, deep cough. Mom let go of my hand and slipped Grandpa's poncho off her shoulder. He smiled and let her help him put it on, and I guess that made him forget the jumps, because when she took his good hand and began to lead him home, he went with her just fine. After we'd crossed the tracks, he started shuffling more and more slowly, and he shivered so hard Colin and I could see him shaking. As soon as we got home, we put him to bed and we covered him with all the extra blankets, but it was a long time before he slept.

We took Mom some dry clothes and a pot of tea and left her sitting there, watching him, while we changed (the second time) and went down to finish making the cocoa. We didn't enjoy drinking it, though; we just sat there, pushing the marshmallows around in the mugs, not looking at each other. Because the house felt the way it had when Mrs Gordon had come to see if we knew where Tiffany was. As if it were waiting for something.

The next morning, Grandpa was so sick he could hardly sit up, and he wouldn't even drink the tea we brought him. I looked at Mom. 'Maybe Colin and I should stay home.'

'Don't be silly,' she said, trying to smile. 'It's a beautiful day – just perfect for a ride – and there's nothing you can do here besides worry.'

She was right, of course, so we went, and at first, we sort of forgot about Grandpa, because Dandy nickered when we came in, and we both hugged him and told him what a wonderful horse he was. But after we started riding, it was different. I got to ride first, and Mr Gordon stood

in the centre of the ring, giving me pointers . . .
but every time I looked at him out of the corner
of my eye, I thought I saw Grandpa. There was
no time to think about it then; Dandy wasn't like
the horses in Faerie – you had to ride him every
second. But when it was Colin's turn, there he
was in the ring with a man in breeches and
boots, just the way he'd always been, even
though he was taller now. I listened to Mr
Gordon's voice giving instructions, and I
watched Dandy's head come down and his
strides get longer, and I was sure – absolutely
sure – I heard Grandpa saying, 'Good, good. A
little more leg, now . . .'

I heard footsteps behind me; it was Mrs
Gordon, holding out a kleenex. 'Want this?'

'Yeah,' I said. We walked away from the fence,
so Colin wouldn't get distracted. 'I'm sorry,' I snuf-
fled. 'It's just . . . I want Grandpa back.'

'We all do,' she said. 'But listen, Sarah,
because your grandfather was who he was, he's
always in the ring, with everybody who trains
horses right. That means you'll never really
lose him.' She put her arm around me. 'And
I'll tell you another thing. Your grandfather
wasn't just a great trainer; he was a great
teacher. I always knew, of course, but today . . .
well, watching you kids ride is poetry.'

'Thanks,' I whispered.

She hugged me, and it sort of helped, because I pulled myself together enough to take the saddle so Colin could hose Dandy off. 'I'll walk him, if you want,' I said.

'That's OK,' he said, but his voice sounded funny, so I walked around the ring with him.

'You all right?'

'No. I miss Grandpa. Not the one at home – our *real* Grandpa.'

'Me too.'

We walked around the ring again. Just before we got to the gate, Colin halted Dandy. 'Um . . . do you think it would be worth it to . . . ask Them if we could go . . . find him?'

I played with Dandy's mane, thinking and thinking. Finally I said, 'No, I don't.'

Colin stared at me. 'You want to chicken out? On *Grandpa*?'

'It's not chickening out. It's that every time we muck around with what the faeries are doing, we mess up – like getting on that crazy bus after we told Mr Crewes, or getting sent to that beach, or getting Tiffany into Faerie. And I think there's stuff going on that we just don't understand, like that guy with the giraffes. So instead of pushing ahead with the wrong theory, like he did, we should . . .'

'Should what?'

'I don't know,' I said. 'Wait, I guess. Until we have a theory that really works.'

He opened the gate and led Dandy back to the barn. I thought he was sore – if there's anything Colin hates, it's waiting – so I put away the saddle and cleaning things instead of going back to Dandy's stall, and I didn't turn around when he came in with the bridle. But he stood behind me like he had something to say, so finally I looked at him.

'Let's go home,' he said. 'And tell Grandpa all about Dandy.'

'Great,' I said. And I meant it.

11 All the King's Horses

The way to the Gordons' looked flat once you passed the tracks, but on the way home, you noticed it was a little bit uphill all the time. Usually, it was no problem; but this time we were in boots and breeches, which are made for horses, not bikes, and our horse-riding muscles were sore from not being used for so long. Between that and the cars filled with dressed-up people who'd been able to go to mass because their grandfathers were OK, we didn't get to our crossing until the 12:15 Sunday express did, though we'd told Mom we'd be home at noon.

'Boy!' puffed Colin, waving to the engineer. 'You know those English bikes – the ones with gears for hills?'

'Yeah,' I said. 'Don't I wish!'

The last car zipped by, and we bumped our bikes across the tracks in the diesel-smelling silence. I was sort of hoping Colin would walk up the hill, but he didn't, so I stepped on the top pedal to give myself a start, which was a good thing, because I just barely passed him.

'Let's leave them here,' I gasped, dropping my bike by the side door. 'We can always—'

'– Not me,' he said. '*I'm* not a slob . . . Hey! Where's the car?'

I stared at the empty space, and the first thing I thought was *oh, no! The faeries have taken it*! But then I thought again.

'Let's go in,' I said, trying not to sound scared. 'There's probably a note on the table.'

We did, and there was. *Sarah and Colin – Grandpa having a lot of trouble breathing. Am taking him to the hospital. Phone plugged in. Will call as soon as I can. Love, Mom.*

Colin took a deep, shuddery breath. 'What do you think we should do?'

Before I could think of what to say – let alone of what to do – the phone rang. We dashed into the hall, and I answered it, squinting in the red, blue and gold sunlight that poured in through the stained-glass window, and holding the receiver so Colin could hear, too. 'Mom?'

'Yes, it's Mom,' she said, and her voice was so

tense I hardly recognized it. 'The emergency room says it's pneumonia, and it's pretty serious, and he has to stay the night. I have to stay here, at least for a while, because he's upset and confused. Will you two be OK?'

I was about to say we'd be fine, but Colin grabbed my arm and turned the mouthpiece towards himself. 'How OK can we be if Grandpa's in the hospital?' he said, choking.

'Now, now,' said Mom, in a fake cheerful voice. 'It's the right place for him; they know just what to do. There's plenty of bread for lunch and leftover chicken in case I don't get home for dinner. But I'll call if I'm going to be late. Take care now.' And she hung up.

I put the receiver down slowly and stood staring at the phone. Colin sat down on the bottom step and rested his chin on his hands. Nothing moved but the dust motes that drifted through the coloured shafts of sunlight and disappeared into the shadows.

Finally, Colin drew a shaking breath. 'And you said we should wait,' he said bitterly.

'Wait for what?'

'Beats me. Inspiration or something. A theory that explained what was really wrong with Grandpa.'

'I just meant there was so much we don't understand—'

'— We don't have *time* to understand! Grandpa's really sick! He might—'

'— But don't you *see*? He's in the hospital, with doctors! *That's* what's going to save him, not a theory we know is a bit off!'

'So our theory's a bit off!' he said, starting to cry. 'Have any of the doctors he's seen had a theory that brought him back to us?'

'That's not the point! He's got pneumonia, and—'

Colin jumped up. 'It is *too* the point!' he shouted. 'Because if our theory is even a little bit right, the Grandpa that's in the hospital may not be the real Grandpa!'

'Don't be a moron! You *know* that's too darned simple!'

Colin whirled around and stomped up the stairs. I thought he was going to his room, but he stopped when he got to the landing. Facing the window, he lifted his arms in a kind of Y, and he tilted his head back so far that I could see the tears on his face. 'You stupid faeries—'

'— Colin! Don't!'

'— Send us to where he—'

I tackled him, and the two of us rolled down the stairs, landing in a heap in the hall. We scrambled to our feet with our fists in a position that would have made Grandpa proud.

But I'd been too late.

Something began to hum, and the pool of coloured light we were standing in flickered with strange-shaped shadows. I dropped my fists, and before they'd even gotten where they belonged, Colin grabbed my hand. Because the faeries in the window weren't mixed in with the trees around its border any more. They were moving – flying, walking, running – all in one direction. As we watched them, the hum got louder and turned into voices, and the faeries got bigger and bigger as the window crept slowly towards us . . . and in a second, we weren't in the house any more; we were in a mountain valley, surrounded by a huge crowd.

It was a crowd of faeries, of course – not the Sidhe, but the other kind. They were all going someplace, but they weren't making much progress because there were so many of them. Most of them were on foot, but some were riding in chariots pulled by the weird creatures we'd seen the night of the bonfires, and the creatures were jigging and shying, and every couple of minutes, one of them bolted into the crowd. Then there was shouting and fighting, and everyone gathered around to watch, so the

267

crowd moved forward even slower than it had before.

'Criminy,' said Colin. 'What a mob! Who would have thought faeries— Oh! I see where we are! And look! They've finished it!'

I braced myself against the crowd and looked where he pointed. Not far from us was a blue-black lake, half-covered with mist and looking as if it belonged to a different world from the noise and colours of the crowd. On its far side, at the top of a marble cliff so high that clouds wisped around it, was the faery palace, its four golden towers shining in the hazy sunlight. I stared at it, blinking as it blurred like a reflection, and thinking of Tiffany: *'Oh! I've never seen anything so beautiful.'*

'Easy there,' said Colin. 'If you lose a contact in this crowd, it'll be a goner.'

'I'm not—!' Suddenly, an idea hit me. 'They were finishing the palace for that coronation, weren't they?'

'Yeah,' said Colin; then his eyes opened wide. 'You mean, you think this is it?'

'Well, They said it was the biggest deal in Faerie, and this sure looks like—'

'– Wow! Cool!' He looked at me accusingly. 'And you tried to stop me!'

I sighed. 'OK, OK. Look, see that willow by

the lake? Let's go and sit in it; that way we'll have a good view and we won't get mowed down by— Look out!' We jumped to the side, and a runaway white bull missed us by inches; the swaying faeries in its cart laughed uproariously.

'Right,' said Colin. 'The willow it is.' And we elbowed and squeezed our way to it.

It was one of my better ideas. Once we'd climbed as high as we could, we could see the whole crowd: two chariots of trolls who'd stopped their long-legged pigs to watch a fight over a goat cart that had just run down four leprechauns; a ramshackle cart of squabbling hobgoblins pulled by a horse-hoofed dog; a bevy of lovely little nixies wafting along in watery dresses; three selkies romping up the hill in seal-skin cloaks; a band of black dwarves marching grouchily in tight formation, with gold chains and sapphire-studded belts.

'Geez!!' said Colin suddenly. 'Do you realize what this means?'

'What *what* means?'

'Our being here. I'll give you a hint: where did I ask the faeries to send us?'

'To—' and suddenly I saw. 'You mean, you think Grandpa's . . . here?'

'You got it.' He bounced up and down on his branch.

'Wait a sec! We don't *know* the faeries send us to where he is. I mean, last time—'

'– was last time! This time's got to be different because everybody in Faerie is here, and so if he's been in Faerie, like our theory suggested, then he's got to be around.'

'*If*. But we aren't sure he *has* been in Faerie. That's what we were—'

'– Oh, great! We aren't *sure*! So there's no need to look for him; we can sit here—'

'– I didn't say that! I just don't want—'

'Hush!' he said. But he didn't need to, because above the noise of shouting and laughing and singing, I heard trumpets. Instantly all the faeries were quiet, and they drew apart in two groups, leaving a wide path between the lake shore a little way from our tree and the top of the hill. All of them looked towards the mountain. Turning, I looked, too. 'Oh wow,' I breathed.

On the lake, the mist swirled and parted; out of the still water rose ten grey horses ridden by tall Sidhe in red tunics and gold cloaks. There was no splashing, and no waves; as they trotted towards us, the water was black and quiet under the horses' feet, and it reflected the Sidhe's streaming cloaks against a perfect image of the palace. When they got to the shore, the riders raised silver trumpets to their lips and blew a fanfare; as it died away, a cavalcade of horses swirled out of the lake. Leading them was a bright chestnut horse, carrying a rider whose silver tunic and gold cloak shimmered in the long sunlight. Behind him came two deep black horses that cast no reflection, ridden by a Sidhe in a black cloak and a magnificent red-haired woman who looked like a queen. Three stocky brown mares came next; Epona, peaceful and lovely, was riding the one in the middle, flanked by a woman with hair that rippled like a stream over the shoulders of her blue cloak, and a grey-haired woman carrying a harp. As they reached the shore, the whole cavalcade began to canter, and one beautiful horse after another flashed past, each ridden by a Sidhe in a different coloured cloak. After the last one had passed us, the company slowed to a walk and the trumpeters blew another fanfare. Whispers spread through the crowd, and the Sidhe halted in two columns up the side of the path, looking back at the lake.

For maybe half a minute, there was nobody; then Mongan and Manannan appeared out of the mist, riding horses the colour of sea-foam, and dressed in sea-green cloaks lined with gold. As they trotted towards the crowd, the mist vanished as if they'd pulled it away, and a team

271

of horses, one white and one black, sprang out of the lake, pulling an ivory chariot decorated with silver and gold carvings, and driven by . . . the king. There was nobody else it could be: he was wearing a deep purple cloak with ermine edges, and everything about him told you he was like the heroes in Grandpa's stories. He was tall, with white-blond shoulder-length hair like Finn Mac Cumhaill's, and his face told you he'd seen terrible things – wars and deaths and maybe even the Underworld – but was past being scared because he Understood. He was past being a show-off, too: his horses were snorting, all set to gallop across the lake and pull up in a cloud of Faerie dust, but he held them in a collected trot as if the reins were threads of silk.

At the shore, his hands moved just a trifle, and the horses stopped, standing like statues. The king looked around him at the eager faces of the faeries and the wonderful, calm expressions of the Sidhe – then he stretched out his arms to the side and said something in a language we couldn't understand. He didn't speak loudly, but his voice spread out over the whole crowd, ringing from the lake to the top of the hill. When he finished, all the faeries cheered, and the roar was so loud that Colin and I pressed our hands over our ears.

Finally, the noise died down, and the king

drove the chariot up the hill between the lines of Sidhe. After he had passed, the trumpeters turned and followed him in pairs. So did the Sidhe – all except Manannan and Mongan, who turned and rode towards our tree through the parting crowds of faeries, their faces very stern and serious.

'Uh-oh,' muttered Colin.

'Yeah,' I said, and I would have stepped in front of him if we'd been on the ground.

The two horses stopped below us. Mongan and Manannan didn't bow; neither did we. We just looked at each other, and when Manannan's sea-green eyes met mine, the sunlit colours of Faerie faded into the background, and I saw caverns so deep and dark that I shivered.

'Children of Lugh,' he said finally, 'the Faer Folk cannot disobey your commands, but you have come here against Our better judgement. Spare yourselves pain; let Us send you back.'

Colin looked at me, then away at the lake. 'You won't . . . I mean, what you're talking about isn't . . . that beach, is it?'

'Surely not, lad,' said Mongan quickly. 'We'll never send you there again.'

That was good to hear, but by now, of course, we knew there were other dangers in Faerie. 'Is it that if we don't go back now, we can't get home at all?' I asked.

'No,' said Manannan. 'We will send you back as We always have.'

'Then why does your better judgement think we should miss this cool stuff?' said Colin.

'Because if your eyes open at the right time, you will see things that terrify all mortals,' said Manannan. 'And even if you look at them courageously, they will cause you grief.'

Colin gulped and gave me a scared 'what-do-you-think' look. And I thought. I thought about all the times we'd told ourselves the faeries were just trying to scare us by warning us against things that turned out to be scarier than we could possibly imagine. I thought about our theory and everything I'd been feeling was wrong with it. I thought about Colin, and how much younger just-turned-ten was than almost-twelve, even in somebody precocious. And I was all ready to say . . .

But then I thought about pneumonia, and the way I'd felt when Mom had hung up the phone, and the way Colin's face had looked when he sat on the stairs. And I thought about the fact that we were here, and that Grandpa *might* be here, and that Darwin and Einstein had gotten from almost right to really right because they'd kept on looking and thinking, even when they'd realized their beginning theories were too simple.

I swallowed hard. 'I'm going to stay,' I whispered to Colin. 'But if you want, you—'

He bit his lip, but he shook his head – twice, because I raised my eyebrows the first time.

I looked down at the faeries. 'Thank you,' I said. 'But we want to stay.'

Mongan looked at Manannan. 'I told you they were loyal.'

'You had no need to,' said Manannan. 'Very well, Children of Lugh. Drop down behind us, and we'll be off.'

Colin gave me a here-goes look and dropped down behind Manannan; I swung down behind Mongan, and we set off, withers-deep in swarming faeries, towards the clear path up the hill. When we reached it, Colin asked Manannan why he wasn't riding Enbharr, and I felt better, because it meant he was cheering up.

'Enbharr has other duties today,' said Manannan. 'All of Faerie honours its king by coming to the coronation – including Faerie creatures. Most of the horses will attend as mounts for the Sidhe; but of course there are mares with new foals and horses too young to ride. So they may honour the king, Enbharr escorts them to the top of the hill after it has been opened.'

Colin stared up at the hill. 'It's going to *open*?'

275

Mongan grinned. 'Not by itself; Cathbad understands the ways of the land.'

'You mean, he——?'

'Patience,' said Manannan, and we cantered up the hill. At the top, the other Sidhe and their horses were standing in a huge circle around a cave like the one the Seer had dreamed in; two tall stones that rose out of the grassy crown in front of it, but two places in front of a double gate to a sort of paddock were empty. We pulled up there, and Manannan raised his right hand. Below us, the noise of the crowd below us died down into an expectant silence.

Mongan grinned at Colin. 'Watch carefully, Son of Lugh,' he whispered.

As he spoke, the crown of the hill began to sink, as if it were a lump of clay and some giant had put his thumb in the middle of it, pressing the centre down, down, down, and pushing the sides outwards. I stared, and I could see Colin was trying to figure out the physics of it, but nobody else seemed surprised; even the horses acted as if having hills turn into valleys was an everyday thing. Actually, it wasn't a matter of hills and valleys; when everything stopped moving, there was a grass-covered amphitheatre with a road winding down it; what had been the top of the hill was now a field at the bottom, with a cave at one end and two stones in its centre.

I was still taking it in when Mongan, Manannan and the other Sidhe on our side of the amphitheatre turned their horses around. 'Look,' whispered Mongan. 'Here they come.'

He pointed towards the lake; I looked just in time to see a herd of horses swirl out of the water in a blaze of grey, chestnut and bay, their manes and tails flying. As they galloped towards us, Enbharr exploded out of the water behind them with an enormous bucking leap. Then he was everywhere, his grey mane flying like foam as he nipped a mare here, cut off a two-year-old there, driving, driving the herd across the quivering reflection of the palace and up the hill between rows of cheering faeries. As they reached the top, he thundered up the near side of the herd with his ears flat back, nipping and shouldering the outside horses so they turned towards us instead of heading down into the amphitheatre. Quickly, Mongan and Manannan moved our prancing horses to each side of the gate that had been behind us – and the whole herd poured between us into the enclosure. As the last mare and foal fled through the opening, Enbharr stopped in two plunging strides and stood across it, snapping at the youngsters who circled back.

Mongan and Manannan reached down to the gate and rode towards each other to close it. When they reached the centre, a little curly-haired faery ran in from the side and shot the bolt.

'Careful,' said Mongan. 'Enbharr's not the creature here that he is in the pastures.'

The faery nodded and looked up with a shy smile.

'Tiffany!' Colin and I shouted it almost together.

The Sidhe turned towards us, murmuring in surprise; Manannan made a sign to hush. But it was Tiffany who hushed us. She smiled as if she hadn't heard a thing, and something was wrong with her eyes; when she looked in our direction, she seemed to look right through us.

The trumpeters blew a fanfare, and Mongan and Manannan pulled their horses back into the circle. I looked over my shoulder, watching Tiffany slip into the crowd of faeries.

'I told you what you saw here would cause you grief,' said Manannan's voice, quietly.

I nodded, sort of frozen. When I finally turned back, I realized Manannan was in the middle of giving instructions. ' . . . then we will leave you and our horses with Epona, as we both must take part in the ceremony itself. You will stay with

Epona until everything is over and ride out when she tells you to do so; and you must do nothing to interrupt the ceremony itself.'

The trumpets blew another fanfare. Mongan drew our horses up beside Manannan's, and we walked down the road into the amphitheatre. The Sidhe followed us, two by two, their cloaks blowing in the breeze. At the bottom, Mongan and I went to the right and Manannan went to the left; we met again at the far end of the field, looking between the strange stones at the cave. Behind us the Sidhe had formed a circle; above them, packed up the sides, sat thousands and thousands of faeries, whispering and giggling or waving to their friends as they waited for whatever was going to happen next. It was perfectly beautiful, but somehow, I felt as if all the colours and expectancy were only reflections on a window that I was looking through – and on the far side was a grey beach and a thousand staring rocks, half-covered by sand. Through the pounding of the colourless sea, I heard a fanfare from very far away. Dimly, I felt Mongan and Manannan slip off our horses, and saw them march across the field like shadows.

A hand touched my arm, and my eyes cleared. Epona had drawn her horse between Colin's and mine, her face full of concern.

'You are distressed,' she said.

'It's Tiffany,' said Colin. 'See, at home, she and Sarah were best friends. And here – well, we just saw her, up with the horses, and it was like we didn't exist.'

'For her,' said Epona, sighing, 'you do not exist. Nor does any other mortal. She has no memory of her mortal life.'

'Omigosh,' I whispered. 'What have You *done* to her?'

'Nothing,' said Epona. 'What was done, was done by mortals.'

'But she was all right when she left!'

Epona looked at me, and somewhere in the depths of her eyes, I saw Tiffany, sitting on the bus, frozen . . . Tiffany, barely able to talk . . . Tiffany, looking out the window . . . Tiffany, looking like the warehouse people, only much, much younger. 'Do you mean, she went . . . ?'

' . . . crazy?' finished Colin, in a whisper.

'Say rather that her spirit was extinguished,' said Epona. 'That is why We let her come here, though a child who comes here permanently is cut off entirely from the world of mortals, and thus from mortal time. She lives here as she would live there: in a world of her own, with no past and no future; but here, she has the horses she loves and cares for.'

I swallowed a couple of times. 'And she's . . . happy?'

'In her way. Yes.'

That made me feel a little better, somehow, and when I looked at Colin, he looked less upset, too. But there wasn't time to say thank you or anything else, because the trumpeters sounded the longest and most brilliant fanfare they'd played yet, and the king stepped out of the cave into the sunlight. He wasn't wearing his purple cloak any more – just a gold tunic, tight-fitting black pants, and riding boots – but you could have told he was a king anyway. When the faeries saw him, the roar of their cheers rolled up the side of the amphitheatre into the clouds above the palace.

Cathbad raised a hand, and the crowd hushed to hear him speak. Epona leaned towards me. 'Because our king has been such a great one, the Sidhe have decided to give him the cloak of heroes. It is a great honour, because only a true hero can wear it; all the troubles in the world are sewn into its seams.'

'What happens if the king isn't a true hero?' said Colin.

'Then the land will swallow him up. There's always that risk.'

As she spoke, two of the Sidhe led a huge

chestnut draught horse out of the cave; over its back was draped a cloak as black as a rainy night. It seemed to be very heavy; the Sidhe could barely lift it off the horse, and Cathbad had to help them unfold it and hold it above the king's shoulders. Slowly, slowly, they lowered it, straining not to let it fall all at once. Not a horse stirred in the circle of Sidhe; all around the amphitheatre, the faeries were completely quiet. The cloak settled on the king's shoulders, looking even blacker against his white-blond hair. He lifted up his hands and fastened its clasp. Suddenly, thunder rolled out of the clouds above the palace, and I closed my eyes, because I didn't want to watch the earth swallow up that wonderful king, even if he wasn't enough of a hero; but I saw a tremendous burst of light on the back of my eyelids, and I heard the crowd roar, so I opened them again quickly. The king was standing right where he had been, but the cloak around his shoulders was shining white. He swept it off and tossed it to the Sidhe, and the faeries cheered and cheered.

Cathbad raised his hand again, and the ten trumpeters began to play – not a fanfare this time, but a melody so beautiful that it made you want to laugh and cry at the same time. As they played, Mongan and Manannan marched slowly out of the cave, bearing a black circlet on a green pillow. When they reached the king and Cathbad, all of them turned and walked to the two tall stones. Cathbad covered the ground with a silver cloth, and the king knelt on it. The trumpeters' melody came to an end, and all the faeries leaned forward, watching.

Carefully, Cathbad took the black crown from Manannan and Mongan's pillow and walked towards the king's stone. Standing in front of the king, he lifted the crown high, and slowly lowered it. As it got closer to the king's head, the crown grew brighter and brighter, first gold and red and green, then a blur of white. As it touched the king's head, it blazed so brightly that even the faeries put their hands in front of their faces. When we looked again, it was simply a gold circlet, decorated with rubies and emeralds – but its light wasn't all gone; it hovered around the king. Slowly, majestically, he stood, and suddenly the air was filled with the music of a harp. The cheer that had started around the amphitheatre died into a wondering murmur.

'What is it?' I whispered to Epona.

'The Gift of the Otherworld,' she whispered back. 'It has been withheld from our kings for so long, only the very oldest of Us can remember its being given. But now it is offered. The king may have his heart's desire – the thing he has wanted most, all his life.'

Colin and I exchanged looks; she must have known what we were thinking, because she smiled sadly. 'What he asks for must be tangible. There are some things that even the Otherworld cannot give.'

I pursed my lips and looked slowly around the amphitheatre at the thousands of faces, all shapes and sizes, still, watching – waiting for the king to state his heart's desire. None of them was the face I wanted most to see.

Suddenly, all those faces changed, and I looked towards the stones just in time to see the king say something to Cathbad and Manannan. The two faeries looked at each other as if they'd been turned to stones themselves, and Mongan, who'd been standing by them, began to argue – you could tell by the way his hands moved. The king said nothing; he just waited. We strained our ears so hard they hummed, and everyone else – even the Sidhe – leaned forward, trying to hear. Finally, Manannan nodded slowly, and Cathbad made some announcement in the faerie language. A ripple of excitement went all the way around the amphitheatre. Next to me, Epona murmured, 'Impossible.'

'What is it? What is it?' whispered Colin.

'The king has asked to ride Enbharr – which no-one but Manannan, faery or mortal, has ever dared to do alone. What's more, as you've seen, today, Enbharr is a ruler himself. Nobody – even Manannan – could possibly lead him away from his herd, so he will have to be brought here by the forces of the Otherworld itself. And those forces strip the training from even the most obedient of horses.'

'Wow,' said Colin, his eyes as round as saucers. 'Does the king know that?'

She was about to answer when the ground began to shake, and the horses in the circle of Sidhe began to stamp and sidle restlessly. Suddenly, the ground in front of the king and the others burst open, and Enbharr leapt out of it, his mane flying and his ears flat back. The ground rumbled shut behind him, and he stood still for a moment, staring at the crowd; then, whirling around to bolt, he saw the faeries grouped around the king. He stopped, his head snaking back and forth, and all of them – even Manannan – backed towards the stones. All of them except the king. He stepped forward, and in the silence, I could hear the murmur of his voice.

Enbharr reared high into the air, striking out, and the king stopped, but his voice went on and

285

on, and eventually, I saw one of Enbharr's ears flick forward. Coming down with a crash, he pranced away, but after a few feet, he turned. Stood. Trembled. Listened. The king started forward, still talking. Enbharr pawed the ground, sending great chunks of turf flying out behind him, but he didn't move away. The king came a little closer, reaching out a hand. Enbharr stopped pawing, but he shrank away from the hand as much as he could without actually moving. The king took one more step, and laid his hand on his neck. I glanced quickly at Manannan; he was standing in front of the stones like a statue, his arms crossed in front of him.

The king stroked Enbharr's neck, straightening his mane and talking. Gradually, Enbharr lowered his head, which was what everybody knew the king was waiting for. He nodded, stroked Enbharr's beautiful grey face, rubbed him behind the ears – then vaulted onto his back. The horse's head flew up, and he half-reared.

'Oh boy,' murmured Colin. 'A rodeo.'

But there wasn't a rodeo. The king sat perfectly still, and when Enbharr came down, he started to walk forward. It wasn't much of a walk – he moved each foot as if he expected the ground to give away under him – but when I glanced at Epona, she was shaking her head in wonder. After ten steps, Enbharr halted. Walked again. Halted. Turned. Walked . . . Then his head came down, his nose came in, and he and the king trotted once around the amphitheatre, each step perfectly spaced.

When they'd gone around once, the king turned Enbharr to the two stones and halted between them, perfectly square, and perfectly still. The faeries began to applaud, but Enbharr looked around uneasily, and the king held up a hand and spoke. Manannan smiled and signalled the trumpeters. Their instruments flashed in the sunlight as they lifted them to their lips, and they began to play. And the king and Enbharr began to dance.

It was dressage . . . except it wasn't. With dressage, even the best horses dance only because their riders have spent hours and hours teaching them how to do it, so though it's beautiful, you always end up having to admire the rider, not the horse. But here, Enbharr moved so joyfully that it seemed he was making up the dance; his neck arched, and his ears shot forward, and he trotted perfectly in time to the music. As he passed the cave, his strides grew slower and higher, until he was trotting in place, his neck perfectly arched, his tail swinging like a dancer's skirt with the movement of his hind quarters.

Then the king signalled to the chief trumpeter, and the music changed to a kind of jig. Enbharr struck off at a canter, and they did circles and figures of eight and serpentines, wonderfully collected but perfectly free, changing leads every ten strides, then every five, then every three – and at last, as they reached the far side of the amphitheatre, every stride. The Sidhe began to clap, and this time, it didn't bother Enbharr at all; he danced back to the centre of the ring and halted between the standing stones.

The music stopped – at least, the trumpets stopped. But as the king and Enbharr stood still, the light from the hero's crown encircled them, and when it reached the dark, terrible stones, there was a new sound . . . not music exactly, or a voice, or a wind, but sort of a combination of all three. It grew and grew, until it filled the amphitheatre, then died away into the quietest silence I had ever heard. The king bowed his head, laying his hand on Enbharr's neck in a kind of benediction.

Out of the silence came Manannan's voice. 'Bravo!' And as if it was a signal, the faeries – even the Sidhe – went wild, laughing and cheering and singing all at once, while the faery animals danced weird dances around the top of the amphitheatre and the Sidhe horses capered on the field. I leaned towards Epona as soon as I had my horse more or less under control. 'What was it?' I shouted over the noise.

'It was the stones,' she shouted back. 'The land of Faerie paying tribute to its king.'

I looked at Colin, but he was still busy with his horse, so I looked back at the king. He had just dismounted. Manannan strode forward to congratulate him, but the king had turned to Enbharr, stroking him. Something about the way he did it seemed almost familiar . . . But when he turned around to greet Manannan, he held out his right hand, and it was whole. I swallowed, looked away – and realized Epona was watching me. But all she said was, 'I think Manannan and Mongan are going to walk out; that means you must ride their horses in the procession, and the order is important. You must stay next to me; your brother will ride next to Boand.' She pointed to the faery in the blue cloak just as the trumpeters blew another fanfare and marched to each side of the road that led out of the amphitheatre.

The king turned towards them, one hand still on Enbharr's neck. I saw him nod at Manannan, and the two of them walked between the trumpeters, one on each side of the great grey horse. Behind them came Mongan; then two by two, the Sidhe in the circle turned their horses and followed. Because of where we'd been standing, we went out last; when we reached the top of the amphitheatre, I looked back. The road we'd been riding on had disappeared, and the last of the faeries who had been sitting in the sides of the amphitheatre were scrambling over its far sides, looking uneasily over their shoulders.

The procession of Sidhe moved down to the lake. At the bottom of the hill, the Sidhe who had left first were crowded around the king and Enbharr, talking and laughing. The king was still wearing the hero's crown, but it was obviously in his way; when we were still fairly high up the hill, he reached up, took it off, and tucked it under his arm in a friendly sort of way, as if it had been a riding helmet . . . Riding helmet. I stopped my horse and stared, feeling the way I had when he'd patted Enbharr. Only this time, I was sure.

Epona touched my arm. 'We can't stop here; the hill . . . oh. You've seen, then.'

I bobbed my head, but I couldn't say anything because I'd started to cry. She moved the brown mare close to my horse and put her arm around me. 'I was afraid you would.'

'Afraid?' I sobbed. 'I think it's the most wonderful thing that ever happened.'

She frowned and started to say something, but I shook myself away and eased my horse up next to Colin's. 'Colin,' I said.

'Hey, come on,' he said. 'Stay in . . . Geez, what is it?'

'Look at the king. Forget the right arm. Forget the long hair. Look at the way he's carrying the crown.'

'Yeah. It's just the way Grandpa used to . . .' He stopped and stared. 'Oh,' he whispered. Boand looked at him the way Epona had looked at me; then she stopped her mare so Colin and I could ride on together. When we got to the bottom of the hill, Epona spoke. Her voice was very soft, but instantly, the crowd made room for us to ride towards the Sidhe closest to the king. He had turned towards the palace, talking to Manannan. But as we halted a few feet behind him, all the Sidhe suddenly became quiet, and he turned around to see what it was.

'Grandpa,' I said. 'Grandpa.'

12 Heart's Desire

The king took a step back, staring at us as if he couldn't believe we were real. Then suddenly his whole face lit up, and he shoved the crown into Manannan's hands. 'Sarah! Colin!' he said, striding towards us with his arms open. In a second, he'd put one arm around each of us and scooped us off the horses, the way he had when we'd been little, and we were hugging him and laughing and crying all at the same time.

Finally, he put us down, stood us in front of him, and looked us over, the way he had at the beginning of every summer. 'It's longer leathers you'll be needing soon,' he said, smiling at Colin. Then he looked at me; and instead of squirming, the way I'd done before, I looked back at him, wondering. He was Grandpa, all right; there was no doubting that, but I could see why it had taken us so long to recognize him. Part of it was his whole arm, which made him stand and move a little differently than the Grandpa I remembered. But it was his face and eyes that were really different. At first, I thought maybe they'd been blank for so long I'd forgotten what they'd been like; but the more I looked, the more I realized that wasn't so. His face was younger, but his eyes kept it from looking like a young man's face. Behind the green-grey they'd always been, they were like faery eyes, wise and deep and without time . . . when they met mine, I saw something in them that even Manannan's eyes seemed not to have. Maybe it was just that he was looking at me a little sadly.

'Has it been so long I've been away, then?' he said, shaking his head.

'No, no,' I said hurriedly. 'It's just the haircut and the contacts. They were Grandmother Madison's ideas, and you know how *she* is! I'm the same old me – right, Colin?'

'Sure you are,' he said. 'Except . . .'

'Oh, come on!'

'There's your proof,' he said, grinning at Grandpa. 'Same old Sarah – see?'

'Same old Colin, too,' he said, laughing. And I felt better, because the laugh got rid of the thing in his eyes that had puzzled me. He put a hand on each of our shoulders and looked at Epona. 'The horses are cool, but it's a long day they've had. Will they stand if we go down to the stones there and talk?'

Cathbad glanced at the sun and muttered something in the faerie language, but Epona smiled. 'I think we can ask them to stand for a few minutes.'

'Thank you,' said Grandpa, bowing slightly. 'And join us, if you will.' He looked at Manannan and Mongan. 'You too, my lords.'

I saw that Colin, like me, would rather have been alone with Grandpa. But we'd never argued with Grandpa, even before he'd been a king; and besides, the air felt the way it does when something is up. So we took his hands, and the six of us walked to the edge of the lake.

When we got there, Grandpa sat down on a long, flat rock and drew us near him. Then, looking at the faeries over his shoulder, he motioned them in front of him – graciously, but as if he expected them to obey him the way the stable boys had at the Smithes'. And they did. Even Manannan. Colin and I stared at each other.

'Sure and I have no fear that anybody in Faerie would dare to choose me as king if they'd harmed my flesh and blood,' he said, quietly, but in a voice that would have made me shake if he'd been talking to me. 'Still, I ask – how do these children happen to be here?'

Colin squirmed as the three faeries looked at each other silently. 'It's OK, Grandpa – really!' he blurted. 'They haven't hurt us at all! We're under Pro—'

'Let Them tell Their own story, Colin,' said Grandpa sharply. 'Lord Mongan?'

'It's a story I'd rather not tell, that's for sure,' said Mongan, with a wry smile. 'But since I must – well, as Your Highness knows, even the greatest hero can't be made king of the faeries until he's in the moment between life and death. That poses Us a serious problem.'

'You mean,' said Colin, 'if You're a split second late getting to him . . . ?'

'We lose him,' said Mongan, shaking his head. 'It happened many a time in the Old Days; Heroes died quickly on the field of honour. That was why We were so happy when you moved into the house Mr Ryan built in Our honour between his fine railroad tracks and the Ring. We could keep an eye on you easily – providing, of course, that your family could be trusted not to meddle with Our powers. And on the Feast of Samhain, these little ones showed Us that they could be trusted, for they gave oatmeal to a faerie.'

'Ah,' said Grandpa, and he looked at us so proudly I couldn't stand it.

'We didn't *know* that's what we were doing,' I said. 'We thought we were just helping the warehouse people – until later, anyway, when Colin did research.' I looked at the faeries. 'Would you really have driven us out of the house if we hadn't? Even with Grandpa there?'

'Yes,' said Epona. 'Even though We had no assurance that he would become our king until the Seer's dream assured us that he would, We felt that the risk of losing him was less than that of losing Faerie. Mortals who do not know the ways of Faerie do it great damage. Think of the cloverleaf, the warehouses – even of Mr Ryan's house itself, now. We can never risk letting those who cannot think beyond their own welfare find the Ways into the Otherworld.'

Her eyes looked deeply into mine, and as I nodded, I saw, in kind of a shade behind her, an old woman with a thousand wrinkles and brown stumps of teeth, wearing a tattered coat from the bottom of a Salvation Army box. 'Jenny . . . ?' I whispered.

She nodded. 'Yes, Jenny. And your charity to me preserved you from great danger later that evening when you followed your grandfather into the Ring to bring him home.'

Grandpa gasped and tightened his arms around us. 'You stepped into a faerie ring on the Feast of Samhain? Dear God, to think that you were in danger like that, and I . . .'

'It should never have happened,' said Manannan, a little shortly. 'We had sent minions to guard all the Ways to the Otherworld, as we always do at Samhain. Unfortunately, the minions at the Ring recognized Your Highness as you wandered towards it in the fog, and led you into it, foolishly thinking they could earn a great reward by bringing you directly to Us before the time had come. They could not, of course; but they were so preoccupied with the effort, they did not see the children until they had stepped into the Ring.'

Grandpa shook his head. 'But if the children had spoken to the minions—'

'— Little would have happened,' said Manannan. 'Their charity, as Epona says, would have protected them from blindness or abduction, though not from terror.'

Terror. I thought of the fog and the way the minions' eyes had glowed. If we'd spoken to them, what would they have done?

'But *of course* we knew better than to speak to them!' said Colin confidently. 'We ignored them, the way the woman in the story should have.'

Cathbad smiled a wintry smile. 'And by ignoring faeries in the ring on the Eve of Samhain – by not trying to use either their charity or their knowledge to gain access to the Otherworld – the children were granted the power thousands have sought. Those are the Rules, and the Sidhe accepted them immediately. We arrived at the Ring too late to discuss the matter with them that night, but when they returned the next day, Mongan and I told them of their Protection and promised to help them with their mission.'

'It's spinning in their graves Oisin and all his kindred must be, hearing this,' said Grandpa, clapping us both on the shoulder. 'Mere babes – breaking the spell of centuries!'

'Um, Grandpa,' said Colin, looking down. 'It wasn't like that. More like an accident.'

Grandpa smiled at him. 'Do you remember how Finn Mac Cumhaill took the first taste of the Salmon of Knowledge?'

'Of course!' said Colin. 'He was cooking it for that hermit who'd finally caught it after years and years, and a bubble rose under its skin, and as he pushed it down, he burnt his thumb and popped it into his mouth!' Then his face changed. 'Oh, I see. An accident.'

'It sure was,' I said. 'We didn't even know the Ring was there; we were hunting for you, and saw the faeries—'

'– and when we *did* see them, we thought they'd stolen the real you and left a changeling in your place,' said Colin. 'So when Mongan and Cathbad told us we were under Protection if we had a mission, we asked them to bring us to Faerie, so we could find the real you and—'

'– Begging your pardon,' interrupted Mongan. 'That's not what you asked. You asked Us to take you where your grandfather was.'

Grandpa's shocked face turned from Mongan to Manannan to Epona. 'They asked that, in their innocence?' he said. 'And You *complied*?'

Mongan looked at him steadily. 'We had no choice,' he said. 'They had broken the spell. The only thing we could do for their innocence was to send them where you were by the route you had taken yourself as you drifted from your world; we hoped that when they felt the horrors that journey had inflicted on you, they would cease to desire its completion.'

'Sure,' said Colin to Grandpa. 'But you can bet we saw that they were just trying to scare us out of Faerie, so we kept on—'

'– Shut up a minute,' I said suddenly. 'I just Saw.'

299

He was about to fuss, but Grandpa waved him to silence, which was awful, because everything was spinning in my mind and I couldn't get it to hold still long enough to look at it.

Grandpa's arm went around me. 'Tell us what you saw.'

'The difference . . .' But it still wouldn't come.

'Ride it at the fence, that's my girl. The difference . . . ?'

'Between asking to go to Faerie and asking to go where you were,' I said. 'That's what was wrong with our theory. Not the logic part. The part you take for granted.'

'Premise,' said Colin automatically. 'But what—?'

'— Let me *think*, will you? OK, our premise was that you were in Faerie, and we never even *thought* of asking if that was right. But you weren't in Faerie – at least, not before this.' I looked at Grandpa for the first time since I'd begun; and I saw the thing I'd seen in his face when we first met. 'You were in the Grey Land,' I whispered. 'Fighting those waves.'

'The Grey Land!' Colin put his hands over his mouth. 'Oh, no!'

Grandpa looked at him, then at me. 'Sure and you're not saying . . . ?'

'Yes, he is,' I said. 'But don't blame the faeries

300

– please! It was my fault! I *made* them send us! They wouldn't have, otherwise! And when we couldn't hear the harp well enough to come back on our own, Manannan rode all the way there to fetch us, even though he was af—' I glanced at Manannan, and shrank close to Grandpa as dark, swirling eddies in the faery eyes swept around me. 'I'm sorry,' I mumbled.

Manannan's eyes moved from me to Grandpa, then back to me. 'You see too well, Daughter of Lugh,' he said. 'No doubt your world will exact a penalty for that; mortals dislike having their dignity undermined by truth. But here, you should not have to apologize for what you see.' He sighed. 'And what you saw when I came to the Grey Land was true. I – Manannan Mac Lir, ruler of all the seas of the Otherworld – I was afraid.'

Mongan gave a little grunt of surprise, but Epona nodded. 'There's no shame in that,' she said. 'The Grey Land floats like a fog around all worlds and all Ways; it's a place that haunts us all.'

'Not quite all,' said Manannan. 'There is one soul who has fought its horrors without fear, and emerged from them in triumph. He stands there.' He pointed to Grandpa with a bow.

'Well, of course!' said Colin. 'He's a hero!'

Grandpa shook his head. 'Sure and I wish you were right, lad – and you too, my lord, for I'd be happy to take your praise if I'd earned it. But you're not right. It's one thing to go to the Grey Land, as you children did, heaven save you, without knowing what it is – that's innocence. It's a different thing to ride there to keep it from hurting the innocent – that's courage, my lord, whether you're shaking with fear or no, and I'll be thanking you for it until the end of time. But to go there as I did, step by step out of the world of man, when you can't recall the step you last took, or recognize the landmarks that tell you where you are, or remember the people who're watching you . . . that's something else again. There's no innocence; just a blur of things seen and not known. There's no fear, even in the Grey Land; it's just one of many unfamiliar places. And no courage; just mindless struggle with no goal or chance of winning.' He gazed out over the lake. 'Oh, little ones! How it grieves me that you've had to—'

The grass behind us rustled; Grandpa glanced over his shoulder and rose slowly to his feet. We jumped up too, and I turned around just in time to see Cathbad's black cloak swish as he bowed. 'Your Majesty,' he said, 'the hour is near. You must prepare to depart.'

'Yeah,' said Colin, looking up. 'We really should be getting back. Mom will be so glad to see you all right again.' His smile faded. 'You *will* be all right at home now, won't you?'

'Colin—' said Grandpa, in a strange sort of voice.

Cathbad frowned. 'You don't understand, Son of Lugh. Your grandfather cannot go home with you, any more than he can stay with us. A man can become king of the faeries only in the moment between life and death. That moment is far longer in Faerie time than in mortal time – long enough for Us to honour him for all that he was in his life. But when it is over, he must go on to the Land Beyond All Lands, and he must stay there forever.'

'Forever!' I said. 'You mean . . . ?'

'Oh, no, Grandpa!' said Colin, clinging to him. 'You can't leave us forever! We need you! That's why we came to get you, all those times!'

Grandpa looked sadly at Cathbad. 'Some things should be explained gently, my lord.'

'Don't worry about explanations!' I said. 'Just come back with us!'

'Right!' said Colin. 'You're king of the faeries now! You make the Rules! Just make one that makes you stay with us!'

'Sure and you know I can't do that,' said

303

Grandpa. 'There are Rules made by neither mortals nor faeries; they're as old as the Earth itself, because they are the Rules of the Earth itself. One of them is that human beings – kings and beggars alike – must travel in the end to the Land Beyond All Lands. That's what it means to be a mortal.'

I closed my eyes, because I knew how Grandpa looked when he said exactly what he meant, and he looked that way now.

'But Grandpa,' said Colin desolately. 'What . . . what'll we do without you?'

'You'll go on with your own stories, just the way you do after you close a book,' said Grandpa. 'And if you want me to be with you again—'

'Oh yes, yes, yes!'

He shook his head. 'If you want me to be with you again, think of the way we used to be, before the time when all there was left of me was the shadow of what I'd been. Think about the barn, and the ponies, and the nights we sat out on the steps and told stories.' He smiled. 'Those were wonderful nights, weren't they? With the stars and the smell of roses, and the sound of the horses grazing in the pastures . . .'

'Oh, Grandpa,' I sobbed. 'Please don't go . . .'

'What I'm telling you,' he said, 'is that when

you remember those nights, and the days that went with them, it'll be as if I've never left.' He paused, then added, 'And it's something else that'll give you comfort too, if you'll dry your eyes and think.'

Something about his voice made us both stop hanging on him and look at him instead.

'Think of the Grey Land and what it does,' he said. 'Steals every quality that makes a man a man, and makes him nothing – right? But some of us . . . whether we deserve it or not, God save us . . . are protected from the horror of that nothingness by the one mortal grace even the Grey Land can't strip away: the dignity of being loved.' He bowed his head and put one hand on each of our shoulders. 'And you have given me that grace.'

'Yes,' said Epona. She swept her arm over the Sidhe, the lake, the horses, and finally, the palace. 'The faeries would not choose a mortal for their king if they didn't know that some mortals are better than they are, though mortal powers seem so weak. This time, we have celebrated, and the land itself has praised, not just the heroism of the Old Days but that great dignity, which only mortals can bestow.' She gave us her wonderful smile. 'Do you understand, Children of Lugh?'

'I . . . I think so,' I said.

'That's fine, for now,' said Grandpa. 'For later – promise to remember what she said.'

'Promise,' we said together.

'That's my loves,' he said. 'And now, we must thank the Sidhe and say farewell.'

I looked at the four faeries, and I suddenly realized he'd meant more than he'd said. 'You mean,' I choked, 'you mean we can't come back?'

Cathbad nodded. 'Your mission is fulfilled. Henceforth, you will have to abide by the Rules that govern all other mortals.'

We looked at Grandpa, but he nodded. 'Cathbad is right,' he said, 'but don't think of it as a loss; you will have lost only what other mortals have never had. As for what remains...' His eyes drifted away, and I felt the way I had in Pennsylvania sometimes – that he was talking to himself, not to us. 'What remains is enough,' he said slowly, 'enough to shelter wasted children, to remind old men there is more in their world than bitterness and regret . . .' He sighed and stroked my short hair. 'Tell your mother I love her.'

I swallowed hard. 'She loves you, too. I heard her say so, and she really meant it.'

'I know she does,' he said. 'And the pity of it

is she had to prove it the way she did, with never a word of blessing from myself, never a glimmer of what she's given me. Be good to her; she's seen only toil and grief.' He bent over us, and for the first time in my life, I saw his eyes fill with tears. 'Tell her – in any way you can – that though I'm king of the faeries and have ridden the horse that has no flaws, *you* have given me my heart's desire. You and she.'

Behind us, we heard a flurry of mounting and getting ready; turning, I saw that the Sidhe were ready to go. The only horses without riders were Epona's brown mare and Enbharr.

Epona touched Grandpa's arm. 'Your Highness, it is time to shed mortal sorrow and ride onward, celebrating what has been and what is to come.'

Grandpa let us go and stood up. 'It was not sorrow I was shedding,' he said. 'But you are right.' He put one hand on each of our shoulders and turned us so he could look into our faces. 'You must not try to follow me; let the Otherworld send you home. Do you understand?'

'Yes, Grandpa,' I whispered. Colin was crying too hard to talk, but he nodded.

'That's my little ones,' he said. 'All right, then . . .'

He hugged us again, and we clung to him until he gently put us away, strode into the circle of Sidhe, and vaulted onto Enbharr's back. Manannan handed him the crown, and Cathbad, leaning from his horse, draped the royal mantle around his shoulders. Epona mounted her own horse, made some gesture with her hand, and slowly, the company of Sidhe rode to the lake – and disappeared, two by two, into the reflection of the palace and the cliffs. There was no ripple in the water, no mist on the far side; they simply vanished, until only Grandpa was left, sitting perfectly on his perfect horse, smiling, whole, wonderful. He raised one hand in farewell; then Enbharr turned, and they were gone.

We both ran forward to wave one more time, but Colin tripped, and I fell over him. When we got up, we were in the Ring, and the trucks were roaring past on Highway 495.

I stood there, staring at them, until a big tanker took the exit and crawled down the ramp onto the 125 Connector, sending a black cloud out of its smokestack as it shifted down. At the bottom of the ramp, it turned towards town, and the gears started the other way: first, second, third . . . It disappeared around the curve, and I turned to Colin. 'Let's go.'

He wiped his eyes with the tail of his shirt. 'OK.'

We turned and picked our way slowly through the junk, blinking in the late afternoon sun. When we got to the yard, Colin stopped and frowned. 'It shouldn't be where it is.'

'The house?' I said blankly.

'The sun. Usually, when we go to Faerie, it's the same time when we come back, right?'

I saw what he meant; it had been a little after noon when we had started home from the Gordons', and now . . . 'Maybe it's different now that our mission's over.' Then I wished I'd held my tongue; putting it in words made it so . . . certain.

We were both standing there, looking towards the sun, when Mom's old car bumped across the tracks. As it got closer, we could see that Mom wasn't driving; Mr Crewes was. I suppose we should have waved or something, but we just watched it pass the warehouses . . . slow down . . . pull into the driveway . . . stop. After what seemed a long time, Mom got out of her door and walked slowly towards us. Her face was completely frozen.

'Children,' she began, 'your grandfather . . .' She stopped, and so did everything else. Well, not really. The birds kept singing, Mr Crewes walked slowly towards the porch, the whistle of the 4:45 sounded far off down the tracks . . . but it was like there was nothing in the world but Mom, all alone, not talking, not crying.

Be good to her, he'd said. I understood now, and I wanted more than anything to tell her all the things he'd explained, but the words just wouldn't come. All I could do was run and put my arms around her. 'Don't feel bad, Mom,' I said. 'He's all right, now . . . and he loved you.'

Mom's frozen expression melted, and she hugged us both – and I guess we all cried, but I don't remember.

13 A Saddle

There were over two hundred people at the funeral; every horse person I'd ever met in Pennsylvania was there, and a lot of other people I'd only seen in pictures. It was great to see them, except they all said the same sorts of things. *It was a blessing. He could have lingered for years. It must be a tremendous relief to have it all over.*

'If I hear one more person say it's a good thing that Grandpa died, I don't know how I'll stay polite,' said Colin, as we climbed into a black limousine to follow the hearse from the church to the cemetery. 'Can't they understand that even a Grey Land Grandpa is better than no Grandpa at all?'

'I guess not,' I said. 'But then, they're not the

ones who have to go into his study and see all his stuff there.'

'Don't,' he said. So I looked out the window.

Mom got into the limousine and sat next to Colin; Mr Crewes got in and sat next to me. He saw I was crying a little, and he put his arm around my shoulder. Which was OK; he'd been really, really great. The thing was, though, it didn't help. Nothing did. Everywhere Grandpa had been, there were empty spaces, and nothing anybody said or did could make them go away. There were even spaces where I knew he couldn't possibly be. Like, when we got to the cemetery, I kept worrying that he might fall into the grave as we watched the funeral people lower the coffin into the ground. And at the wake, as I passed the food and said 'thank you', when people told me how grown up I looked, I kept worrying that the noise and confusion would upset him. It all seemed like a bad dream, and I was very glad when we finally went back home with Mr Crewes, the Gordons, and the Smithes, who had come up from Pennsylvania.

After I'd helped put the leftovers away, I changed and lay down on my bed, hoping I'd go to sleep or something; but I stayed awake and hurting. Outside, the 5:15 express shot past, and in the silence it left behind, I heard Colin's sneakers padding down the hall to the front stairs. When I looked out my door, he was sitting on the top step with his chin on his hand, and he didn't turn around. I tiptoed to the stairs and sat down next to him, feeling sort of guilty. All through the wake, he'd been looking just fine, and I'd thought he'd let everyone cheer him up. After a while, he looked sideways at me. 'That was awful,' he said.

'Yeah,' I said, 'but like Mr Crewes says, you have to do *something*.'

'The faeries do it a lot better.'

'I'll say.'

We sat there, listening to the grown-ups' voices float up the stairs from the living room . . . not words, just questions, answers, mutterings . . . and watching the colours in the stained-glass window flicker in the shadows of the leaves outside. They were the same colours they'd always been, but the pattern around the border was just vines, trees, and flowers. No faeries.

'Do you suppose They knew when we were there?' said Colin after a while. 'About the house, I mean?'

'Maybe. Epona said something about it . . . I can't remember exactly what.'

He looked up at the dingy bronze chandelier and the cracked ceiling. 'You'd think they'd fix

313

it up instead of tearing it down,' he said. 'It could be a great house.'

'Not with four lanes of Route 125 running through it.'

'Well, yeah, but it's a shame. And then there's the warehouse people. I suppose they'll find other warehouses, but . . .'

I nodded. 'Lots of them have gone already – have you noticed? – even though they've got until September.'

'Sure I've noticed. And it's not *fair*, pushing us all out just to build a stupid road! Grandpa never would have let it happen!'

I wasn't sure Grandpa could have stopped a four-lane road from being built, any more than the faeries could. But I might have been wrong, and anyway, this wasn't the time to say so.

Colin looked sideways at me. 'You thought about where *we're* going to go?'

'Sort of. They haven't said anything, though.'

'Yeah, but they're going to. Right? Some big, sappy announcement—'

'– I thought you *liked* him!'

'I *do* like him! I just wish they'd stop treating us like babies and get it over with.'

'Think that's what it is? I kind of thought . . . well, he's patient. Like when everything was so

314

crazy, and you asked him to watch you flip that penny a hundred times—'

'– I just wanted to see if the faeries were really gone, and nobody else would—'

'– OK, OK. Anyway, you can see how tired Mom is, with the house thing happening in the middle of the funeral and all. And I thought maybe he was being patient about her, too.'

The big sliding doors to the living room slipped back, and the grown-ups walked out, talking, the way they do when everybody's leaving. We smiled politely and started down the stairs, bracing ourselves for being kissed.

'There they are!' said Mrs Smithe. She turned from Mom to us. 'We've got a present for you – just the thing, from what the Gordons have been telling us about the horse you're working with them.'

'She means Dandy,' said Mrs Gordon quickly, as we stared at each other. 'It seems that there's almost no chance of Tiffany's coming back. Her parents have skipped town, and the police are pretty sure they sent her on ahead somewhere and then went to collect her. And since we have no legal claim . . .' She sighed, and Mr Gordon put his arm around her.

'In any case,' he said, 'Dandy is standing in our barn, and your mother and Jim agree with us that you're the perfect people to work him, if you want to.'

'*Want* to!' said Colin, his eyes shining. 'Criminy!'

I nodded, trying to look enthusiastic. And I was – really. But somewhere in the back of my mind, I saw Tiffany, patting foals, brushing mares, riding young horses in a huge green field. Her face was completely happy, but . . . I glanced at Colin, and I prayed that his face would never look like that.

'So,' said Mr Smithe. 'Let's go get your present.'

We all trooped out to the cars, and he pulled a carefully-covered saddle out of the plush back seat of his Cadillac. 'There you go,' he said, handing it to me.

Colin slipped off the cover – and we stared at each other. It wasn't just a saddle; it was the very, very best jumping saddle you could buy – so good, you wouldn't even *think* of buying one if you weren't a rider like the famous ones who'd been at the funeral. And though it wasn't new, it was beautifully oiled, all supple . . . I ran my hand over it gently, and in the empty space next to me, Grandpa . . . not the Grey Land Grandpa, but the real one . . . nodded in approval.

'It's really gorgeous,' I said, looking up at Mr Smithe. 'I . . . thank you.'

'It's nothing,' he said, looking a little embarrassed. 'It's been sitting in the tack room for years, and just before we came here, one of the senior stable boys asked me who it belonged to, because he'd been cleaning it as long as he could remember, but nobody ever used it. Well, that seemed a waste, and I remembered that you kids had used our kids' saddles when you rode, and so . . . enjoy it.'

'Thank you,' we said – and boy, did we mean it.

Mr Smithe clapped Colin on the shoulder, and Mrs Smithe kissed me on the forehead. Then they said goodbye to everyone and took off for Pennsylvania.

Mr Gordon stepped over to look at the saddle. 'Wow,' he said. 'If I were you kids, I'd get down to the barn right after school tomorrow and try it out.'

'All *right*!' said Colin, looking up at Mom. 'Can we?'

'*May* we,' she said. 'You may indeed.'

'Great!' said Mrs Gordon. 'We'll take the saddle, and when you come—'

'– Um . . .' I said, looking down. 'I'd really like to clean it . . . not that it needs it . . .'

'That'll be fine,' said Mom, smiling at Mrs Gordon. 'I'll bring it over in the morning, and we can talk over boarding arrangements.'

Mrs Gordon said not to even *think* of arrangements. Mr Crewes and Mom said not to be silly . . . Mr Gordon looked at his watch and said it was past feeding time, and we'd settle things tomorrow. Then everybody laughed, and the Gordons jumped in the truck and left.

Mr Crewes looked around the yard, the way you do after everybody has gone; then he offered to go and get a pizza from a place that had started making them so people could take them home – because Mom had been cooking for days. Colin wanted to go along, to make sure it was the right kind of pizza, and they took off, thick as thieves. Which left just Mom and me.

'Your arms getting tired?' she said, holding hers out towards the saddle.

'They're fine,' I said. 'You'll get your dress dirty. Is there any saddle soap?'

'Blocks of it. Dad insisted on bringing it all up here with him, and I didn't have the heart to tell him he wouldn't need it. It's in the cellar.'

I zipped in the door and down to the cellar, leaving the saddle on the back of a kitchen chair. When I came back up with a new glycerine bar and a sponge, Mom was standing there, looking at it.

'Saddles in the kitchen,' she said, with a funny sort of smile. 'Just like home.'

I nodded, but what I was really thinking about was taking the stirrups off. When I turned around, there was a bowl of water on the table, all set to go; I dampened the sponge, scrunched it around on the bar of glycerine, and tipped the saddle up, to start on the bottom, the way Grandpa had always made us . . . and stopped. On the inside of the tree was scratched neatly, 'D O' B.' Deirdre O'Brien.

I stared and stared, feeling the kitchen dissolve into another kitchen, cluttered with boots and bridles and newspapers. In one corner was a big chair and a table, with a copy of Yeats or whatever with a riding glove shoved in it to keep the place. And at the sink, peeling potatoes with an expression that said he was really thinking of what stories to tell us after dinner . . .

I blinked and looked up. Mom was standing at our sink; her hands were completely still.

'Mom . . .' I said. 'Um . . . someday, would you like to go riding? Just you and me?'

For a long time, she just stood there; then she turned around and smiled. 'Yes,' she said. 'Yes, I would.'

THE END

ABOUT THE AUTHOR

Laura Stevenson grew up in Ann Arbor, Michigan, the University town in which she was born, but 'home' to her was the Vermont farm that became her parents' summer place when she was five years old. During her Vermont summers, Laura began the day by practising the violin for three hours in the loft of the barn; in the afternoons, she, her horse and her dog explored all the trails and back roads within thirty miles of that farm.

As a child, Laura dreamed of being a novelist, but as she grew older, her family's ties to England developed her interest in English history. After studying at the University of Michigan and at Yale, she became a historian and published articles and a book on Elizabethan literature and culture. Gradually escalating deafness, however, forced her to retreat to Vermont, where she began to write fiction for her two daughters (collectively, she and her husband now have seven children and fourteen grandchildren). Laura's books *Happily After All* and *The Island and the Ring* have been shortlisted for nine children's books awards and have been translated into Danish and German. *All the King's Horses* is her first book to be published by Corgi Books.

Laura and her husband, the poet F.D. Reeve, live in Vermont, where she teaches at Marlboro College. They have spent two of the past five years in London, where Laura has been working on a book about Victorian children's literature.